I'd like to thank Marcia Schlossberg, Matthew Schlossberg, Rachel Schlossberg, Ruth Schlossberg, and Judy Janec for their ongoing support of my writing, and the folks at Denver Horror Collective—Desi D, Gary Robbe, Henry Snider, Hollie Snider, Jeff Wood, and Joy Yehle—for their invaluable critiques.

CHARWOOD is dedicated to the following torch-bearers of culture and ecology:

Gloria Schlossberg (1920-1995), my Bubby. Rabbi Erwin Zimet (1912-1989), spiritual leader of Temple Beth-El. Art Spiegelman, author and illustrator of MAUS. Tim Hermach, my former boss and president of Native Forest Council. Shannon Wilson, my friend and director of Eco-Advocates Northwest. David Brower (1912-2000), exiled environmentalist and the inspiration behind my advocacy.

Madness Heart Press
2006 Idlewilde Run Dr.
Austin, Texas 78744

This is a work of fiction. Names, characters, places, and incidents either are the product of the author's imagination or are used fictitiously. Any resemblance to actual persons, living or dead, events, or locales is entirely coincidental.

Copyright © 2023 Josh Schlossberg
Cover by Don Noble using a photo provided by Scott Beahan of Shutterfly Perfect Photography

All rights reserved. No part of this book may be reproduced or used in any manner without written permission of the copyright owner except for the use of quotations in a book review. For more information, address: john@madnessheart.press

First Edition
www.madnessheart.press

Charwood

Josh Schlossberg

An Aggadah Try It Publication

"His mouth is full of lies and threats;
trouble and evil are under his tongue.
He lies in wait near the villages;
from ambush he murders the innocent.
His eyes watch in secret for his victims;
like a lion in cover he lies in wait.
He lies in wait to catch the helpless;
he catches the helpless and drags them off in his net."
–*Psalms 10:7-9*

"The clearest way into the Universe is through a forest wilderness."

–John Muir (1838-1914), *John of the Mountains: The Unpublished Journals of John Muir* (1938)

"For the average person, being in the woods means nothing, and that's because it's the equivalent of an illiterate standing in one of the world's great libraries."

–Richard Gavin, "Primeval Wood," *Sylvan Dread* (2016)

CHAPTER 1

Orna Tannenbaum's bones rattled as her Forester climbed the steep washboard road. To her immediate right was a ragged rock face that had been blasted out of the side of the mountain many decades ago. Down to her left, a hundred-foot drop to the wooded valley, mostly in shadow as evening drew near. Sitting up straight, hands tight on the wheel, music off so she could focus, she thanked God for the warm, dry October, as even a dusting of snow on the near-vertical slope may have slid her off into the void.

The "All Hallows Climate Action Bonfire" was scheduled to start at dusk near the historic mining village of Silvercleft, Colorado. Barely fifteen miles outside Meadbury—the bustling college town Orna called home for the last couple of years—the narrow dirt track winding up into the Rocky Mountain foothills had already plopped her in the middle of nowhere. A queasy peek out the window to the spiky tree canopy below, and she shot her gaze back to what she prayed was the right road, drops of sweat breaking out at her hairline.

Soon, the road leveled out for a short stretch, and Orna came to a stop. In her native state of Vermont even the most desolate back ways eventually took you past a farmhouse or some sign of humankind. But as she'd discovered on her many solo camping trips around the Centennial State during the pandemic, a wrong turn out there could strand you in the wilderness.

She grabbed her phone from the passenger seat and pulled up the map app. Sure enough, the white route coiling like a snake through grey nothing on her screen was the only way to Silvercleft and the event she wasn't even sure she wanted to go to anymore.

Glancing in the rearview mirror, her face was stark white. Not out of fear but from the makeup she'd caked on for her golem costume—her go-to as a kid, and the easiest one she could think of—the Hebrew word אמת (truth) scrawled in eyeliner across her forehead above thick brows and piercing green eyes. Still, she had to keep going. Setting her jaw, she toed the gas and followed the road as it pitched upward again.

A year and a half of COVID near-isolation, with a constant background of dread, had triggered a newfound anxiety in Orna. For thirty-one years she'd dodged the stereotype of the neurotic Jew only to fall victim to random, awful panic attacks once or twice a month.

The road made a hairpin turn, and, ears popping from the elevation gain, she navigated the switchback warily. Lucky for her, not only was the grade gentler, the drop-off to the prior section of road was barely twenty feet down. Relaxing back into the seat, she loosened her death grip on the wheel and eased up the mountain.

Moving to Meadbury two months before the pandemic hit, and having sensibly avoided most public gatherings, she'd yet to make any local friends. Now that the virus—after several nasty variants, millions of deaths, and immeasurable suffering—no longer felt like much of a threat to young and healthy folk like her (fingers crossed), she craved human contact.

Unfortunately, with all that time alone, her mind

had begun eating itself like digestive acids in an empty stomach. Suffering an embarrassing panic attack at an outdoor bluegrass concert over the summer, she'd been too afraid to socialize again, basically holding herself hostage at home. Finally, it was time to get out—of her condo and her head.

Three more switchbacks and the road crested the hill to flatten out onto a ridge, the tall dense pines a comfy buffer to either side. High as she was going to get according to the map, she'd reach the village soon.

The key to breaking the curse of anxiety, a number of YouTube videos insisted, was to focus on things other than yourself. While Orna had never been much of an activist outside a handful of Take Back the Night marches in college, she could think of few bigger and more important issues than climate change. Searching online for local environmental groups, she found the bonfire, which she figured might also be a good place to meet new people. Two birds with one stone.

She chuckled at the absurd and grisly image of tossing a rock at a flock of crows in the sky, and two of the birds dropping to the ground. How was that even possible? It wasn't like you could hit—from around the curve, a huge pickup truck barreling towards her in the middle of the road.

Heart in her throat, she jerked the wheel to the right, the side of the Forester scraping up against hanging conifer branches. At the last second before the truck smashed into her, it swerved—horn blaring—back to its rightful side of the road to race past in a plume of dust.

Braking, Orna pulled over, and, panting, braced for a panic attack. But her breathing steadied and her pattering heartbeat slowed. Usually, the episodes didn't come during moments of stress but days or even weeks afterward. It was anyone's guess when this shock would catch up to her.

Much as she wanted to go home, bailing would only make things worse. The more she gave in to her fears—simply her unconscious mind trying a little too hard to keep her safe—the stronger they would get. On the other hand, if she went on with business as usual, the anxiety wouldn't find anything to feed on and would let up. At least in theory.

Reminding herself all was well—just some reckless backwoods driver, no harm, no foul—she kept going, if a bit more slowly. For the next mile, as if to comfort Orna, the woods wrapped its lush green blanket around her, a carpet of seedlings sprouting from the needle-strewn forest floor.

Then all turned to black as she rolled into a landscape of charred trunks, bark burned away to the skeletons beneath. The bare soil, layered with grey ash, was littered with crispy logs and fallen branches. A jolt of unease turned her guts to stone.

She remembered news reports from last summer about two of the largest wildfires in Colorado history—one of which raged not far outside Meadbury—but hadn't put two and two together. She drove in tense silence, as if through a graveyard, until a half-mile or so later the green forest cheerily came back to life, like the return of spring after a long hard winter.

Another few hundred yards, and then a wooden sign on the side of the road:

SILVERCLEFT
EST - 1859
ELEV - 8463
POP – 34

Off to her right, several slab-wood shacks so crooked

and collapsing they might've dated back to the gold rush. If it weren't for the woodsmoke pumping from a few of the stovepipes, along with cordwood stacked on porches and dirty pickups in driveways, she might have guessed she was in a ghost town.

To her left, a two-story log building, its windows dark, a boardwalk out front. Its lot empty, she swung in, parked, and grabbed her phone to check the directions. The Evite, however, wouldn't load. No reception, of course.

Orna chewed her lip, annoyed at herself for not writing down the address. She turned off the ignition and got out of the car, reaching in her pocket for the fob to lock it, out of habit. Grey woodsmoke hung in the unseasonably warm evening air, prickling her nostrils as she walked behind the inn, sun below the pines, clouds like cobwebs on fire.

Skirting a huge heap of cordwood partly covered by a tarp, she wandered into a small grassy clearing at the edge of a grove of leafless aspen, everything smelling like fresh sap. She spent the next few minutes holding her phone over her head at different angles and pacing around. Shadows pooled under the slender, chalky trunks where black eyes stared out from old branch scars, but she couldn't summon a single bar. A few names and dates had been carved into the bark, like BRODIE 2011, ZACK + LIZ 4EVA inside a heart, and FUCK THE T.

On her way back to the dark parking lot, she pictured herself at her condo watching something funny on Netflix. Relief washed over her and then a pang of guilt, as that's what she'd done nearly every frigging night for the past year and a half. If she couldn't find the bonfire, fine, but first she'd drive down the road a bit. Then, and only then, could she head home without feeling like a failure.

A car door slammed. At the edge of the lot, a long silhouette in a what looked like a cape gliding towards her from a pickup truck that hadn't been there before. Body tensing, Orna picked up her pace to close the distance to her car, but the door was locked. The figure slowly approached her, scuffing the heel of its boot as it got closer. She refused to make eye contact. All she could picture was Leatherface.

She snagged the keys from her pocket and pushed the button on the fob. No beep. Over and over she thumbed it, but the battery was dead. Blood rushing in her ears, Orna stuck her housekey between two knuckles and whirled around to face her attacker.

"Here for the bonfire?" A reedy, seemingly male voice from the tall lean figure. Though he stood maybe ten feet away, she couldn't quite make out his features.

"How'd you know?" she croaked, throat dry, key-hand shaking.

He chuckled in the darkness. "The Subaru. I'm Rowan, with the Tenders."

Remembering his name from the Evite, she sighed in relief. She wasn't going to be dismembered after all. "Oh, hi, I'm Orna. Where is this place?" She put the keys back in her pocket.

"Charwood's not far down the road, but people get lost. Good thing I did one last sweep, eh?"

"So, you guys do climate stuff?" she asked.

He scuffed his feet on the gravel. "Like they say, renewables are the future."

"You make solar panels or—?"

"We're late, so I'll fill you in at the bonfire. Sound good?"

Seemed legit. Still, Orna wasn't about to drive off

into the night with a stranger whose face she hadn't even seen. She slid her phone out of her back pocket. "What's this building, here?" she asked, swiping the screen to glowing life.

"Silvercleft Inn," he mumbled.

"Is it open?" She pushed the flashlight icon and shone the beam in Rowan's face. He squinted and held up a hand, but she saw what she needed to. Narrow face with pointy nose and bushy beard, thinning hair in a ponytail, checkered flannel and jeans under some sort of hobbit-cloak costume. Late thirties, maybe early forties. Not her cup of tea, exactly, but probably halfway cute if he cleaned up a bit.

"Sorry," she laughed, as if it had been an accident, and switched off the light. "All right. Guess you'll lead the way?" "Yep, it's not far!" He turned on his heels and waltzed off into the gloom.

Ducking back into her car, instead of the nervous wreck Orna thought she'd be, she was actually excited. Rowan seemed nice, and hopefully his friends would be, too. His pickup pulled ahead into the forest, splitting the dark with its headlights, and she followed close behind. If only she could keep it together, maybe she'd finally find a place she belonged.

CHAPTER 2

Leaving the inn behind, Orna drove past ten or so small cabins to either side of the unlit dirt road. While half of the chimneys billowed smoke, faint light seeping through drawn shades, the other half looked abandoned.

Right before the road plunged back into forest, the Subaru's headlights swept across a boxy plank building like a child's treehouse fallen to the ground, a sign for SILVERCLEFT STORE over the door. More primitive than quaint, the village felt like a desperate—and failed—attempt to a hack a bit of civilization out of the wild.

After a quarter mile of potholed road cutting through pitch black woods, Rowan's brake lights flashed red, and his pickup turned into a driveway. As Orna followed, the tops of tall conifers met overhead for roughly a football field until they opened into a few acres of tallgrass meadow, in the middle of which raged a massive bonfire. A dozen or so people stood in clumps around the dancing orange flames. She smiled. No crazy rager here, thankfully, just a mellow get-together in the woods. She could totally handle this.

Six vehicles—mostly pickups and a motorcycle—were parked in the dirt driveway ending at a sprawling two-story lodge with houselights off at the fringe of the forest, trees brushing up against one whole side and what had to have been two years' worth of cordwood piled on the porch. Charwood.

Rowan stopped his pickup behind a dusty blue Prius, and Orna pulled in a car's length behind. After she killed the engine, but before her headlights dimmed, a pair of yellow eyes glowed from the bed of Rowan's truck. She froze, skin tingling. Then Rowan opened the tailgate, and a big shaggy dog with pointy ears leapt down. She could barely see in the dimness, but it had a bunch of bald patches across its back and legs, like a bad case of mange.

She undid her seatbelt, wondering for the first time whether going to a backwoods party thrown by a bunch of strangers was such a good idea. *C'mon Orna, that's your anxiety again,* she thought. *All you gotta do is stay cool and make small talk for an hour or two.* Then she could go home, having taken a major step back to normal.

She zipped her fleece, took a deep breath, and flung open the door. Despite being full dark, the air was almost balmy and smelled smoky. *Let's do this!*

Rowan was waiting for her in his silly cloak at the edge of the driveway, bouncing on his heels like a schoolboy eager for the recess bell, holding some sort of straw mask shaped like a triangle. The dog, an old black German Shepherd without a collar, stood in front of his human the way Orna once saw a mother moose do with her calf.

"This is Lottie, my rescue." Rowan patted the animal's neck. "Might not win any beauty contests, but she's got a heart of gold."

Orna offered the dog her hand to sniff. "Hey there, puppy." But the dog didn't budge.

"C'mon, let's head over to the party." Rowan led the way across the crunchy, knee-high meadow grass, Lottie keeping to his heels, Orna a few steps behind, into a scene straight out of her University of Vermont days. Folks standing around a fire or sitting on logs, plastic cups in hand for the keg of beer, a half-dozen lit jack-o-lanterns with slit eyes, pinprick nostrils, and a crude line for a mouth guttering on the ground.

Closer to the giant blaze, the grass trampled and thinner, Orna got her first good glimpse of Lottie. Her breath caught. Other than the missing patches on the dog's body, something was wrong with the poor thing's face. Blotches of pink skin instead of black fur, like someone had splashed her with acid.

Orna shuddered. Who would do something like that to a dog? And what a good guy Rowan was to adopt her. Rowan brought Orna over to the bonfire, and Lottie lay down in the grass not far away. "Let me introduce you to my friends," he said.

A skinny someone swayed by the flames in a floppy hemp hat, ash-smeared sweater, and long skirt, a fat, stinky joint burning between thin fingers. Rowan tapped their shoulder and they turned around. Like the jack-o-lanterns, the triangle mask had tiny slits for eyes, dots for nostrils, and a crooked gash mouth, all woven out of dead pine needles like a Native American basket.

"Isabel," Rowan said, "meet Orna."

Isabel stopped swaying and stared at Orna through the weird, unsettling mask.

Rowan cleared his throat. "Say hi, Isabel," he said, as if to a child.

Isabel lifted the mask, and she was beautiful. Her face angular as if chiseled from stone, a hard-to-place mix of backgrounds that might've included Middle Eastern, African, and/or Asian descent. Orna had a glimpse of the twentysomething as Eve, the first woman—that is, if Eve had been a stoner with bloodshot, far away eyes.

"Hi, Isabel," the young woman deadpanned in a smoker's voice. Then slipped her mask back on, faced the fire, and started swaying again.

"Always a kidder." Rowan chuckled and led Orna to a short, muscular man with a shaved head in hoodie and jeans sitting by himself on a log staring into his cup, mask beside him. Nearby, a giant heap of branches, blackened like the trees she saw in the burn on the drive up.

"This is Silvio, our newest Tender," Rowan said.

Silvio had a perfect smile, the irises of his eyes the same shade of caramel as his smooth skin.

"Nice to meet you," was all Orna could say before Rowan took her by the elbow—the man smelled of sweat but not in a bad way—to a cluster of blue-collar types at the edge of the gathering.

Five middle-aged "good old boys" in work clothes and boots, and one wiry, grey-haired woman probably in her seventies, stood there grimly, cupless and without costumes. Rowan introduced them as "some folks from town," and that was it before spiriting her off to a pair of triangle-masked men—one wearing it backwards—by the fire.

"That's Ray." Rowan pointed to the guy with his mask on the right way, a thick-necked, burly bruiser of medium height in a scuffed leather jacket, jeans splotched with grease, and black boots. He turned towards her, cigarette burning from the mouth slit of his mask—a dumb thing to do since it was made of kindling.

"Hi," Ray said in a quiet voice, waving a massive and horribly scarred hand, like he'd gotten it caught in a meat grinder.

"Nice to meet you," Orna said.

The slightly built kid with his mask on backwards looked to be in his late teens, messy dirty blond curls falling over big ears to frame a chubby baby face, peach fuzz on his chin. He was dressed in a colorful Baja hoodie, surfer shorts, and sandals.

"Yo, I'm Dougie," he said with a grin and gave Orna one of those "cool guy" handshakes she could never quite pull off.

"I'll get you a drink," Rowan said, leaving her with the strangers, Lottie shadowing him as he went for the keg. Orna smiled awkwardly and toed the grass, not sure how to break the ice—it'd been that long since she'd talked to new people. She hoped she could keep everyone's names straight.

Thankfully, Dougie was friendly as all get out. "Where you from, girl?"

"Vermont, originally. Now I'm in Meadbury."

Dougie's face lit up. "No way! I go to the college!" Followed by a shrug and sheepish grin. "Well, used to." He shared a story about a party-turned-riot he threw last spring with his fellow frat brothers that was broken up by cops and got them all expelled.

Silly as Dougie seemed, there was something about his lack of self-consciousness she liked. Not romantically, of course—he was just a kid—but maybe a good sidekick?

Rowan came back with two plastic cups and handed one to Orna, which she feared was some Coors Light swill she'd have to pretend to drink. Instead, to her pleasant surprise, it was a thick, smoky stout, the perfect choice for a fall night, even if such a warm one.

Silvio joined them, and they chatted about Colorado living, mostly the legal weed, the influx of "transplants," and the high rent.

A few minutes later, Ray took off his mask. The man had widely spaced bloodshot eyes on a round, crewcut head, a broad flat nose, and a gap between his front teeth whenever he grinned, which was often. He didn't have much to say, just a few monosyllabic words here and there in a low voice. Every few minutes he stepped away to toss armloads of branches into the already gigantic bonfire. Meanwhile, Silvio kept eyeing her, and though she wasn't quite ready for dating yet, she couldn't say she minded the attention.

"I gotta know," Orna finally said. "What's up with the masks?"

"Isabel likes her arts and crafts." Rowan jerked his head towards the young woman rocking back and forth by the fire, puffing on yet another joint.

"But what are they?" Orna asked.

Rowan smiled. "You'll have to ask her."

"How about yours?" Dougie asked. "What are you supposed to be?"

"The golem," she said, earning blank stares from Silvio and Dougie. "An old Jewish legend about a clay monster brought to life by a rabbi to protect his people."

"The hell does *that* mean?" Dougie squinted, pointing at her forehead.

"*Emet*." She swiped away a frizzy curl, leaving her fingers sticky white from the makeup. "It means truth in Hebrew, and it's how the rabbi wakes the thing up."

"And when he wants it dead," Rowan said, "he erases the first letter to spell the word, *met*, or death."

Though Orna had turned her back on the Orthodox faith she was raised in almost a decade before, she was still impressed. "You're Jewish?"

"No." Rowan shook his head and cracked a goofy smile full of bright white slightly crooked teeth. "I just appreciate the culture. All the hardship you put up with and made it through."

"But you speak Hebrew?"

He shrugged. "A few words here and—"

"I'm Jewish," Silvio blurted.

"You are?" Orna said doubtfully, regretting the words as soon as they left her mouth.

Silvio nodded and shrugged one broad shoulder. "Well, not practicing. But my folks are Sephardim. From Syria."

"I know Sephardim," Orna said quickly, glad her golem makeup covered what was almost certainly blushing cheeks. Originally from Spain and kicked out around the fifteen century, Sephardic Jews spread out across Europe, the Middle East, and Africa. While not what most people thought of when picturing a Jew—Orna included, to her embarrassment—they were every bit as legit as Ashkenazis. Often more so.

Eventually, they asked Orna what she did for work, and she told them about freelancing for a dozen local media outlets. She left out the fact that she had to write at least three articles a day, every day, to *barely* pay her bills, student loan debts hanging over her head the whole time.

"You're not gonna do an exposé on us, are you?" Dougie joked.

"Nah, tonight's off the record," Orna said, and everyone laughed like it was the funniest thing ever. Overall, she felt relaxed and was close to actually enjoying herself. It had been the right choice to come, after all.

"When do we get into the climate action part?"

"You're looking at it," Dougie gestured towards the fire into which Ray had just heaved a hefty branch.

Orna gazed at the crackling flames, no clue what he was talking about.

"We're renewable energy advocates," Rowan said

brightly. "Bioenergy, in particular."

The term rang a bell. "Like ethanol?"

"Our focus is woody biomass." Rowan beamed, blue eyes shining. "For electricity."

She remembered that her hometown of Burlington, Vermont had one of those biomass plants tucked away on the industrial side of town by the railroad tracks. Some ugly factory with a smokestack and piles of woodchips out back.

"But don't trees store carbon?" she asked, going back to her eighth grade Earth Science class.

"Yes, they do!" Rowan said. "That's why we only use waste wood from unhealthy forests at risk of wildfire."

Sipping her beer, Orna took in the dark woods hemming them in at the edge of the meadow. Burning trees wasn't something she would've thought of as "clean energy," but Colorado certainly had plenty of trees. And if it was true they were all going to catch fire anyway, she supposed they might as well get something out of them first. Still, it felt so...backwards.

"Fitted with state-of-the-art pollution control technology, of course," Rowan added, as if reading her mind.

She shrugged. New to all this stuff, she was there to learn. Any drawbacks aside, biomass had to be better than fossil fuels.

Before she knew it, she finished her beer, and Rowan took her cup to fill it at the keg and bring it back again. A warm rush as she realized she'd made it close to an hour without feeling anxious. Was she finally over all that nonsense?

And, of course, that was the moment Dougie chose to make his announcement. "So glad to see everyone!" he called out to the group, all of whom turned to face the fire, townies included. "Tonight is a special night for two reasons. One," Dougie held up a finger, "it's frickin' Halloween!"

Whistles and claps from Rowan, Silvio, Isabel, and Ray, which Orna joined in on. A rude silence from the townies. If they were such party poopers, why hadn't they stayed home?

"Bonfires like this go way back," Dougie went on, "where our ancestors burned wood in hopes that the old gods would bring back the spring."

Ray picked up a thick branch from the pile and chucked it into the fire, sparks floating overhead like fireflies. Rowan and company cheered again.

"And two," Dougie made the peace sign as everyone quieted down, "we've got ourselves a guest."

Oh no. Oh no. Orna's cheeks were hot but not from the fire.

"As is the Charwood tradition," Dougie went on, "we'd like to ask Orna to say a few words."

Frozen stiff, she was barely able to shake her head. A welcome, fine, but a speech? No way.

Rowan took her hand. "Just something about why you're here," he whispered, breath minty. Unable to think of a good excuse, Orna let him lead her in front of the fire, where he left her alone.

Beer hand shaking, she peered out uneasily at the dozen or so strangers, no idea what she was supposed to say. Then a flash of anger—at herself. What was she so scared about? It wasn't like she had to impress any of these people. Heck, she'd never even have to see them again if she didn't want to. Enough was enough, already, this anxiety crap was getting boring. Plus, the beer buzz could only help.

"I don't know a ton about climate change," she

called out, surprised by how well her voice carried in the dry air. "But one thing I do know is, if we don't so something soon, all the progress we've made in the world won't amount to a hill of beans." Orna wasn't sure where the phrase "hill of beans" came from, but Rowan gave her a thumbs up, and Dougie hooted and hollered like he was watching his favorite jam band.

Unsure what else to say, she blurted the next thing that came to mind. "If the pandemic's taught us anything, it's that if we mess with nature, it'll come back to bite us. Our choices have consequences, and we can't keep ignoring the harm of fossil fuels."

Rowan nodded enthusiastically and spun his finger in a "keep going" gesture.

"That's why what you all are doing is so important." Sweat trickling down her ribs, bonfire roasting her backside, she kept going. "As I see it, we've got two choices." She held up her pointer finger like Dougie had done. "One, we move forward with renewable energy and save the world." Then her middle finger. "Or two, we don't, and end life as we know it."

Loud applause from all the Tenders, Isabel and Ray included, the latter of whom turned towards the townies until they started clapping as well.

Orna curtsied and left the "stage" to plop down on a log, proud of herself for the first time in a long time. Not only had she left the condo, she'd made an impromptu speech in front of an audience!

Rowan sat next to her, Lottie standing an arm's length away, runny eyes on her master. "Have you done this before?" Rowan's brow crinkled, which she could see in the firelight was wild with long, crazy strands.

Her heart sank. "Was I that bad?"

"You're a goddamn natural!"

Surely, he was exaggerating. "I don't even know what I'm talking about."

"Yeah, you do. But most important, it came from the gut." He smacked his own belly through the cloak.

Without saying goodbye to anyone, the townies stalked off through the meadow towards their pickups. Lottie got up from her spot in the grass to watch them go.

Orna laughed to hide the hurt. "Looks like I chased them away."

"Nah." Rowan waved a hand. "Mountain folk are early risers."

"You really think I did okay?" She wasn't usually big on compliments but somehow wanted praise from this man she barely knew.

"More than okay." He met her eyes, the firelight glinting off his very blue ones. "Would you be open to more of this?"

"Of what?"

"Spokesperson. Paid, naturally."

"You're joking, right?"

Face grave, Rowan shook his head. "Public speaking, lobbying politicians, that sort of thing. We've been looking for the right person forever."

"Isn't that what you are?"

"I freeze up around strangers." He looked down into his cup and let out a breath. "As in, freak the fuck out."

"You get panic attacks, too?"

Frowning, he nodded. "Bad."

"But you're talking to me just fine."

Rowan leaned in and whispered, beard brushing her ear, "Because I felt like I knew you right away."

Heart aflutter, she sipped her half-empty beer.

Flattered as she was, none of it made any sense. "What about everyone else?"

He held up a large sooty palm. "Don't get me wrong, they're all great at what they do. Just not outreach."

"I've got a job."

"This'll be steady. And pay more."

"How do you know how much I—" Orna flinched as a chunk of wood popped in the bonfire.

"A grand a week. How does that sound?"

A longer swig of beer. Obviously, it sounded amazing but was too good to be true. "Where do you get that kind of money?"

"Environmental foundations are tripping over themselves to fund anything renewable," Rowan shrugged. "We just got a grant for thirty-K."

"That's amazing!"

"It would be, but it's earmarked for public and legislative outreach. So, if we don't find someone to fill the position, we'll have to send it back."

Maaaaybe, she could see herself handing out brochures or getting signatures for a petition. But spokesperson? "Much as I appreciate the offer, I can't."

Rowan raised his eyebrows. "Will you at least think about it?"

She already had. "Sorry, it's not for me." It came out snippier than she intended.

Rowan's face went slack, and he slumped on the log. "Okay. No big deal," he said flatly and waved the dog over. "Lottie, come." The dog joined her master by his side. "Now, stay."

Leaving his beer and mask, he got up without another word and moped over to Dougie and Ray standing by the fire. Lottie stayed put, watching Rowan as he slid his arm around Dougie's shoulders, and the two men walked off across the meadow towards the lodge.

Irritated, Orna sucked down more beer. "Typical dude, eh, Lottie? All smiles when he wants something from you, and when he doesn't get it—"

Lottie swung her ugly mug towards Orna, a startling awareness in the ancient pup's eyes. Come to think of it, Orna hadn't once seen the animal bark, wag her tail, or do anything else, well, doglike. Sadly, the abuse from her former owners must've triggered a kind of canine PTSD. She related.

Maybe ten minutes passed, Silvio, Ray, Isabel huddling together on the far side of the fire, Lottie stinking up the fresh mountain air with her farts. Orna ground her molars. If this was how they treated people who wanted to help, who needed them? She guzzled the rest of her stout, threw down her cup, and got to her feet.

Lottie growled, the dog's black lips curling back to a mouthful of jagged yellow teeth.

"Easy, girl." Heart pounding, Orna scanned the meadow for Rowan, still nowhere to be found. Afraid of being chomped, Orna dropped her butt back on the log, and Lottie stopped growling.

She thought about calling the other Tenders over, but they were gone now, too. Searching the ground, she snatched up a stick and waved it at the dog. "Wanna play fetch?" Orna flung it into the dark. "Go get it!"

Lottie's intelligent eyes never left hers. "You'd think a mutt like you would have some retriever in you," Orna grumbled.

Just when she was about to shout for help, Rowan came loping across the meadow from the lodge, acoustic guitar strapped over a shoulder. He walked up to her with a shit-eating grin and strummed an out-of-tune chord. "Now the party's really about to start!"

"Your dog growled at me!" she snapped.

His smile didn't budge. "Oh, she just doesn't like being left alone. Do ya, Lot?" He patted Lottie on the head, and had it been possible for a dog, Orna would've sworn the German Shepherd shot him a sullen glare.

"It's late." Orna knew she was pouting but didn't care. Whether or not Lottie would've actually bitten her, she'd been really scared.

Rowan laughed. "What? It's barely nine. This is Dougie's big night, you know."

"His birthday?" she muttered. The kid *had* been nothing but nice to her.

Rowan nodded.

"Fine." Softie that she was, she picked up her cup. "One more drink."

Rowan let out a Homer Simpson "Woo-hoo!" and held out a hand. Still mad at him, Orna took it. He pulled her to her feet, and they joined the rest of the Tenders who'd come back to the fire, Lottie curling up on the warm ground a bit too close to the flames.

Dougie, holding a bottle of Wild Turkey, sat at the edge of one of the logs wearing a wreath of blue spruce sprigs around his head like a halo.

"Nice party hat!" Orna yelled over to him as she filled her cup from the keg. "How old are you, man?"

"Almost twenty," Dougie said, and took a long pull from the bottle.

"Well, happy almost-birthday." She raised her cup, and they both took a drink.

As Rowan tuned his guitar, Orna took a seat next to Dougie, and Silvio joined them on her other side. Ray— his mask back on—and Isabel stayed by the fire taking turns feeding it wood. Rowan ran through some classic rock songs including The Beatles, Zeppelin, and The Who, in a high, halfway decent voice, only flubbing a few chords here and there.

Silvio kept smiling at her while Dougie drained his bottle, to the point where Orna felt like she should tell the kid to slow down but didn't.

It was getting late, yet every time she was about to go, Rowan toasted the birthday boy again. Having actual fun with people for the first time in over a year, Orna couldn't help but join in on the chorus to "Rocky Mountain High."

Then, in the middle of a Grateful Dead song, Rowan snapped a string, and Orna took that as a sign to call it a night. Except when she stood up, she was woozy and had to steady herself. While not a large woman, she was hardly petite, which meant two and a half beers should only mean a decent buzz. So why did she feel so wasted?

She went over to the keg, knelt down, and in the flickering light of the bonfire squinted at the label. No ordinary stout, this was an imperial with an ABV of 12.5 percent. Which basically meant she downed a six pack.

"I can't drive like this," she slurred more to herself than anyone.

"Plenty of room at Charwood," Rowan said.

A bed would be nice, but even though Orna didn't get bad vibes from anyone other than the dog, she didn't know them well enough to sleep inside. Luckily, she always kept her camping gear in the back of her Forester. Warm as it was, it would make a nice night out. "Cool if I set up my tent?"

"Anywhere you want!" Rowan said.

"Sweet, thanks." She stumbled off across the meadow

towards her car, and then shouted out, "See you guys in the morning!"

Everyone waved back. Could this be her new group of friends? She smiled all the way to the Subaru, where an old, beat-up black motorcycle—TRIUMPH in white letters on the gas tank—had wedged itself between the front of her car and the tailgate of Rowan's pickup. Her Forester had probably been blocking one of the townies from getting out and Ray—who else's could it be?—must've moved it there.

Even with her headlamp, it took about fifteen minutes of fumbling to set up the one-person tent at the far end of the meadow by the woods. One by one, the Tenders went inside, leaving the bonfire going strong on its own—only Lottie out there snoozing by the flames—all the jack-o-lanterns dead. But finally, the tent was up, and Orna unrolled her sleeping bag and blew up her pad. Too tired to wipe off her makeup, she zipped the doorflap, stripped down to bra and panties, slid into the warm bag, and laid her head on her little camping pillow. *Mmmm, cozy.*

Just as she started to drift off, crunching footsteps in the dry grass coming her way.

"Knock, knock." It sounded like Ray.

She sat up straight in her bag, mouth sour. Her drunk fading, she wasn't feeling so bold anymore, and wished she'd chosen to sleep in the car. What if he tried something?

"Will you move your car?" Ray asked in his quiet, dopey voice. "Need my bike."

See? Everything's cool. "Yeah, shoot, sorry about that." She unzipped her bag.

"Need my bike," he repeated.

"Of course." As she put on her clothes and donned

the headlamp, she wondered why he couldn't move his motorcycle himself. But by the time she poked her head out of the flap to ask, he was gone, the unattended bonfire shrunk down to half its size.

The night air mild as midsummer, she trudged over to the driveway, tripping here and there on grass clumps. She got in her car, pushed the ignition, shifted gears, and toed the gas. The vehicle revved but didn't move. Because she was in neutral.

Laughing at her buzzed self, she put it in reverse and pushed the pedal. The car rolled backwards and then bucked as the rear tire ran over something. Orna stomped the brake, her stomach a squirming bucket of worms.

Someone yelled.

CHAPTER 3

Orna slammed the gearshift into park and shut off the engine.

Please, let it be the dog. Please, please, let it be the dog.

Adrenalin cutting through the alcohol, she sat there in shock, hands frozen to the steering wheel, knowing life might not be the same when she opened that door. A wild impulse to drive off into the night, stop at the condo for supplies, and head straight for Mexico. But that was just a fantasy.

Lottie was the first thing she saw when she stepped outside, and how Orna burned with hatred for that big dumb animal standing a few feet away, safe and sound. Ray knelt by the rear tire, tending to something in the shadows. Except for the distant crackle of the bonfire, the night was silent.

Oh my God.

Numb, like she wasn't in control of her body, Orna stumbled over to see how bad it was. Before she could get a good look, Ray took her firmly by the shoulders—she struggled, but he was too strong—and turned her around. But not before she saw a pair of bare calves and feet in sandals sticking out from under the car. Dougie.

"Is he alive?" Orna cried as Ray escorted her across the meadow, legs rubber. While this was no panic attack, it felt like someone had kicked her straight in the gut.

"Shhhh," Ray said.

Silvio jogged over and met them halfway across the sea of grass. "What the hell happened?"

"Dougie got hit by her car. Take her to her tent." Ray let go of her and went back towards the driveway.

Silvio propped her up as they slogged across the field. Maybe it was a nightmare. It *had* to be a nightmare. Just outside her tent, Orna fell to her knees and puked.

Nope. This was really happening. She'd run over someone with her car. She heaved until nothing was left. Then kept gagging, as if her belly wanted to get rid of whatever made it hurt so badly.

Silvio helped her take off her sneakers, and Orna unzipped the doorflap. She crawled inside and curled up in the fetal position on her sleeping bag, warm tears streaming down her cheeks.

"I'm a murderer." She tore off her headlamp and flung it against the tent wall, where it landed face down. "A fucking *murderer*."

"No, you're not." Silvio's voice from outside the tent was calm, soothing. "It was an accident, right? He may still be fine."

She shut her eyes tight, wishing she could disappear. Of all the people in the world, why did this have to happen to *her*?

A few minutes later, footsteps in the grass. Ray muttered something, and then Silvio's soft reply followed by someone running off.

Heavy breathing from the open flap.

"Please say he's okay," Orna whimpered.

A pause that felt like an eternity, until Ray said, "Not your fault."

"Ambulance?" Her throat was so clogged with snot she could barely get out the words.

"Too late."

Dead. He was *dead*! She shook with sobs. "I'msosorry. I'msosorry. I'msosorry."

"He was black out drunk."

"Doesn't matter," she whined. "I still did it."

"It is okay."

"They're gonna arrest me and take me to jail." Orna hated that she was so focused on herself but couldn't help it. She pictured her father weeping into his hands when he heard the news; she was almost thankful her mother wasn't alive for this.

"No, they will not," Ray said softly. "I did it."

"What do you mean?" She opened her eyes and rubbed away the tears, Ray's silhouette blurry against the night. "Did what?"

"We will say it was me."

She got to her knees. "What are you talking about?"

"We need help." Ray was a broad shadow, his face little more than an ink blot. "I take the blame, you take the job."

"What job?" Orna's mind was reeling. None of this made any sense. *Wait.* "The spokesperson thing?"

"Yes."

"That's crazy!" But a part of her wouldn't let it go. "For how long?"

"One year."

On one hand, a year at a job was forever, especially one she didn't have the skills for. On the other, how many years of jail would she get for turning herself in?

"What about his family?"

"We are it. No one else."

"But..."

"It is not like we can bring him back," Ray said. "No

need for your life to end, too."

Orna rubbed her eyes. "I don't get it. Why do you even want me?"

"Rowan needs you. We all do. For the cause."

Guilt a hot coal in her chest, she couldn't believe she was even thinking about going along with this. But Ray was giving her a way out, and she'd have to be stupid to refuse, right? Her usually sharp brain felt like mush, and she simply didn't know the answer.

"So, we keep this a secret?" she peeped.

"Yes."

"And Dougie?"

"I will make the phone call."

Orna wasn't sure what, if anything, put her over the top. But she heard herself saying, "Okay."

"Thank you," Ray said and set off like a dark ship sailing off into the darker night. "You get some sleep."

Incredibly, despite all the stress—or maybe because of it—she found herself exhausted and lay down. Before long, she felt herself fading.

Orna jolted up from a dream where she'd been tossing a stick for a dog, who kept bringing it back to her. Except it wasn't a stick but a long white bone.

Head swimmy, she couldn't figure out why her mattress felt so thin. Then it all rushed back—where she was, what she did—and the weight of the world crashed down on her.

Hunched up in a ball, stuck in her own personal hell, a voice called from far away. And then a second time.

She unzipped the tent and poked her head out into the warm, dark night. No one there, the bonfire smoldering ashes, a three-quarters moon hanging over the lip of the forest like a smudged thumbprint. Still a tiny bit drunk, she must've imagined the voice.

It came again, some sort of atonal singing from the forest. *What in the world...* And then it hit her. A memorial service for Dougie. A kid whose last name she didn't even know. All at once, she needed to be there, to tell everyone what really happened.

She slipped her headlamp on, jammed feet into sneakers, and set off straight into the pines towards the singing...or was it chanting? Though she didn't know the area, she couldn't get lost so long as she kept the voice in earshot.

Orna hadn't gone far under the trees when, out of the corner of an eye, motion. Something dangling from a low branch. Curious, she got closer. A tiny stick doll about six inches from head to toe, face made of a pinecone scale, two evergreen sprigs sprouting from its shoulders like wings. It reminded her of a Christmas ornament. As she headed deeper into the forest, a few more of the dolls hanging from branches, and then dozens. A little weird, but all that mattered was finding the gathering. She cocked an ear, yet there was only silence. And then a stick cracked. And footsteps.

"Who's there?" she called out.

The footsteps came quicker, closer.

Alarm bells ringing in her head, Orna whirled and ran back the way she came. She didn't know what she was afraid of, but every shred of her being told her to get out of there. Thank God for the moon lighting the meadow and guiding her out of the trees.

Still in flight mode, she headed straight to the tent and inside, sneakers and all, zipped it up, swatted off her headlamp, and huddled in the darkness. She held her breath, listening. Nothing. Whatever it was—probably some harmless critter like a chipmunk—had stayed in the woods.

The impulse to confess her crime no longer as strong, all she wanted to do was hide for a while in sleep. She'd deal with things in the morning. Wriggling into her sleeping bag, she forced her eyes shut. But all she could see was poor Dougie's body splayed out under her car.

She kept awake for maybe another hour, tossing and turning on her thin pad, knowing she deserved every minute of suffering. Until, finally, the kinder part of her mind had mercy on her and released her into slumber.

CHAPTER 4

Orna peeled open gummy eyes with a groan. The morning sun lit the tent like a lantern. Head pounding, throat dry, the bitter taste of ashes in her mouth, the last thing she wanted to do was face her first day as a taker of human life, but the longer she put things off, the worse they'd get. Nothing to do but head straight to the police—county sheriff, probably—and turn herself in. She tore herself out of the sleeping bag like a gooey caterpillar too soon from its pupa.

Wasting no time, she unscrewed the valve on her pad, pushed out the air, rolled it up, and crammed it in her pack with her sleeping bag. Unzipped the flap and stuck her head out into the toasty morning air, meadow glowing yellow as the African savannah and smelling faintly of straw and soil.

Ray's motorcycle was gone from the driveway, which meant he was probably already at the sheriff's— maybe even sitting in jail. She assumed Dougie's body had been taken away in the middle of the night either by ambulance or hearse. The only other vehicles were Rowan's pickup, Silvio's Prius, and her Subaru. The murder weapon.

"Shut up," she barked at herself as she heaved her pack outside and scrambled from the tent. Freak accidents were a dime a dozen: lightning strikes, construction cranes falling, bathtub drownings. Dougie's death, while a horrible tragedy, was just a fluke where she happened to be in the wrong place at the wrong time. Dougie more so, obviously.

She knelt down to yank a tentpole from its loop and had to shut her eyes against the dizziness. As she unhooked the other pole, a bird's harsh cackle from the lodge, making her headache worse. She collapsed the poles, rolled them sloppily in the tent and rainfly, and jammed it all into the stuff sack.

The raspy squawk kept up as she cut through the meadow to the driveway. On Charwood's porch a large bird with black head, white belly, and long black tailfeathers perched atop a stack of cordwood cawing its head off. A magpie, she was pretty sure. Except this one looked sick, its body splotchy with crusted sores, tailfeathers chewed up or missing, like someone had started plucking it but gave up halfway. Its sharp black beak opened and closed as it let out a grating call.

Orna's stomach swirled. She bent over to dry heave but couldn't bring anything up. Wiping her mouth with the sleeve of her fleece, she made a beeline for her car, the magpie still squawking. A deal was a deal, but right now, all she wanted was to go home.

Her whole body tensed as she closed in on the Subaru, bracing herself for the sight of blood, gore, chunks of brain. But no, her rear tire had been scrubbed, the dirt swept clean all around. Grateful for everything Ray had done for her, it was time to pay the piper. She opened the hatch and tossed in her pack.

Just as she slammed it shut, the lodge's front door swung open, and Rowan stepped outside. She ground her teeth in dismay—she'd been so close to skipping out without talking to anyone.

Wearing the same red-and-black checkered flannel from yesterday over a pair of jeans, Rowan walked over, reaching out his long arms for a hug. She let it happen and was surprised how nice it felt to be held. She choked back a sob.

"You okay?" He held her shoulders at arm's length, sad eyes blue as the morning sky.

"I'm fine. I just can't believe it." She swallowed the lump in her throat, the horrible bird still squawking. "Seemed like such a good kid."

"He was. But accidents happen." He frowned and let his hands drop to his thighs. "Ray is in pieces about the whole thing."

"About that…" Orna took a deep breath. *Here goes nothing.*

"The dummy shouldn't have been in such a hurry to move your car." He shook his head.

"Has he been charged with anything?" Why was she beating around the bush? *Come out and say it, already!*

"I'm about to head down to the station to find out," Rowan said. "Believe it or not, the guy's got a spotless record, so there's a good chance it'll turn out okay."

"There's something I need to tell you," she blurted and then couldn't find the words.

"I already know." Rowan smiled, taking her hand and squeezing. "And you have no idea how happy we are to have you on board as an official Tender. It would've meant a whole lot to Dougie." Then he turned, walked over to his pickup, and got in.

"Rowan, wait!" Orna said just as he was about to close the door, and then fell silent. If Ray was going to get off anyway, how would turning herself in make things any better? Not only would she be charged with lying on top of everything else, she might be putting Ray in deeper water than he already was. "I'm so sorry."

He shook his head, ponytail bobbing. "Nothing to be sorry about."

Orna felt like puking but from somewhere deeper than her stomach. "There going to be a service or anything?"

"We had a small one last night while you were sleeping."

So Orna had been right about hearing voices in the woods. Maybe it was a good thing she hadn't found them; it would've been impossible not to confess.

"I'll email you soon." He shut the door, started the ignition, did a three-point turn, and rattled off down the driveway.

Dazed as if from a blow to the head, Orna stood there a minute, the messed-up magpie on the wood pile giving her the side eye as if judging her. What else could she do but get in her car and head home?

CHAPTER 5

Orna rode the brake the whole way down the mountain, the road steeper and twistier than she remembered. The more she told herself the deed was done, and there was nothing else she could do, the queasier her stomach felt.

She'd never so much as cheated on a test before and now she was, what, a manslaughterer? If only she'd gone straight to police first thing in the morning, she could have already taken that first step to redemption. Unfortunately, this wasn't even something she could talk to a therapist about. No, she was going to have to carry the burden the rest of her life.

Not until the grade leveled out and dirt turned into Meadbury's paved main drag did she feel vaguely like herself again. For once she was glad for the constant stream of traffic flowing in and out of town. The familiar sights of red brick buildings, cyclists in rainbow spandex, and clumps of wandering tourists brought her halfway back to sanity. Yes, something terrible had happened up in Silvercleft, but she was on the downslope of it all—both figuratively and literally.

Her head weighed at least fifty pounds, and all she wanted to do was nap. After, she'd set the rest of the day aside for yoga and meditation. All that would give her the space she needed to put together the jumbled puzzle pieces of her mind. And hopefully make sense of her new job as spokesperson for the Tenders, something she was dreading as much as a biopsy. She'd also have to email her editors that she was taking a sabbatical from freelancing.

By the time she pulled onto her quiet, tree-lined street, her stomach was growling with hunger, a good sign her system was getting back to normal. She'd jump in the shower, heat up some leftovers, and then crash out. On to her complex's private road, past the row of narrow, cookie-cutter condos, and she was home. Except parked in her space was a yellow taxicab.

Growling in frustration, she pulled into one of the guest spots where idiots like this were supposed to park. Any other day, she'd have knocked on their window and told them to move, but she was too wiped to deal. As she strolled by the cab on the way to her unit, the passenger door opened and a shorter, bearded man in a *kippah* who looked a lot like an older version of her dad got out.

"Hello, Orna," her dad said. He was leaner with less hair on top, his once salt-and-pepper beard almost white. Not surprising, as the last time she'd seen him had been at the funeral over six years before. Since then, they'd talked on the phone maybe ten times—his old desktop computer didn't have a webcam—and sent a handful of emails back and forth. But no visits.

It wasn't that she never planned to. In fact, she'd been toying with taking a trip back to Vermont in the spring—he was her *Abba*, after all, even if she didn't call him that anymore. But she wasn't ready yet. And he couldn't have picked a worst time.

"What're you doing here?" It came out harsher than she meant.

"Took the red eye." His stern face with its high brow and narrow nose didn't twitch; like Orna, the man could handle blunt. "I wanted to see my only child."

"You could've given me a heads up." She ran a few fingers through her knotty, unbrushed hair, made worse by the fact that she still had her golem makeup on.

"Would you have let me come, if I had?" he asked.

No, she would've come up with some excuse. Which was crappy, she knew. But not as crappy as showing up out of the blue like this.

They stood in silence for several awkward seconds, avoiding eye contact. Could he tell that something was off with her? Then she sighed. He was already there. What was she going to do, send her elderly father away after coming two thousand miles to see her? No, the best thing was to power through, and in a day or two he'd be gone. "C'mon inside."

She knew she was supposed to hug him, but there was no way. Instead, she took one of his suitcases from the open trunk. Her dad leaned into the cab, thanked the driver, and fell in behind her as they went up the sidewalk to her two-story end unit.

"When did you get in?" She climbed the steps to her deck and grabbed the keys from her pocket.

"About an hour ago. The cabbie kept me company on his lunch break." On the surface, an innocent enough comment. But beneath it the obvious subtext, *Where were you?*

None of his business, but she said, "I was camping out for Halloween."

A pause. "By yourself?" Again, from anyone else, a harmless question. But from him, an accusation.

"No." If only she'd been alone last night, things would've turned out very different. But that wasn't a train of thought she was about to board right then.

She unlocked the door and stepped into her messy

living room—piles of paper scattered across the kitchen table, clothes strewn over the couch, a faint whiff of rotting compost—and wished she'd cleaned that week. When he scrunched up his nose, she almost apologized but then thought better of it. It was her place, darn it, she could leave it however she wanted. She dropped his suitcase on the carpet with a thump.

"I'll give you the tour." After they took off their shoes, Orna led her father through the open living room with its high ceiling into the roomy modern kitchen, sink piled with dishes. Next, off to the small but tidy guest room with its private bath—the cleanest part of the house since she never used it—and back to the living room. She almost took him upstairs but needed to put a few things away in her bedroom and bathroom first.

"How long you planning to stay? You're staying here, right?" Despite having done well as an elder care lawyer before retiring last year, there was no way he'd pay for a hotel if he didn't have to.

"That's up to you."

"Make yourself at home," she said as chipper as she could, knowing three days was likely the max for this rigid man who hated leaving the comfort zone of his house and close-knit orthodox Jewish community.

But something about him was different, and it wasn't just the grey beard and thinning hair. His once fierce, almost arrogant gaze had softened and turned sad. For a second, she felt sorry for this lonely widower. Until, with a surge of molten anger, she reminded herself how *he* was the one who let his wife die. That if only he'd joined Orna in demanding Eemah continue her treatments, she might've still been alive today.

"Gonna hop in the shower," Orna blurted before she said something mean and went upstairs, ignoring his confused—and was that hurt?—look.

The just-short-of-scalding water felt amazing on her skin as she washed away the stink of woodsmoke from her hair, makeup from her face, dirt and sweat from her body. She basked under the nozzle, tightly wound muscles unspooling.

As she picked up the bar of lemon soap, a big round bubble formed. When it popped, she thought of Dougie's head getting crushed under her tire, and she cried like she hadn't since her mother's death. Kneeling on the shower floor, tears and snot streamed down her face and washed into the drain.

First the panic attack at the concert over the summer, and then the tragedy at Charwood. Was this some curse that would kick in every time she tried to make friends? Had she been right to stay a shut-in the last couple of years? She kept on her knees—hating life, hating herself—until the hot water ran out.

Toweling off in the steamy bathroom, she knew the only chance she had to even come *close* to paying back what she'd done was by trying to be a good person from there on out. And what better way than making nice with her father? After all, his weakness when it came to doing the right thing about Eemah was no different than her own—and maybe *that* was the reason it bugged her so much.

After putting on a hoodie and sweatpants she went back downstairs. Her dad, lounging on the couch, snapped shut the hardcover book he was reading. Before he did, she caught the title, something *Zohaf* or *Zohan* traced in gold leaf.

"What's that?" she asked.

"Oh, nothing." He set the book face down on his lap. "Just some research."

"For what?"

He waved his hand as if fanning away a bad

smell. "Writing a book on scripture. You wouldn't be interested."

Smug as the comment was, it was true. While she honored the plight of her people over the ages, after years of forced study and prayer, Judaism bored the heck out of her. "Gonna heat up some soup."

"I trust everything is—"

"Yes, of course." While she didn't keep kosher, herself—eighteen years at home was plenty—she knew the drill. From out of the fridge, she got the glass container and set it on the counter. It took a minute to find Eemah's kosher pot in the back of the cabinet—kept around for sentimental rather than practical reasons, of course—into which she poured in the matzah ball soup. Next, she scoured the crusty burner with steel wool pad and cleanser. Setting the pot on simmer, she stood on tiptoes to grab two of Eemah's china bowls from the overhead cabinet, and from the back of the utensil drawer she fished out a pair of silver spoons and matching ladle.

Once the soup was hot, Orna ladled out generous portions into each bowl and brought them to the table. Steam rising from the fragrant soup, saliva pooling in her mouth, for the first time in years she mumbled the *bracha* along with her dad. "Baruch atah Adonai, Eloheinu Melech haolam, ha motzi lechem min ha'aretz," the English meaning, *"Blessed are You, God, our Lord, King of the universe, who brings forth bread from the earth."* Or the modern-day translation, "Rub a dub-dub, thanks for the grub."

Finally, she sliced a matzah ball in half, spooned it into her mouth, and moaned in pleasure. Three days of the dumpling soaking in broth had saturated it with salt, pepper, dill, and cumin; heavenly.

They ate quietly—only the scraping of spoons and

slurping of soup—until they both finished.

Her dad wiped his mouth with a napkin. "Just like your Eemah used to make."

Orna frowned. It still hurt to talk about her. "Hers were fluffier."

"Let's just say yours are more…" He made a fist. "Substantial."

"Yeah, as a rock."

He chuckled, and so did she, and she sat back in her chair. Maybe she'd get through the visit, after all.

"Been following some of your journalism online." He rubbed his beard and gazed at her, his eyes deep brown as melted chocolate.

"Oh." She was both flattered and a little embarrassed. Her political stuff she could see him liking, the fashion and pop culture pieces not so much.

"What are you working on now?" he asked.

She'd been kicking around a few ideas—a new music venue in Denver, a top ten list of local food carts, women in tech—but she'd have to put them on hold so she could focus on the Tenders. Dark thoughts about the accident rose up from the back of her mind, but she was able to push them down. "I've got a new job."

He raised his bushy eyebrows. "Doing what?"

"Renewable energy." She stood up and started to clear the dishes, anything to avoid talking about that place.

"And it pays…?"

"Quite well, actually." Orna darted into the kitchen and dug around in the pantry until she found an unopened container of macaroons she'd bought for some Passover seder she never went to. She put several of them on a kosher dish and brought them to the table, hoping there would be no more talk about the Tenders.

He smiled and popped one in his mouth. "Oh, I almost forgot," he said, mid-chew, then stood up and shuffled into the guest room. He came back holding a small box sloppily wrapped in green tissue paper.

"I know your birthday isn't for another few months." He sat in the chair next to her. "But I figured, why risk the mail when I can deliver it myself?"

"Thanks." He had used so much tape she had to shred the soft paper with her fingernails to get to the cardboard box. Inside that was a gorgeous rectangular slab of fine-grained wood, stained dark brown and polished to a shine.

On its face were carved ten spheres connected by a latticework—one circle on top, under that, three horizontal rows of two, then splitting that, a vertical column of three more circles. A Hebrew word was engraved in silver in the center of each sphere. She didn't know the point of the image, but it sure was beautiful.

"What is it?" she asked, touched that he'd thought of her.

"The Tree of Life."

"The tree of good and evil? From the Garden of Eden?" Squinting at it, it looked more like a canoe.

"Yes, but it's also a map of creation, showing the descent of the divine into the physical world, and how we might reconnect through prayer." He reached over and carefully picked up the slab as if it were brittle glass. "Each of these ten circles are *sephirot,* or spiritual principles. You can still read Hebrew, I assume?"

She rolled her eyes and made a gagging sound in the back of her throat.

"Just checking." He pointed to the top sphere. "What does this say?"

It read, כתר. "*Keter,*" she said.

"Which means?"

Easy-peasy. "Crown."

He nodded. "*Keter* signifies *Ein Sof Aur*, or infinite energy, the light out of which all things are created." He slid his finger one sphere down and to the right. חכמה.

"*Hokhmah*," she said proudly. "Wisdom."

He smiled. "The stage where hot masculine energy expanded into the universe."

"And this?" He pointed at the circle to the right. בינה.

"*Binah*. Understanding."

He patted her knee, which felt a bit patronizing. "The primordial feminine energy, the mother of the universe which cools *Hokhmah* and nourishes it, turning it into everything we see. In other words, the beginning of time itself."

With his fingertip he traced a triangle around the top three spheres. "These are known as the Supernal spheres, the cosmic energies of the universe. They also represent the intellect."

"Cool." Probably the only time Orna had enjoyed one of her father's lectures on Judaism. If only Hebrew school had been this magical and weird, she might still be practicing.

Then, to her surprise, he opened the box to an empty space with a dozen or so compartments of different sizes lined with blood-red felt. "For your jewelry." He held up the back of his hand, golden wedding band gleaming from his ring finger.

Instead of thanking him for the gorgeous gift, she heard herself mumble, "I don't wear jewelry." While true, she didn't know why she said it; they were both well aware she inherited all of Eemah's earrings, necklaces, bracelets, and rings.

"What, your boyfriend hasn't bought you any?"

For some reason, his joke rubbed her the wrong way. "I don't have a boyfriend." Nor had she even dated since she broke up with a teary-eyed Seth before leaving for Colorado.

"Remember Avi Shaw's son Omer from summer camp?" He drummed his fingers on the table. "He's in Denver. Very successful insurance practice."

"Yuch." The only thing Orna hated more than someone playing Jewish cupid was when that someone was her father.

"If you're thinking of having kids…" He held up his palms as if surrendering, while clearly doing no such thing. "You're not getting any younger, you know."

A hot flare in her chest, she barely stopped herself from throwing a macaroon in his bearded face. "How about *you*? You seeing anyone?"

He pressed his lips together in a thin line.

"It's been six years," she said icily. "You're not getting any younger, you know."

"That is not a father-daughter conversation."

"Oh, but my dating life is?"

He stood up. "Thank you for the delicious meal. Now, I must rest."

Stiffly, he walked to the guest room and closed the door behind him.

Orna traced her fingers along the carving. The next sphere down and to the right read חסד, *Hesed*, which translated to "mercy." How quickly she'd forgotten—but no one she'd ever met pushed her buttons like that man.

Dead tired all of a sudden, she dragged herself upstairs, fell into bed, and was out like a light.

CHAPTER 6

Wobbling on the high heeled pumps she never wore, Orna clip-clopped from the Meadbury University parking lot toward the theater, a huge blocky red brick building looming like a cliff face, the sunset behind it pink as attic insulation. Gaggles of students in every shape, size, and shade strolled, biked, or skated past her, most wearing backpacks or messenger bags, earbuds in all but a few ears.

Her guts wriggled, either from nerves or the three-day old pizza she scarfed down before leaving the condo. Even though she had her talk down pat—Rowan's email included the slideshow he put together—a part of her hoped no one would show.

Incredibly, despite the accident and her dad rooming with her all week—the man still hadn't told her when he was leaving and had already found a local *shul*—she felt mostly sane and more or less in control. A major part of that was the fact that Ray was out on bail after being charged with only the minor crime of reckless endangerment, according to Rowan. And poor Dougie's funeral had apparently come and gone. Plus, she'd gotten pretty good at pushing away the bad thoughts, though she worried it might be a false calm, the ocean sucking back from the beach before the tidal wave.

Throwing her purse over a shoulder, Orna lugged

open the heavy wooden door, and, to her shock, stepped into a buzzing beehive. Scores of kids milled around the spacious lobby, the walls lined with tables cluttered with pamphlets and colorful signs like, WIND POWER 4 EVERY 1, COMMUNITY SOLAR INSTALLATIONS, and LEASE AN ELECTRIC CAR TODAY! From the other side of the theater's closed double doors, over which hung a banner reading, MEADBURY GREEN ENERGY CONFERENCE, a gravelly woman's voice boomed over the P.A. about something called a "smartgrid." A much bigger deal than Rowan had let on.

And speak of the devil, a grinning Rowan in his red-and-black flannel and jeans came out of the bathroom. He went in for a hug and held her against his lean, toned body; she inhaled a strong whiff of sprucy aftershave or deodorant along with a hint of woodsmoke.

"Why didn't you tell me there'd be so many people?" She pulled away from him, not because the hug made her uncomfortable but the opposite. She liked being touched by this man.

He put on an *I'm sorry* grin. "Didn't wanna make you nervous."

"Yeah, well, too late."

"You're gonna be great."

She shrugged. "If you say so."

Smile gone, he stared down at her. "If only you had half as much faith in yourself as we do." A hokey thing to say, but it also felt genuine. "C'mon, I saved us a spot."

Orna followed him into the theater where she gaped in horror at the roughly two hundred people filling nearly every seat. Anywhere else in America, a renewable energy conference would be a major snoozefest, but in the hippie town of Meadbury it was the next freaking Woodstock. Goose pimples sprouted on her calves from the air conditioner, making her wish she'd worn slacks instead of a skirt.

On stage, a grey-haired woman in a pantsuit droned on about megawatts, an overhead projector casting a flow chart with solar panels, wind turbines, and batteries onto the ten-foot screen behind her. A solid young woman with turquoise hair sat at a small desk behind the speaker, laptop in front of her.

Orna tried to keep up with Rowan's long steps as they made their way to their seats, which were, of course, in the middle of the front row. When she sat down, she had to crane her neck to see Pantsuit.

"You're next," Rowan whispered in her ear, and she tried to figure out whether his breath was spearmint, peppermint, or wintergreen. "They've already got the slideshow queued up."

"What if I freeze?" she whispered back, hoping her breath smelled half as good as his.

"The trick is to pick three faces in the crowd. One in the middle—that can be me—one on the left, and one to the right. Focus on one at a time, and then every ten seconds or so switch to the next. That way it's like you're only talking to a few people."

"What happened to picturing everyone naked?" she joked, digging out her note cards from her purse.

"Well, it's a bit cold in here," he deadpanned. "So, I'd rather you not."

She snorted, which earned her an annoyed look from Pantsuit. Orna clapped her hand over her mouth and elbowed Rowan in the ribs.

Finally, Pantsuit ended her lecture to healthy applause and left the podium, quickly replaced by Turquoise Hair. "Next up, Orna Tannenbaum, communications coordinator for the Tenders, presenting on biomass energy.'"

Handing her purse to Rowan, Orna launched up from her seat to the most applause since her Bat Mitzvah.

"Kick some butt up there!" Rowan said.

Like an out of body experience, Orna found herself floating down the aisle and up the steps to the stage. Behind Turquoise Girl, the title of her slideshow in leafy vine font filled the giant screen, THE FUTURE OF CLEAN AND GREEN.

Feeling every one of the hundreds of eyes on her, she walked jerkily across the stage, somehow forgetting how to swing her arms naturally, pinching the notecards between sweaty fingers. Halfway to the podium a few cards slipped out of her fingers and fluttered to the stage. Impossibly, one of them sailed off the edge.

Face hot, Orna knelt down to pick up the cards, reminding herself that she'd memorized her talk and didn't need them, anyway. Only when she was standing at the podium did she peer out at the audience, a tapestry of faces rippling as if in a high wind.

Her heart skipped a beat before she remembered Rowan's trick. She found him up front nodding and giving her the thumbs-up. Half a dozen rows back and to her left Orna's eyes fell on a pretty young brunette. And then towards the back, off to stage right, a guy with bushy hair and slight build dressed in baggy surfer clothes. She squinted to bring the childish, somehow familiar face into focus. The instant she recognized him, the entire room swayed.

Dougie.

Impossible! He was *dead*. Pulse pounding in her temples, Orna shuffled the notecards, hoping that when she looked up again he'd be gone. But he kept staring at her from the back of the room. Was this really happening?

A saying from her college theater days bobbed up: *The show must go on.* If that was indeed Dougie—it couldn't be!—there was nothing she could do about it until her talk was done.

Hands shaking, she picked up the remote control, turning her body sideways so she could look at the screen and talk into the mic. Careful not to drop the remote from her slick fingers, she pushed the FORWARD button, and a picture of a red-barked tree with sprays of light green needles—ponderosa pine— lit the screen.

She read from the first card quaking in her hand like an aspen leaf, "Ecologically, trees give us oxygen, shade, and wildlife habitat." The P.A. system and bad acoustics made her voice nasal and squeaky.

Keep going, Orna. Keep going.

The next slide was of a heavyset man in helmet, safety goggles, and work clothes posing next to a conveyor belt with a large circular saw blade about to bite into a log. She recited from the card, "Economically, trees give us lumber to build houses, furniture, and so many of life's essentials."

She risked a look up. Rowan beaming like a proud father. Pretty Girl's head cocked in a way that seemed like she was paying attention. And Dougie—*Dougie*?!— glowering at her from the back of the theater.

"But trees have so much more to offer. Such as..." She switched the slide to a young boy in a hospital bed, arm hooked up to an IV. "Electricity to save lives."

Another slide of a burly man with a mustache staring at computer screen, FBI on the back of his jacket. "Power to solve crimes." Followed by a mother, father, daughter, and son curled up on a couch watching TV. "Or just binge watching your favorite show. How can a tree do all that?" Orna asked into the mic. "Two words." In the leafy vine font the next slide read, BIOMASS ENERGY.

Rowan was still smiling. Pretty Girl fiddling with her phone. And Dougie had his arms folded across his chest. Did anyone else see him or was it just her? Sweat poured from her armpits, and she wanted to run screaming out of the building.

No way out but through, the voice in her head said. And so she carried on.

Clicking to new slide, a wide-angle shot of a dense thicket of conifers with tight green bristles: lodgepole pine. "Thanks to decades of fire suppression across the western U.S., we're left with hundreds of millions of acres of unhealthy, fire-prone forests, sitting ducks for the next catastrophic megafire," she read from her card in a single rushed breath. "Most of these tinderboxes are on national forests, tens of millions of acres in Colorado alone."

A "ssssss" from the audience like air leaking from a tire. Dougie was shaking his head furiously. Heckled by a ghost? This had to be a dream. *Just hurry up and get this over with, girl!*

On to a blackened forest that looked a lot like the one she drove past on her way up to Silvercleft. "Here's a glimpse at the havoc these unnatural conflagrations wreak on our precious forest resources." She clicked to a fresh slide of a bearded man in fluorescent safety vest chainsawing a small lodgepole. "We have a moral imperative to tend to these matchbook forests by sustainably thinning out the dead and dying trees before they're set ablaze by the next killer fire. Not only will we save lives and property, we'll be providing jobs and boosting local economies."

A repeating GIF of a logger feeding branches into a

bulldozer-like machine, wood chips spitting out from the other end into the open bed of a tractor trailer. "Fireproofing our forests alone would be a win-win for the environment and rural communities. But when we use this waste wood to power carbon neutral biomass energy plants to break our addiction to fossil fuels, we're talking nothing less than a win-win-win-win."

Rowan and Pretty Girl were all eyes and ears, but Dougie let out a low "Booooo!" When someone shushed him, Orna's breath caught—she wasn't imagining him!

Please God, don't let me have a panic attack up here.

But she was in the home stretch. She could do this. Breathing slowly from her belly, she changed the slide to a squat factory, cylindrical tower to one side and smokestack to the other, set against a backdrop of bare scrubby hills. "The Hawk Valley Clean Energy Center, about ninety miles west off I-Seventy."

Then quickly on to a map of the U.S., hundreds of tiny green cartoon conifers dotting the nation. "Right now in this country, two hundred and thirty-two industrial-scale biomass plants generate almost eleven thousand megawatts of power—not counting tens of millions of residential woodstoves, wood pellet systems, and wood boilers."

While Orna was rushing, her practice had paid off and the spiel came out perfect; though at that moment she couldn't have cared less.

"But over the next decade with the right subsidies, we could be up to two thousand plants." She switched to a slide with ten times as many tree icons across the map. "And in thirty years…" In the following slide pretty much the whole map was blotted out with cartoon trees. "…tens of thousands of green energy plants, producing more than half of our domestic electricity needs."

A bitter laugh from Dougie, which got several

people to turn around. Rowan didn't seem to hear, just mouthed something to Orna that might've been, *You got this.*

Then, like an oasis in the desert, the last slide. "In closing, we'd like to ask you to contact your U.S. Senators and Representative." She waved her hand at the rows of names, websites, emails, and phone numbers on the screen. "And demand that they protect human life and the environment by opening our national forests to responsible, sustainable tending and offering more subsidies for clean, green, renewable biomass energy. Thank you."

Orna set the remote on the podium to polite if not enthusiastic clapping. Rowan, however, beat his palms together as if she'd conducted a symphony.

Just as she was about to hurry off stage, a sharp voice cut through the dying applause. "You killed me!" Dougie shouted.

The cards fell from Orna's hands onto the stage, and, woozy, she leaned against the podium for support. Maybe this *wasn't* real, after all! But then why had everyone had gotten quiet, all eyes on the kid?

Rising to his feet, Dougie yelled again, "You killed me!" Then kept prattling on. But Orna's body went numb, and all she could hear was "wahwahwah" as if she was underwater.

Had she just injured Dougie when she ran him over? Was this his way of getting back at her for her drunken carelessness? Was Ray in on it, too? Was Rowan? But the head Tender, wearing a mild smile, merely shrugged, as if it was all par for the course. What in the world was going on?!

Squinting hard as Orna could, Dougie's head and body looked intact, impossible for someone who'd had a ton and a half vehicle run over him. Heck, she'd *felt* the tire bucking over his skull like a frigging speedbump!

But the more she stared, the more she realized this Dougie was taller. Hair a few shades darker. Cut of his jaw blockier.

"It's not Dougie," she mumble-laughed to herself, and the dark cloud hanging over her broke apart.

"—not only are you clearcutting forests for this fake green energy, you're fucking up the air with particulate matter and pumping out more carbon dioxide than a coal plant!" Not-Dougie spat, throwing up his hands. "You're killing me, over here, just *killing* me!"

He sat back down to more applause than Orna had gotten, herself.

Then Turquoise Girl appeared by Orna's side and said into the mic, "We'll be taking a fifteen-minute intermission."

Punch-drunk from the ordeal, Orna walked offstage casually as she could. Then straight up the aisle, frozen smile pasted on her face, until she made it to the lobby. She barreled into the bathroom which, thankfully, was empty.

It was obvious what was going on. Her guilt over the accident had finally gotten to her. The longer this went on, the more she'd see Dougie everywhere. Only one way to end this, and that was by turning herself in. She glared at the pale, wide-eyed face in the mirror over the sink and splashed herself with cold water from the faucet.

No more beating around the bush. She had to tell Rowan she was quitting, and then get in touch with Ray to let him know the gig was up. It was possible she'd get jail time, but a couple of years in a cell had to be better than fifty hallucinating dead people.

Orna gazed into her eyes, pupils tiny black umbrellas

opening and closing.

CHAPTER 7

Pumps in hand, Orna strolled barefoot with Rowan along the dimly lit path next to the hissing creek, fat willows trailing naked branches into the water from the opposite bank. Rowan had been so pleased with her talk that he insisted on celebrating with a drink. As much as she wanted to head home, the walk from the university to downtown Meadbury would be a good time to tell him she was quitting.

"Like Jordan on the court! Yo-Yo Ma with his cello!" Rowan tossed up his hands, raving on and on about her performance.

The wad of cash Rowan had tucked away in her purse was certainly something Orna was going to miss. Because she did the math; if she stuck with the Tenders for the next year, not only could she cover bills and pay off her student loans, she'd have a little nest egg to put away for the future. But was the money worth her sanity? Not if being yelled at by corpses had anything to do with it.

"Doesn't seem like people are really that into biomass," she said, figuring that would be the best way to weasel out of it all.

"Plants."

"Huh?" Her feet were achy from the hard, cold pavement.

"They were plants. Paid operatives," Rowan

growled, face shadowy and grim. "From the fossil fuels industry."

"You're joking."

A small gang of whooping college boys came up from behind. Shoving one another and laughing way too loud, they paraded past.

"Biomass is the number one threat to coal, oil, and gas. You think they're just gonna let themselves become obsolete?" Rowan threw up his hands. "Exxon, Shell, BP," Rowan raved on, the boys' hollers fading in the distance. "All dumping millions into fake grassroots campaigns to smear biomass as bad for forests, air pollution, whatever."

"So, that guy wasn't a student?" All Orna really cared about was the fact that he wasn't Dougie.

"Doubt it." Rowan shook his head. "But even if he was, he's been brainwashed by the disinformation."

They reached the part of the path where it and the creek dipped down into a tunnel under Broadway, cars whizzing back and forth on the elevated section of road above. Inky black inside, the tunnel was the main reason Orna never took this route at night on her walks around town.

This was it. The end of the line. She stopped and grabbed Rowan's ropy forearm. "I can't do this anymore.

"Orna."

"I gave it a try, and it's not for me." She longed to reveal her part in the accident, but not until she talked to Ray first.

"Will you sleep on it?" His face was dimly lit, but he didn't sound angry or even annoyed.

"That wouldn't change anything." She sighed. "I support what you're doing and all, I just think you should find a better fit."

"Okay, no big deal," Rowan said casually. "Can I still buy you that drink?"

Some of the weight off her chest, she was actually up for a beer. "No, but I'll buy you one."

Rowan gave her an awkward high-five and led the way into the dark tunnel. Grimy footlights made small glowing islands every ten feet or so as the invisible creek flowed past stinking of algae, its trickles echoing off the cement walls. Cars rumbling past overhead sounded miles away. Halfway through the tunnel, Orna realized she was holding her breath and let it out.

A patter of footsteps from behind, yet another jogger in the city ranked as America's fittest. She and Rowan moved to the side of the path, and she winced as she squished something slimy between her toes.

Then the jogger rammed into her side, and Orna staggered back to slam against the cement wall, a galaxy of stars exploding in her head. A rough tug as her purse was yanked off her shoulder, and the jogger sprinted down the tunnel.

"What the hell!" Orna shrieked, more angry than afraid, her whole body pulsing with adrenalin. Not only were her keys, credit cards, and cell in her purse, so was her fat wad of cash.

Without a word, Rowan took off in hot pursuit. After a few dazed seconds, Orna got it together enough to drop her pumps and trot off behind him. But her stumpy legs were no match for his super long ones, and by the time she left the tunnel for the open air again, Rowan was yards ahead, the mugger out of sight. When Rowan veered off the sidewalk to lope across an open park, she followed, grass prickly under her feet.

As she huffed and puffed along, Rowan turned a corner at a well-lit cinderblock parking garage and disappeared. A stitch burning under her lower rib, she had to slow down and feared she'd lost them.

But as she came around the bend into a narrow alley, Rowan stood over the mugger—who lay on his side dressed in a black sweatsuit, face hidden behind a neck gaiter—kicking him in the stomach over and over with the toe of his work boot. The sight of Orna's purse slung over the Tender's bony shoulder was both a relief and slightly absurd.

Leaning over to catch her breath, hands on knees, Orna thought about how Seth, her ex, probably wouldn't even have chased after the guy, much less fought him.

Moaning in a deep man voice, the mugger curled up into the fetal position as Rowan went on kicking his ribs.

"I think he's had enough," Orna said halfheartedly, a wicked part of her enjoying the beat down.

"He's—" Kick. "Not—" Kick. "Getting away—" Kick. "With this!"

Rearing his leg back like a place kicker, Rowan delivered a sweeping punt to the back of the mugger's head. Worried he'd kill the guy if she didn't step in, Orna grabbed Rowan's bicep and tried to wrench him away. Before she could, he lifted his massive boot and brutally stomped the side of the guy's skull. After that, the mugger lay still, hopefully just unconscious and not dead.

Rowan turned towards her, a thin stream of blood trickling from a nostril, and handed over her purse. "You okay?"

"Me? You're the one bleeding." She unzipped her purse and dug through it—phone, card case, cash all still there—and pulled out a mini package of tissues.

"He got in an elbow before I could knock him down."

The mugger shifted and groaned—still alive, thank God.

"Hold still," she said, and dabbed Rowan's blood with a tissue. As much as Orna hated violence, this man had risked his life for her. From out of nowhere, she felt a crazy, overwhelming desire to kiss him. Instead, she used all her willpower to crumple the dirty tissue and cram it in her purse. Cell in hand, she pulled up her phone app.

"What are you doing?" Rowan demanded, an edge to his voice.

"Calling nine-one-one."

He circled her wrist with a giant hand. "No police."

"This guy should *not* be out walking the streets."

"They'll want to question me." He frowned, still holding her tight. "It was self-defense."

"First Dougie, and now this? You think that'll help Ray's case?"

Shoot, he had a point. What if the cops connected it to what happened at Charwood? Two incidents in roughly a week with the same players involved? Not until she talked to Ray.

"The least we can do is call an ambulance."

"Not from your number. We can find a payphone."

Shrugging, Orna stashed the cell in her purse, wondering if payphones even existed anymore. "Shouldn't we find out who he is?"

"No time." Rowan gave her hand a little pull. "Quick, before someone sees us."

After one last look at the mugger groaning on his back, Orna let Rowan led her down the alley, grateful this would be her last adventure with the Tenders.

CHAPTER 8

Sweat beading on her forehead, Orna steered the Forester to the shoulder of the narrow mountain road, straining her eyes for any hint of headlights around the blind curve.

"Completely blocked off, no way down," Rowan said excitedly from the passenger seat, finishing his hair-raising tale about escaping last year's wildfire.

Barefoot driving aside, the tomblike darkness was actually safer than daylight, as Orna would be able to see any oncoming headlights well in advance this time. A moot point thus far, as they'd been the only ones heading to or from Silvercleft.

Having just quit her gig with the Tenders, she couldn't believe she was on her way up to the creepy-ass mining town yet again. But after Rowan almost literally kicked the crap out of her mugger—an act equal parts horror show and turn on, she couldn't deny—he complained of dizziness and asked her to drop him off at Charwood; tomorrow, he'd have Silvio bring him back into town for his pickup.

It was perfect, really—she could let Ray know what was happening and make a clean break with these people. A good night's sleep and then turn herself in first thing in the morning. Jail or no jail, she was done rehashing everything. The only way out was through.

"Luckily, the winds blew the fire away from the

lodge," he said, as the Subaru's headlights lit up the burnt forest to either side of the road, dead trees merging with their shadows. "Though about half our forest—just over fifteen hundred acres—is pretty much toast now."

It dawned on Orna that she knew next to nothing about this strange man she'd never see again. "How long have you lived up here?"

"All my life," he said proudly.

"At Charwood?"

"Me, my parents, and no less than a dozen others at any given time. Charwood was basically a commune back then, though we didn't call it that." Though Rowan hardly came across as a hippie, himself, now it made sense where he got his love of the outdoors.

"Your parents still local?"

"In a sense," he said. "Buried out back."

"Oh, that's awful," Orna said, avoiding the "s-word"; after her mother's death, so many people had said "sorry for your loss" she bristled every time she heard it. How the heck could you be sorry for something you didn't do?

What about running over someone with your car? Could that be worth an apology? She pushed away the sickening thought and waited a few seconds to see if he'd volunteer anything else about his family. He didn't, and she was the last person who'd pry.

"How's your head feeling?" She toed the gas as they cruised past the sign marking the Silvercleft town limits.

"A lot better, now that I'm home." He buzzed down his window, fresh air rushing in. "It's weird, but I hate being in the city that long. Kinda like a reverse altitude sickness, you know?"

She did not know and frankly couldn't wait until she

was heading down the hill again to Meadbury. As she'd texted her dad before she'd gotten in the car, she aimed to be back at the condo by ten.

They rolled through the silent village, a second story window lit up at the inn. The general store was dark, as were most of the cabins, the ever-present woodsmoke puffing from stovepipes. Into the murky forest again, and then she swung onto the driveway through the tunnel of trees out into the open meadow. A bonfire was burning, though much smaller than the other night, someone standing beside it.

Orna was calmer than she thought she'd be coming back there. Even when she parked behind Ray's motorcycle and Silvio's Prius, feet away from where the accident happened.

"Well, I guess that's it." Rowan unbuckled his seatbelt.

"That Ray out there?" she peered at the fire across the tall grass.

"Think so."

"I should say goodbye." Orna got out of the car, and a delicious scent wafted over on the warm air. From the days of the Israelites wandering the desert and getting sick from parasites, kosher law has forbidden Jews from eating pork. But ever since Orna's first taste of bacon her freshman year of college, hardly a week had gone by without at least a taste of sausage, spareribs, or pork dumplings.

"Pig roast tonight. Ray's specialty." Rowan swept his arm grandly towards the front door. "Stick around for a bit and you can have some."

"Oh, I really need to get back."

"Come in for that drink, first."

"My dad's waiting," she faked a teenager's annoyed tone, rolling her eyes even though it was too dark for him to see.

"Oh." The disappointment in his voice thick as oil. "I thought we could do one last toast to Dougie."

A wave of guilt crashed over her, and she shut off the engine. "One drink," she said, knowing full well what had happened last time she'd said that.

Charwood's front hallway was narrow with low ceilings, the floor scuffy with ash and sharp scraps of tree bark under Orna's bare feet. And the fact that it was smoky and had to be at least eighty degrees only made it more claustrophobic. The den, thankfully, was open with high, beamed ceilings and a little cooler, windows open to let in a cross breeze.

Antique axes and handsaws hung on one of the wood panel walls. On the other, a six-by-six foot lattice of what looked to be dead pine needles woven in concentric squares over a stick frame—a God's eye, she was pretty sure it was called. Or, just as easily, the web of a giant spider. A staircase curved up to the second floor and a closed door led into what she guessed was the kitchen.

On one end of a leather L-section couch, Isabel, in her hemp hat and patchwork hippie dress, gave a nod as she puffed away at a finger-sized joint. She was using a bottle of glue to make one of those stick dolls Orna had seen hanging in the forest. On the other end, Silvio, in T-shirt and jeans, looked up with a smile from his game of solitaire on the coffee table.

Lottie, the ugly old German Shepherd, sat on a recliner a few feet away from a stone fireplace stuffed full of blazing logs, a thin layer of blue smoke hanging in the air. Several cords of split, blackened wood were stacked high against the wall, a hatchet sunk into a tree stump, splinters strewn on the floor around it.

After a quick stretch of her front legs, Lottie leapt

out of the chair and stalked towards Orna and Rowan. Orna took a nervous step back.

"Lottie doesn't get up for everyone, you know," Rowan said as the dog came over, its runny, bloodshot eyes on Orna's. He scratched Lottie's head. "I think she wants you to pet her."

Orna's pity for the poor animal greater than her fear, she reached out a hand, ready to pull away at the slightest lip curl. But when she gently patted the dog's fat head—avoiding the gross bald patches—Lottie closed her eyes and grunted with obvious pleasure.

"Good girl, Lottie," Rowan said. "Now, go lie down."

Lottie shot a look at Rowan before plodding back over to her chair, jumping up, and curling into a ball.

"Don't keep us in suspense." Silvio cocked his head. "How did it go?"

"Grand slam!" Rowan said, heading off behind the kitchen door. Orna caught a glimpse of a granite counter before it closed again.

Instantly, Silvio got to his feet. "Wanna show you something."

"What is it?" Orna asked.

"Upstairs." He held out a hand, a wild look in his pretty eyes. "Just come."

Maybe ten years ago Orna would've fallen for the old "head upstairs with me" trick. Cute as Silvio was, it was Rowan—self-assured yet humble—she felt drawn to. A moot point, since she'd never see either of them again, anyway. Instead, she sat at the corner of the L, while a sullen Silvio took his seat again at the end of the couch.

Seconds later, Rowan came back into the den with a mason jar full of brown liquid in one hand, a small stack of tumblers in the other. He plopped down between her and Silvio, set the glasses on the coffee table, poured a finger's worth into each, and passed them around.

Orna swirled the thick amber fluid around the bottom of the glass. "What is this stuff?"

"Whisky."

She sniffed it, and her eyes watered. "What brand?"

"No brand."

"Moonshine?"

Rowan nodded and grinned. "I barter with some of the locals."

"Can't that stuff blind you?" she asked.

Rowan laughed. "Only if it's garbage. This, I assure you, is not." He raised his glass. "To Dougie!"

Just in case, Orna waited until everyone else had taken a sip—Isabel gulping hers in a single swallow while letting out a loud fart—before she wet her lips.

By no means an aficionado, Orna had tried enough whisky over the years to know the difference between bottom shelf swill, drinkable mid-grade, and high end select reserve. Once she even sampled a hundred-dollar glass of scotch some drunk investment banker bought her at a Burlington cocktail lounge.

But this batch was unlike anything she ever tasted before, a smoky blend of butter and cinnamon, like liquid French toast. She took a bigger sip and swished it around her mouth, hints of oaky sweetness waking tastebuds she didn't know she had.

"You like?" Rowan asked.

"Incredible."

"So are you." Rowan got to his feet. "Wish you guys could've been there tonight."

For the next few minutes, Rowan paced the room, droning on about how great Orna's talk had gone.

Ashamed, Orna sipped from her glass so she didn't have to look at anyone. Soon as it was empty, she'd be out of there.

In the meantime, Isabel's joint burned down to a roach. Setting the finished doll—which resembled a crude angel—down on the arm of the couch, the gaunt young woman got up to flick what was left of the spliff into the raging fireplace. From the breast pouch of her gramma dress she plucked a fresh one and lit it in the flames. Then came back to sit right next to Orna, so close Isabel's bony hip poked up against her fleshier one. Seemed the woman was warming up to her. Too bad they'd never see each other again.

After a long drag from the joint, Isabel blew a massive dragon hit right in Orna's face. Coughing, Orna sprung to her feet to get out of the cloud.

"Isabel!" Rowan swatted the joint out of the stoner chick's hand, which rolled under the coffee table.

As Rowan rushed into the kitchen, Isabel slid off the couch, scurried on all fours across the floor, and snatched up the still-burning weed. Then stuck it in her mouth and dropped back down on the couch like nothing had happened. As she did so, her hat slipped back a few inches. And before she could tug it back down, a nauseating blotch of gummy red and yellow scalp that reminded Orna of Freddy Krueger.

Lottie's face. Ray's hands. And now Isabel's head. *What happened to these people?*

Rowan came into the den with a glass of water, which he handed to Orna. She guzzled it down, ending her coughing fit.

"Isabel has a sick sense of humor," Rowan said. "But she's sorry. Isn't that right, Isabel?"

"So sorry," Isabel said, the joint tucked in the corner of her mouth.

"No big deal," Orna said, pleased to find that the creeping second-hand high was actually calming her tornado brain. An occasional pot smoker since her twenties, she'd gone cold turkey when COVID hit, not wanting to risk her lungs. Since then, she hadn't touched the stuff, afraid it would trigger her adult-onset anxiety. But maybe she'd been overcoddling herself.

"Mind if I have an actual hit?" she asked Isabel who, not seeming to hear her, kept on toking.

Rowan cleared his throat. "We share in this house. Don't we, Isabel?"

A shrug, and then Isabel held out the burning joint on the palm of her hand.

Orna pinched it between her fingers and took a solid draw. No coughing this time. To the contrary, it tasted like pine sap and the smoke felt good inside her, like a warm bath for her lungs.

"Want some?" she asked Rowan, who nodded and took a couple of practiced hits before offering it to Silvio—who refused—and then back to Orna. After one last drag, Orna returned it to Isabel who sucked deep as if she were on top of Mt. Everest and the joint her oxygen tank.

"I don't know about you guys, but I can't stop thinking about that pig," Silvio said.

"Mmmm, pig," Rowan said in his dumb Homer Simpson voice, making everyone laugh.

Including Orna, who realized this was her cue to talk to Ray and skedaddle. "I'll go see if it's ready," she said, getting up and skating across the den floor before anyone could stop her.

Goodbye, weirdos! It's been real!

CHAPTER 9

Outside, the tepid air—low sixties, if she had to guess—was a feather on her face, the full moon a fluffy dandelion gone to seed. She bounded barefoot through the meadow, the tall dry grass tickling her soles and back of her calves, towards the lone figure by the flickering fire. As she got closer, the heavenly smell of frying pork made her stomach growl. Maybe she'd stay for that bite after all.

Ray, in his leather jacket, worn jeans, boots, and cigarette, turned a crank that slowly rotated a naked pig on a spit above the fire. Both horrible and fascinating, the animal's pink skin shiny as laquer, split in a few places and blackened in others, dripping fat into the flames with a sizzle.

"I can't do this anymore." She could barely keep her voice steady.

Ray didn't look up, just kept cranking.

"I'm turning myself in," she said.

He met her eyes, and in the shadows his face almost looked black and blue. "I dug his grave."

"You mean at the funeral?" Rowan hadn't told her much other than it was a small service and they sprinkled Dougie's ashes in the forest. "I thought he was cremated."

Ray shook his head. "That night. Here."

"What're you talking about?" She wasn't hungry

anymore.

"I told you I went to the cops. I did not."

Orna gasped. "Rowan said you were out on bail."

"He does not know. Isabel went in for him."

Just like that, Orna's pot high fizzled, and she felt sick to her stomach. "What?! Why?!"

"We will not risk our work."

That clinched it. Now she had no choice but to go to police.

When Ray reached out a hand, she took a step backwards, terrified he was going to grab her. Instead, he pinched the pig's haunch with bare fingers, tore away a chunk of smoking flesh, and popped it into his mouth.

It hit her like a train. This wasn't only about the accident or her lying about it anymore. Now there was a missing body, she wasn't flirting with a couple years in prison but much longer.

Unless… "I'll tell them I didn't see," Orna said. "That you took my keys while I was sleeping. And threatened to kill me if I told anyone."

"All on tape," he said through a mouthful of pork.

"What?"

Swallowing, he pointed towards the lodge with a thumb. "Take a look."

Orna turned and ran across the meadow, hoping it was a bluff. Halfway across, she peeked to see if Ray was chasing her, but he'd gone back to turning the spit. When she made it to the lodge, sure enough, a glint of glass in the moonlight from a small camera hanging from the porch eave aimed at the driveway. And a second one further down.

The nightmare wasn't about to end, it was just beginning. Orna's chest was tight, like breathing through a soda straw. A panic attack on its way, and there was nothing she could do about it.

She lurched towards her car. The driveway stretched away under her feet like taffy, and she knew she'd never make it in time. Like a dying animal, she felt drawn to the darkness, and staggered around the side of the lodge towards the forest.

A screen of grey smoke blew in her face from a kind of metal outhouse at the edge of the trees, a one-foot diameter tin tube snaking into one of the lodge's back windows, big pile of cordwood on the ground beside it. Not an outhouse but one of those wood boilers she'd seen as a kid in Vermont. A rectangular storage shed was next to it.

Hands prickly, heart bounding against her ribs like a runaway horse, she dropped to her knees, straining for breath as the thick cloud fouled the air around her.

Vision blurry, she was a fish yanked from the water and left to smother on shore by a sadistic fisherman. No matter how hard she tried to drink in the air, it wasn't enough. Teetering on the brink of unconsciousness, she held on tight but felt herself slipping over the edge.

From a million miles away, a hand reached out and touched her shoulder.

"Asthma?" Rowan asked in a soft voice.

"Panic," Orna wheezed through the lasso around her torso, "attack."

"Breathe out slowly."

She shook her head which had become a burning coal. *I need more air, not less!*

"You're holding in too much carbon dioxide," he said calmly. "You need to exhale."

On all fours, now, she blew out the precious air through her lips like a leaking balloon.

"Good. Deep breath in, slow breath out," he guided.

She did as she was told, but it wasn't helping. Dizzy. Evaporating like a drop of water on a griddle.

"Good." Rowan's voice was far away. "Close your mouth, pinch one nostril shut, and breathe in through the open one."

There was no way she could get a full inhale doing that. But desperate for anything that could end this, she gave it a try.

"Pinch the other nostril," he said, "and exhale."

She did it, and the invisible belt strapped around her breastbone loosened a notch.

"Good," he said from right beside her. "Keep at it, and look off into the sky," he whispered.

Weird thing to suggest, but okay. She craned her neck and stared into the blackness between the winking stars. A breeze picked up, sighing coolness across her cheeks, and the smoke from the boiler twisted and tumbled in white loops and furls. It was beautiful, like ripples on a stream. Her breath came easier now, as if her lungs remembered how to work again.

From inside—but also somehow part of—the flowing smoke, a ghostly, man-sized figure with feathery wings, somersaulting and corkscrewing like a slow-motion high diver, triangular face smooth as a stone.

What. The. Heck? The thing was otherworldly, a being of smoke and vapor, translucent enough to see dark tree trunks through it but real as the nose on her face. Was this what dying people saw?

Then the wind shifted, breaking up the smoke. And it was gone.

"Did you—did you see that?" she asked.

"See what?" Rowan squatted nearby, features soft in the moonlight.

"In the smoke? The-the…" She couldn't find the words. Then remembered the weed. And how a few hours earlier she'd hallucinated a dead Dougie. And how during her one college mushroom trip, saw elves in her lava lamp. There was even a name for it—pario-something—the mind wanting to turn random shapes and patterns into faces and bodies. That or insanity. Orna brushed back sweaty strands of hair from her forehead. "It was nothing."

"You sure?"

"Yeah." And suddenly everything was back to normal, just a girl kneeling in the grass on top of a mountain. Her dad was surely waiting up for her, worried sick. Might've even already called the cops. "I need to get home."

Rowan stood up and held out a hand. Orna took it, and he hoisted her to her feet with what seemed like no effort.

"Sure you're okay to drive?" he asked.

Orna nodded. She felt fine. A kind of brain puking, her panic attacks were awful, but they got out the poison. And she then remembered what Ray had done with Dougie's body. And how he was blackmailing her.

"I want to give the Tenders another try," she choked out, the words like ashes in her mouth. For the next year she was a slave, like her ancestors in Egypt millennia before.

"Oh, Orna, I'm so glad." It was too dark to see for sure, but his voice sounded thick with tears. He opened his arms for a hug, and she fell into him.

Orna's nose nuzzling Rowan's armpit, she sniffed his earthy musk and her groin tingled. Shaken, she pulled away. Way too much, far too fast. As with everything at Charwood.

The head Tender escorted her to her car and stood there waving as she got in and drove off. No matter how hard she tried, she couldn't stop crying the whole way down the mountain.

CHAPTER 10

Panting, Orna's dad leaned against a massive boulder at the side of the trail, Red Sox cap shoved down over his eyes, JCC T-shirt soaked with sweat. Pale, hairy calves bulged from his running shorts, once-white tennis shoes coated in red dust. "How much further?"

"Another quarter-mile or so," Orna said. Dead ahead, a steep hillside dotted with thousands of young ponderosa pines where a wildfire had burned almost twenty years earlier, according to a sign by the trail. Higher up at treeline, a hundred-foot red rock slab tilting at a forty-five-degree angle. Above that, the autumn sun beat down like August—her phone read seventy-nine degrees—the end of the drought nowhere in sight.

"If I have a heart attack," her dad shoved himself off the boulder with a grunt, "I hope they make you *schlep* out my body."

Orna faked a laugh which came out like a witch's cackle. More than she'd done all weekend since coming back from Charwood with her sanity hanging by a thread. "Elevation takes a little getting used to."

He gave her a searching look. Though she'd been trying to put on a good show during the last days of his visit—he was flying out tomorrow morning after a long week and a half—he'd seemed to notice something was up but had wisely given her space.

"You okay?" he asked.

Orna nodded, though she wasn't even close. Three nights in a row she'd either dreamed about Dougie splayed out under her car or that floaty thing in the smoke, to the point where she almost booked an online therapy appointment. But couldn't. Because she was caught up in something very dark. And very illegal.

How could Ray have buried a body without telling anyone? Anyone except Isabel, it seemed. Then the sickening, unforgivable thought: If Dougie really didn't have any family, it wasn't like making it official would bring him back.

"No wonder people are so fit out here," her dad called out over his shoulder as he set off at a decent clip. "Everyone else has dropped dead."

Shuddering at the joke, Orna waited for him to get a little ways up the trail before following. Barely in his sixties, the man was in better shape than Orna thanks to his regular tennis matches, swims at the Jewish Community Center, and walks to shul for Shabbat services on Saturday mornings. Only two miles from the front door of her condo, her last—only?—good deed of the visit was to share the view from her favorite local trail. Plus, hiking was always her best antidote for nasty thoughts.

Meandering along, she took in the fresh, evergreen-spiced air, hoping for the inspiration to write that letter to the editor on biomass, her latest assignment from Rowan via that morning's email. Fluffy clouds streamed over the ridge, one clump like a bear's head with a long snout, and another a seahorse—neither anywhere near as lifelike as the figure she'd seen in the plume. While she had good reason to stay away from Charwood—if Ray could dig a secret grave for his friend, what else was he capable of?—she had the compulsion to head there soon to see if that thing showed up in the boiler smoke again. If so, she could skip the therapist and go straight to the asylum.

Throat dry, Orna stopped to slide an aluminum bottle from her backpack pouch. She unscrewed the cap and took a long swig, the water cold and sweet.

There was one bright spot in all the gloom: Rowan. This man had talked her down from a panic attack, something she hadn't thought possible. Because he, too, was struggling with anxiety and had picked up a few tricks along the way; not only able to protect her from muggers on the street but her runaway mind as well.

Another drink, and she put the cap back on the bottle.

Unfortunately, not only was the power dynamic off with him being her boss, too much chaos was swirling around to kindle real romance. Still, she was thirty-one, and literally one hundred percent of the men she'd chosen had been the wrong ones. If she was going to start a family someday, maybe it was time to start doing things differently.

She reached back to shove the bottle in its pouch but missed. It clunked to the stony, sloping ground and rolled towards a drop-off at the edge of the trail. Luckily, a rock stopped it before it fell into the gully below. Shaking her head at her clumsiness, Orna knelt down to pick it up, carefully stowed it away in the backpack, and continued up the trail.

Finally, she topped the rise and was treated to the sweeping view of a yellow meadow valley split by a sparkling stream, the Rockies' snow-capped peaks beyond, all underneath a flame blue sky.

Her dad stood next to a wooden bench gazing out at the landscape, hands on hips like some old-time explorer. "I understand why you live here." He nodded.

"It's like the whole state's a national park."

"It's your fault, you know."

He jerked his head around with jaw set, lips tight, clearly bracing himself for another of her unkindnesses.

Quickly, she added, "What was I, twelve when we came out here?"

His face relaxed. "That was a good trip."

"Remember we went fishing, and I kept catching all those rainbow trout?"

"They were stocking the stream that day." He smiled. "Jingo, Jango, someplace like that."

"Durango."

"That's it. Little cowboy town. Your Eemah loved it."

Orna's good feelings soured like wine left out too long, and she shrugged off her backpack to sit on the bench. Unzipping it, she pulled out a paper bag and dumped the contents on her lap: two packaged strips of salmon jerky and a couple of peanut butter and honey sandwiches in baggies. After handing one of each to her dad, she unwrapped her sandwich as he unpeeled the jerky.

They ate in silence for several minutes.

Done with the jerky, her dad broke into his sandwich and took a bite. "What kind of bread is this?" he grimaced through a mouthful.

"Sprouted whole wheat," she snapped. "It's healthy, just eat it."

He rolled his eyes. "Sure tastes healthy."

Seething, she crammed her half-finished sandwich and baggie into the paper bag. The bread was a little dry, but nothing was ever good enough for this man. She felt a crack somewhere deep inside her, and then the dam broke. "Why did you give up on her?"

He hunched over like he'd been punched in the gut. "Oh, *bubala*."

"We had options," she growled.

"God had other plans."

"God works in mysterious ways!" Orna mocked in a stupid voice. "Let go and let God!" She tossed the paper bag down in the dirt and stomped it with the heel of her boot. "Always the same old *bullshit*!"

A puff of wind blew a few strands of hair across her lips, which she angrily spat away.

"She didn't want to," her dad mumbled, the corners of his mouth drawn down, crumbs in his beard.

"What?"

"I begged her to hang on. To keep fighting. To have faith."

Orna shook her head, not believing him.

"Three years of radiation. Two of chemotherapy. Experimental cocktails. She didn't have it in her anymore." His eyelids drooped as if he was growing sleepy. "*She'd* come to peace with it. *I* was the one who hadn't."

Orna sat staring at her hands for what had to have been a full minute, digesting what she'd heard. He was lying. Had to be. Head bowed, her dad nibbled his sandwich.

But what if he was telling the truth? That would mean she'd been holding this grudge for no reason, punishing him for something he hadn't even done. Punishing them both. "If so, then why didn't you tell me?"

He tore off his cap, *kippah* still pinned in place on his sparse, matted hair, and glared down at her. "Why didn't I tell you that all the joy in her life was gone?! That the treatments not only weren't helping, they made her feel worse?!" His cheeks were red, nostrils flared, sandwich crushed in a fist. "Why didn't I tell my only child that her mother was in such pain—such terrible pain—that some nights before bed she prayed for death?!"

He slammed his hat back on and chomped down on the mashed sandwich.

Orna closed her eyes, mind whirling like a merry-go-round. He'd been protecting her. But Eemah had been gone for years. "After she died…You could've told me."

"Better mad at me than her."

Orna's heart melted like a snowball in the sun. Shakily, she got to her feet and hugged him. Her *Abba*. "I don't want to be mad at anyone, anymore."The hike back was a breeze, gravity pushing them down the trail in half the time it took to climb it. They didn't talk much, but now the silence was comfortable. Her father marching an arm's length ahead, she realized she'd actually miss the guy when he left in the morning. This spring she'd have to take a trip back to Vermont.

About a half mile from the road, he veered off the trail to scoot behind a low pile of boulders. "Gonna take a quick pee."

"TMI." Orna walked on a bit and bent over to stretch a hamstring.

A yelp. She scanned the rocks, but her father was nowhere to be seen. She jumped atop the boulders, and there he was, kneeling on the sand, gripping his ankle. "Did you twist it?"

He pointed at a yellow-brown snake thick as her forearm oozing under a rock, a bony segment at the tip of its tail. Rattlers were common around the Front Range, though she'd never seen one before in the wild. They should've been hibernating this late in the season, but apparently with the warm weather they were still active.

She leapt down and ran over to him. "You got bit?"

The somber look on his pale, sweaty face said all she needed to know. Furious, she bent over, snatched up a small stone, and whipped it at the rock. Though she couldn't see the snake anymore, its terrifying dry rattle—like a hundred crickets chirping—sent a shiver up her spine.

"Leave her alone," he said. "She doesn't know any better."

Right or not, never before had Orna so wanted to snuff out a life. It actually scared her how badly she wanted to kill that disgusting thing.

Her father reached out a hand. "Help me up." She took his sweaty palm and yanked him to his feet. "How far's the nearest hospital?"

"A few miles from the trailhead."

Two wet red dots glistened on his calf, the skin around them pink and raised. Orna's mind raced with movies she'd seen where they sucked the venom out of the wound. But she was pretty sure that didn't work, nor did tourniquets, and that the best thing to do was get him antivenom soon as possible.

Her arm around his midsection, his arm over her shoulders, she helped him hop back onto the trail. It took almost twenty minutes of limping and stumbling among the dust and rocks before they made it to the road. At that point, her dad was out of breath, face white and shiny with sweat.

"Stay here." Orna eased him down to sit on the curb. "Be right back." Then sprinted off to the condo faster than she'd ever run before. Hopped into the Forester. Slammed the gearshift to DRIVE. Booked it past the other condos. Swerved onto the road. Mashed the brakes where her father sat waiting, hat on knees, *kippah* hanging off the side of his head.

Parking the idling car in the middle of the street, she got out and helped him into the back, where he lay with his legs out. In the driver seat again, she floored it, and they took off with a squeal of rubber.

"Heyheyhey! You wanna kill us both before we get there?!" he shouted.

"Sorry." She feathered the brake.

"What did I always tell you when you got upset?"

"Respond, don't react," she said in a monotone, feeling like a little girl again.

"That's my Orna."

Driving no more than five miles per hour over the speed limit down the clogged Meadbury streets, she had to keep resisting the urge to lean on the horn at the slow-ass drivers, probably all baked on weed. Every time she snuck a nervous peek in the rearview mirror, her dad's face was more ghostly.

"How you doing back there?" Her voice trembled. *People hardly ever die from rattlesnake bites. Except when they do.*

"Oh, you know," he said feebly. "Living the dream."

"Hang in there. We're close." The green light at the intersection turning yellow, she punched the gas and blew through as it switched to red. Surprisingly, her dad didn't scold her. Glancing back in the rear view, his eyes were closed.

Orna stomped the accelerator and sped the rest of the way to the hospital. Screeching to a halt at the emergency room entrance, she jumped out of the car and dashed inside to the front desk.

"Mydadgotbitbyarattlesnake!" Orna shouted at the redheaded nurse in scrubs and ran back outside.

By the time Orna had gotten her groggy, sweaty dad out of the car—his leg swollen and dark purple around the bite—a hefty orderly with tattooed forearms was there with a wheelchair. Together, they sat him down, and, way too slowly it seemed, the orderly wheeled him inside. Orna followed along, but when she passed the front desk the nurse said, "You gotta move your car, ma'am."

"Then tow it, bitch," Orna snarled, and followed her dad—no, *Abba*–through the swinging doors down the hallway, holding her breath against the stink of antiseptic.

CHAPTER 11

Orna followed the orderly pushing Abba down the hall and around a corner into a small room with an examination table, desk, chair, and counter with an array of medical implements. Abba was fully conscious, but his eyes were filmy, and he slumped limply in the wheelchair.

Within seconds a thin blonde nurse stepped into the room, and the orderly left. The nurse bent down to untie and slip off Abba's shoe from his bitten side and roll down his sock. "Sure it was a rattlesnake?"

"Yes," Orna said patiently as she could, which wasn't very.

"Doctor should be in any minute." Nurse Blondie picked up a temperature gun from a rack on the wall and pointed it between Abba's closed eyes. "In the meantime, we need you to go up front and check in."

"How you doing?" Orna touched Abba's shoulder, and he jerked up as if waking from a nap. Forcing a smile more like a grimace, he gave a thumbs up.

Orna went back to the front desk and—after apologizing—gave the redheaded nurse all the info she could about Elon Tannenbaum, sixty-three, then hurried back to the room. Not a minute later a fortyish Latino woman in scrubs, stethoscope around her neck, strode in, eyes glued to an electronic tablet.

"Mr. Tannenbaum?" the woman said to Abba,

ignoring Orna. "I'm Doctor Morales." She set the tablet on the counter, knelt next to his wheelchair, and gently lifted his swollen leg so she could look at his calf.

Abba screwed up his face and squeezed his eyes shut but didn't make a sound.

"How long ago was he bitten?" The doctor turned hard hazel eyes to Orna.

"Maybe forty-five minutes?"

Dr. Morales stuck the tips of the stethoscope in her ears and slipped the metal disc over Abba's chest. After a moment she said, "We'll need to run a few tests."

"Tests?" Orna blurted. "Give him the antivenom!"

"Ma'am, I've to check to make sure—"

Orna's hands shook with rage. "There's nothing to check! He's got poison in his veins!"

"I assure you we're well versed in—"

"I'm not sure that you are, though!" Orna was white hot. "Cuz you're wasting time with procedural crap when my dad's dying!"

"Ma'am, if you're not able to get yourself under control." Morales made eye contact with the nurse, who slipped out of the room.

"Calm?" If she called her ma'am one more time… "I'll calm down soon as you DO YOUR JOB!"

"Hollis, please escort this woman to the waiting room so I can tend to the patient."

Someone grazed Orna's elbow, and she whirled around to slap at the orderly from before. "Don't you touch me!"

Hollis held up meaty hands and in a quiet voice said, "We're trying to help him, but you need to let us."

Something about the orderly's chill vibe cooled Orna down—her anger, after all, only a mask for her worry.

She took Abba's cold, sweaty hand. "Love you," she whispered, and he nodded weakly. Feeling two feet tall, she followed Hollis out of the room and down the hallway, to the waiting room.

"You gonna be okay?" Hollis asked.

"Yep." The beep of a truck backing up. Shoot, her car!

By the time Orna raced outside, the tow truck was parked in front of her Forester, the operator lowering the ramp.

"I'm sorry, my dad—" Orna made the tears come, easy enough in her current state of mind.

Nodding his head, the operator immediately reversed the tow ramp.

"Thank you." She got in the car, feeling a little bad about the fake crying. But what other choice did she have?

She puttered around the circular driveway and into the garage, parked, and hurried back to the front desk. "Any updates on Elon Tannenbaum?"

The redheaded nurse—who'd probably called the tow truck—stopped her typing and looked up from her monitor. "Nothing yet," she said curtly and went back to clattering away at the keyboard.

Orna plopped down in one of the thin-cushioned chairs, legs out in front of her, exhausted. Half a dozen patients sat as far away from one another as possible: a college-aged bro-type who couldn't stop coughing; a skinny teenage boy holding an icepack to his jaw, frowning mother beside him; a fifty-something woman with grey streaks in her raven hair rocking back and forth, staring at a spot between her feet; a confused-looking elderly couple holding hands.

After five minutes of staring into space, trying not to

imagine the worst, Orna went to the desk again.

Nurse Redhead smiled blandly. "I promise you'll know soon as we do."

Orna guessed the nurse probably dealt with hundreds of patients a day, but she still felt like the woman should be more concerned about Abba.

She sat back down, and, to avoid thinking, picked up a beat-up *National Geographic*. On the cover, a teenage girl in flowing green dress and matching headscarf leaned against a brick wall holding a sign, STRIKE FOR CLIMATE, in large neatly painted letters. The caption over her head read, "The New Face of the Climate Movement."

Orna had seen a YouTube video of this Nigerian girl, Bishiya, speaking at some United Nations summit, and was impressed by how fearless she was, boldly calling out politicians in a way no adult ever would.

She opened the magazine and started reading. Bishiya had quit school in the sprawling city of Lagos at age sixteen to raise awareness of climate change. However that worked, the girl was trying, and that was more than almost anyone was doing. Despite all the madness at Charwood, what if the Tenders gig actually did some good?

A ding from the overhead speaker, and then a voice saying, "Code blue. Code blue." Two nurses speedwalked out of one hallway, across the waiting room, and down the other leading to Abba's room.

The magazine slipped out of Orna's hands and fluttered to the floor. *Please, no.*

Mouth dry, Orna darted across the waiting room, snuck past the front desk, and jetted down the hallway. She came to a skidding halt outside Abba's room and burst inside. Empty except for his *kippah* on the floor, the room zoomed in and out as if through the lens of a broken camera.

Mechanically, she bent over to pick up the *kippah* and kissed it, per tradition. Then she darted out of the room and jogged down the hall, nearly running into an empty gurney pushed by an extremely tall male nurse.

"Where's the man who was just in there?" Orna pointed in the direction of the room.

"Older man with a beard?"

Orna nodded.

Looking surprised, he pointed down the hall.

Pressure building behind her temples, Orna blundered down the corridor, holding Abba's *kippah* tight. Room after room, she threw open doors and popped her head in. An older woman with dark circles under her eyes lounging in bed watching TV. A heavyset man standing facing the window, hairy butt sticking out of his hospital gown. A teenage girl in a chair sucking down a pudding cup. But no Abba. A sinking in her stomach told her Abba was gone.

She only had one thought: If they let him die, she would burn the place to the ground.

Finally, she barged into the last room at the end of the hall. Abba lay propped up in bed, pillow under knees, one calf swathed in a bandage. Face sagging and eyes shut, his skin was pink, and his chest rose and fell rhythmically. As if sensing her standing in the doorway, her father opened his eyes.

"You're alive!" was all she could say, high with gratitude.

"I should hope so." Abba cocked his head. "Though, when I get the bill, I may feel otherwise."

"Did they give you antivenom?"

He nodded. "And muscle relaxers. And pain meds."

She remembered the *kippah* and handed it to him.

"Dropped this."

"Thank you, *bubala*." He set it atop his head.

"I'm really glad to see you." Her voice was thick, but she was not going to cry. *Not* going to cry.

"We'll see if you feel that way next week," he said.

She squinted at him, confused.

"They said my leg should heal up fine." He tapped his knee. "But they want me to stay off it for a bit."

She chuckled. Funny how the man couldn't come out and ask her. So, she saved him the trouble. "Stay as long as you want."

"Careful." He stroked his beard and smiled. "I just might take you up on that."

CHAPTER 12

"Your destination is on the right," the feminine robot voice said from Orna's cell phone as she sped along the tree-lined mountain highway outside the posh ski town of Ferndale. Hitting the brake, she pulled over onto the turnout where a dirt road cut through a stand of lodgepole pine which, according to her map app, led into the Bluff National Forest.

It was 8:41 a.m., twenty minutes before she was supposed to meet Rowan and U.S. Senator Tasha Palmer for a short hike through some beetle-killed forest. The hope was to get the Democrat to pass a bill that would open public lands west of the Mississippi to restoration, the glut of waste wood sparking the construction of hundreds of new biomass plants. Not only would this save forests, Rowan claimed, the electricity would replace over a dozen dirty coal-fired plants.

Since Ray, that sociopath, had made sure this was going to be Orna's life for the next year, she might as well do things right. And who knows, maybe it was her calling after all? Plus—smart or not—it would bring her closer to Rowan…so long as he didn't find out the truth about Dougie.

She got out of the car to stretch her legs from the hour and a half drive. The air at ten thousand feet was sweet with conifers but fifty-one degrees and sunny, nowhere near as cold as it should've been in mid-

November. With no snowpack other than a few crusty patches under the pines, even the staunchest climate denier would have to admit something was off when ski resorts had to make all their own powder.

Orna pulled up the text thread with Abba and wrote, "Back before sundown. Making shepherd's pie."

Almost a week into recovery, her father's leg was healing up nicely, though he was supposed to keep on the crutches for at least another week. Something about her playing the caregiver role had shifted the energy between them, and they hadn't argued once since the hospital. Observing Shabbat for the first time in forever was mostly a gift to him, but she was actually looking forward to it.

Moments later, Rowan pulled up in his pickup. He waved at her through the windshield and butterflies flitted around her stomach. Could things really work out between them, or was she being silly? Five years ago, when she believed the supply of suitable men to be endless, she probably wouldn't have bothered, judging him too old, too rough around the edges, too this, too that. But these days she was starting to wonder how much that stuff mattered.

"Hey!" Rowan got out dressed in his usual lumberjack garb, flashing that crooked-toothed smile. She went over to him, glad to have a few moments alone. But as she was about to lean in for a hug, a black SUV with tinted windows veered off the highway and came to a dusty halt beside them. The front window buzzed down and a middle-aged baldie in mirror sunglasses jutted his chin at them.

"Site's just a mile up the Forest Service road." Rowan pointed. "You can follow behind."

The driver nodded and buzzed up his window.

"We'll catch up later," Rowan said and got in his

pickup.

Orna moped back to her car, a bit miffed he hadn't asked her to ride with him.

Rowan leading the way, the SUV second, Orna in the rear, they started up the road. Rough and studded with rocks, it was no problem for the Subaru, though her old sedan would've bottomed out right away. Gouged into the soft dirt was a single thin tire track, probably a dirt bike. Annoying as the noisy machines were, the motorized recreation industry was a strong ally of the Tenders, since forest restoration meant plenty of new access roads.

Their caravan passed through what Orna swore was the same stand of lodgepole over and over again, like God had run out of landscape and was repeating the same scene. Then they topped a rise, and the green needles gave way to orange rust; the mark of the infamous pine bark beetle. Orna was shocked to see how much damage the tiny insect could do, nearly every other tree dead as a doornail.

Rowan parked at a small turnout, the SUV angling in next to him, Orna squeezing into the last few feet of space. A wooden sign read, COLORADO TRAIL, and though she'd never set foot on it, she knew the world-famous hike went 500 miles from Denver to Durango.

Everyone got out of their vehicles, and the SUV driver, dressed in a black suit like some hit man, opened the rear door. Out stepped a tall, willowy woman, probably in her late twenties, dressed in a loose white blouse, pencil skirt, and—unbelievably—low heel pumps. She had the perfect skin and delicate features of a Bollywood actress, a glossy black braid hanging between her shoulder blades. Not the senator.

A jolt of jealousy ran through Orna as Rowan went over to give the woman a hug. What the hell happened to his social anxiety? Though she supposed if he already knew her…

"How was the drive, Kathy?" Rowan asked, peeking behind her into the SUV.

"Long." Kathy shook her head. "And spotty reception the last twenty minutes. I was worried we weren't going to find you."

"Sorry about that," Rowan said cheerfully. "Where's the senator?"

"Oh, something came up." Kathy shrugged. "But don't worry, I'll take photos."

Rowan's face fell and his shoulders slumped. Orna felt bad, knowing what a big deal this was supposed to be for him.

"How long's this gonna take?" Kathy asked.

"Less than an hour, if that's okay?" Rowan said with a weak smile.

"I guess." Kathy shuddered. "It's cold as a witch's you-know-what up here." Kathy leaned into the SUV for a fancy white silk coat which Rowan helped her put on as if she was royalty.

Tired of being ignored, Orna stepped forward. "Hi, I'm Orna Tannenbaum. Communications coordinator for the Tenders."

"Oh, okay." The aide looked Orna up and down and then shifted her attention back to Rowan. "Let's get this over with, shall we?"

"First, let me give you an idea of what we're looking at." Facing the orange-brown trees, Orna started her spiel, per the plan she and Rowan had agreed on. "These trees were killed in a pine-bark beetle infestation that started in the state about seven years ago due to a combination of—"

"A combination of drought, fire suppression, and

lack of proper management," Rowan broke in, as if Orna had missed something, though she'd just barely gotten started.

"Ugly," Kathy said.

"Not only is it an eyesore," Orna picked up where Rowan left off, "which impacts recreation and tourism, major drivers of Colorado's economy, it's a huge—"

"A huge tinderbox," Rowan cut her off again. "The smallest lightning strike could send the whole national forest up in smoke."

Orna tried to catch Rowan's eye and give him a *What are you doing* look, but he ignored her.

Kathy wrinkled her nose. "The bugs still here?"

Orna knew the answer to that one, too. "The epidemic peaked three years ago and has since petered off into—"

"What she means," Rowan blurted, "is that while this local outbreak may be winding down, it's getting worse across the state."

Orna clenched her fists, fingernails digging into her palms. That was *not* what she meant, because it wasn't true. The beetles weren't totally gone—they'd always been there and probably always would—but recent studies proved they were barely a blip on the radar anymore in Colorado.

She was about to say so when Rowan clapped his hands together. "Let's go for a hike!" His hand on the small of Kathy's back, he escorted her along the needle-strewn trail.

Orna paced along several yards behind, muttering "ridiculous" over and over under her breath. Of course, the minute Orna set her sights on a possible match, some hussy would swoop in and try to take him away.

The thrumming of a woodpecker drew Orna out of

her sulk, the black and white-spotted bird with a red patch on its head hopping up the side of a naked snag. From her research she knew dead trees like this were full of insects, a kitchen pantry for countless species of birds. Hopefully some of them would be left after they thinned the forest.

Hurrying around a bend in the trail to catch up, Orna found Kathy holding on to Rowan's elbow, balancing herself as she plucked a twig from her pump.

Chewing her lip, Orna passed by without a word and kept going, the only sound the crunch of needles underfoot and the creak of trees in the light breeze. No way she was going to throw herself at Rowan like this woman. Hopefully, he also found Kathy's desperation pathetic and was simply being nice to get in with the senator.

The patch of forest Rowan wanted to showcase was supposed to be about a half mile in. And after ten minutes of fast hiking, the forest gave way to a jewel of a meadow, hundreds of burnt orange trees ringing the dry grass. Obviously, the spot they'd talked about.

Above the trail, the trees looked different, their needles dense and blue. Spruce? Curious, she scrambled up the slope into a very different forest, the light a soft purple, trees fatter, branches strung with pale, wispy lichen. It felt magical in there, like an elf could peek its head out behind a trunk at any moment.

She made her way over to a large boulder. Since the lovebirds still hadn't caught up, she climbed on top of it, and the whole valley spread open beneath her. While a few hundred acres or so were cinnamon brown, thanks to the beetle, the rest of the forest—unbroken miles of it—was pure emerald. Just an isolated outbreak, it turned out.

Laughter from below as Rowan and Kathy strolled

into the meadow.

"Be professional," Orna grumbled to herself, and went down to join them. Besides, Kathy—phone out to take photos—was far too high maintenance for a woodsman like Rowan.

"The Hawk Valley plant takes a hundred thousand tons of wood per year, all from the Bluff National Forest," Rowan said, acknowledging Orna with a smile that almost—but not quite—melted her icy mood. "But trucking in chips outside a seventy-five-mile radius from our ten other national forests isn't economical. We need more power plants."

"How many more?" Kathy took a selfie, duck lips and all.

"At least one per forest."

"And how many jobs would that be?"

"About thirty people work at Hawk Valley." Orna stepped in front of Rowan to finish the pitch; it was what he was her paying for, wasn't it? "So, around three hundred."

Kathy lowered her phone. "Not very many."

"Three hundred at the plants themselves." Rowan put his hand on Orna's shoulder as if to say, *I got this*. "But if you count the logging contractors, the mill jobs, and the lumber sales, we're talking *thousands* of jobs and tens of *millions* of dollars pumped into struggling rural communities."

"What do you mean, lumber?" Kathy creased her forehead, the only lines on an otherwise smooth face. "I thought we were talking about thinning for *biomass*?"

"Taking out the dead and dying, which are only sometimes of lumber quality, makes sense for your typical doghair stand," Rowan said. "But with beetle-kill, where everything's dead, regeneration harvest is the only option."

"Clearcutting?" Kathy asked, which was news to Orna.

"We try not to use the c-word," Rowan said with a giggle. "But the only way to recover some forests is to start from scratch."

"As you know, logging on public lands isn't exactly a hit with the voters." Kathy crossed slim arms across an ample chest.

"This isn't commercial logging. It's restoration." A slight edge to Rowan's voice beneath his smile. "And remember, we're not just talking about jobs but new energy sources, which I know was one of Senator Palmer's campaign promises."

Kathy raised an overplucked eyebrow. "That's why I'm here."

"Well, the facts are, if the senator wants to claim growth in the clean energy sector, solar and wind are a drop in the bucket compared to biomass, the latter making up about half of all renewables."

"I've certainly learned a lot today." Kathy rubbed her hands together, bright red fingernails glinting in the sun. "But I need to be getting back to civilization."

Rowan's smile gone, he gestured towards the trail with a hand. "After you."

Kathy in the lead, Rowan close behind, and Orna picking up the rear, they crunched along the path without speaking. Though Orna was glad those two didn't seem to be as friendly as before, it probably meant that neither she nor Rowan had won the aide over to the cause. Maybe if the head Tender hadn't kept interrupting Orna, she could've done a better job. Still, her fault or not, she couldn't imagine Ray being pleased, and a shiver went up her spine.

They were most of the way back to the trailhead, when something creaked overhead. In a flash, Rowan snatched Kathy's arm and yanked her back as a small tree crashed across the trail not ten feet in front of them.

"The fuck!" Kathy shrieked.

Rowan let go of her arm. "You okay?"

"No, I'm *not*!" Kathy's hand clutched her chest, eyes wide. "A fucking tree almost fell on my fucking head!"

Though a part of Orna wanted to laugh, she couldn't pretend she wasn't a bit shaken up herself. While the dying pine was only about ten-feet tall, if it had hit any of them it could've done some real damage.

"I'm so sorry," Rowan said. "I should've been more careful."

"It's fine," Kathy pouted, craning her neck up at the canopy. "Just get me out of this deathtrap."

Rowan bushwacked around the crown of the fallen tree, and Kathy scurried along behind. Orna was about to join them when something on the trunk a few shades lighter than the brown bark caught her eye.

A rope was tied two feet up from where the butt had snapped off its stump, the other end trailing into the forest. She bent down to pick it up; it looked brand new.

"Lost the trail?" Rowan appeared behind her.

She shook the rope. "What do you make of this?"

"Probably some camper setting a bear bag," he said.

Except, no one set a bear bag that low. And the fact that he wouldn't meet her eyes clinched it. "You did this."

He paused a few seconds then peered up with a hangdog look. "Technically, it was Ray."

Heart hammering, Orna thought back to the single-wheel track on the road. Not dirt bike, motorcycle.

"You could've hurt…"

"No, Orna. We know how to safely fell a tree."

She had no words. Hiding dead bodies. Beating up muggers. Now dropping trees on what could've been a U.S. senator? Blackmail or not, Orna had been a fool to have ever signed on to this madness.

"A last resort." Rowan scuffed the needles with the toe of his boot. "The only way to prove to them that these trees need to come down."

"It's not…ethical."

"And the fossil fuels industry is?" His eyes were hard, jaw set. "The game is rigged, Orna. Playing fair means we keep losing."

"Doesn't seem right."

"I know it doesn't. And maybe it isn't." For the first time since she met him, Rowan seemed annoyed at her. After all the praise, it felt awful. "But ask yourself this: What's the difference between killing the Earth yourself or standing by as you let someone else do it?" He walked off, leaving her standing there.

They both agreed what he did was shady. But, as with the pummeling of her mugger, wasn't it justified? If, like Rowan said, the bad guys had no problem playing dirty, wasn't it up to the good people to do the same? A breeze sprinkled a handful of needles into her hair, and she brushed them off.

After all, freeing slaves, letting women vote, and gay marriage were all illegal until activists broke the law to show how wrong it was. Now everyone *knows* those things were evil. And this time, nothing less than the future of the planet was at stake.

Unsure whether she'd come to her senses or was letting Rowan off too easy, Orna broke into a jog to catch up.

CHAPTER 13

Orna sneaked behind Charwood as the sun set in the western sky, shadows drawn to the ground like metal filings to a magnet. Rowan's text from a couple of hours earlier hadn't said much other than, "I need to see you tonight." So, after letting Abba know—he was busy working on his book anyway—she drove straight up to Silvercleft, almost giddy.

Soon as Rowan had promised after the field trip not to pull anything like the tree-felling stunt again, she'd felt the spark between them rekindle. Though he'd obviously invited Orna up for romantic purposes, she didn't go all the way on a first date. Before all that, though, Orna had to prove to herself that what she'd seen in the smoke the other week was nothing more than a hallucination from a super potent strain of cannabis.

As she approached the boiler next to the storage shed, its grey cloud billowing despite the warm, almost stuffy evening, she got why the things had been banned in Vermont. They were filthy. She stared into the plume hunting for shapes or figures, to no avail. Straining her eyes for anything the least bit like that strange, winged creature, minutes passed with nothing but churning smoke.

And that settled it. Just a hallucination. Nothing more to see.

Feeling ten pounds lighter, she skipped around the

front of the building and up the porch steps to knock on the door, which was hung with a spruce wreath, like poor little Dougie's birthday crown. No one answered. She rapped harder and winced when a small splinter lodged into her knuckle. Biting it out and suckling the salty wound, she turned to make sure Rowan's pickup and Silvio's Prius were still in the driveway—they were, though Ray's bike was not, thank God.

She raised her other fist to knock again, when something moved out of the corner of her eye. A tall rangy form that could be none other than Rowan, loping from the far side of the meadow into the forest.

"Rowan!" she yelled, but he was already gone. She jogged across the grass to the edge of the trees, searching for some sort of trail. But either there wasn't any, or it wasn't light enough to find it.

"Rowan!" she called again as she threaded between the trunks. Almost right away, the terrain sloped downhill, and she stopped to listen. There it was, the cracking of sticks underfoot. She almost shouted his name a third time, but something about being in the woods in the dark made her not want to call attention to herself. Besides, how romantic would it be to have their first kiss out there?

She followed the decline for maybe a hundred feet until the ground flattened out and she could pick out a faint path. A minute tracing it before accepting that Rowan had probably circled back and was waiting for her at the lodge wondering where she was.

Just as Orna was about to turn around, she almost stumbled into a dry, shallow streambed worn into the hillside. Instead of backtracking, she followed the lip of the slight gulley uphill towards the meadow.

Indeed, she'd barely broken a sweat when the gloomy forest opened up into a brighter patch. She sighed, knowing she'd be inside Charwood soon, sitting before the fire with Rowan, maybe sipping more of that delicious whisky. But as she got closer, to her dismay, it wasn't the meadow at all but a burned patch of forest, the last of the daylight filtering through naked branches. Heart pounding, she gathered with some alarm that the streambed hadn't led straight uphill, as she'd assumed, but veered off at an angle. Not that she was lost or anything, just temporarily misplaced.

She whipped out her phone and pulled up the map app, praying for just one bar. No dice, of course, the whole freaking mountain a dead zone. Luckily, she was on a ridge, which meant that so long as she stayed at the same elevation, she'd reach Charwood, or the village, eventually. Plus, the moon would be up soon. Worst case scenario, she'd come across a private road leading to some hunting cabin. *No, Orna. Worst case scenario is you'll wander in the wild until you die.*

"Shut up," she growled at her stupid, useless anxiety—with the temperature hovering around sixty and wearing a wool sweater, it wasn't like she was going to freeze—and switched on her flashlight app. Then quickly turned it off when she saw she only had eleven percent battery. Keeping the dying embers of the sunset over her left shoulder, she trudged north.

A couple of football fields later the burned forest thinned into a clearing. But her high hopes fell as she came across a kind of tree plantation instead of the meadow. Several rows of knee-high pines spaced a few feet apart growing gradually larger—waist-high to head-high to taller—until they merged with the natural forest. In an empty space at the center of the trees, a massive heap of dirt or sand, like a giant anthill.

She was about to check it out when a twig snapped. Rowan? Then something grunted from the woods. She held her breath, listening. The grunt again—actually, more of a snort. She smiled. Bucks sometimes did that to warn the herd of danger.

She clapped her hands to scare it away. A few seconds of silence and then more snorting. And the crunch of footsteps heading her way. Again, she clapped, but whatever it was kept coming.

Spooked, she spun around and speedwalked back into the burn, aiming to circle the plantation. After maybe a minute she stopped and cupped a hand to her ear. The footsteps closer, faster, the snorting louder.

Switching to full-on flight mode, Orna barreled downhill through the burn into the dense living forest, her best bet for losing whatever was chasing her. An elk? A bear? What the hell else made sounds like that and wasn't afraid of people? The same thing that was after her the night of the accident?

Branches yanked her hair and slashed her cheeks, until she tripped on some root or fallen branch and tumbled face first into the soft duff. Spitting bitter pine needles from her mouth, she shoved herself up to standing, straining her ears for any sound of her pursuer. Other than the thud of her heart, silence. Whatever had been after her had given up, or more likely hadn't been chasing her at all.

Unfortunately, now she had even less of an idea where she was. All she could do was head uphill—giving the plantation a wide berth—and hope for the best. Otherwise, she'd have to spend the night, which as far as she was concerned, wasn't an option.

She popped on the flashlight to make sure she was going the right way, the once lovely evergreen forest now menacing. No, menacing wasn't the right word, as that would've meant it gave a crap about her. The truth, she realized with a sinking stomach, was the forest had no idea she was alive, and, therefore, didn't care for her any more than a gnat or pebble.

Guided by the circular yellow beam, she struggled uphill back into the burnt forest until she was winded. Pausing to catch her breath, throat dry, she was relieved to see a stick lean-to propped up against a large rock. She was on the right track after all!

This one was square and three-sided, not unlike a sloppy *sukkah*, the makeshift hut Jews built during the harvest festival of Sukkot, like the ones their ancestors made while wandering the desert. For the heck of it, she peeked inside. A body-sized depression in the thick carpet of needles, like someone had slept there. Smiling, she imagined Rowan in his sleeping bag playing Boy Scout.

Towards the rear, a small pile of something. For no reason at all, she crawled into the cramped space. Just a bunch of pinecones, each the size of a child's fist. But with little white flecks in them. She picked one up and shone the light. Tucked between each of the dozens of scales were teeth.

What kind of animal could those be—the light winked out—phone dead!—and darkness smothered her like a sackcloth. A prickling of her skin, and she no longer wanted to be anywhere near this hovel, in case whoever was using it came back.

She scurried out of the shelter and rushed up the slope, night vision coming back. Then a swath of grey in the blackness. The meadow? Her heart swelled, and she blundered from the forest cover into a moonscape of bare soil pimpled with tree stumps; an enormous clearcut far as the eye could see. Hideous as this scar on the Earth was, it brought tears of joy to Orna's eyes. Civilization!

Sure enough, she didn't have to wander far before a

distant voice called. Then again, "Orna!" It was Rowan!

"Over here!" she shouted, running across the clearcut, leaping and tripping over jagged stumps, past the grey ash pit of what seemed to have been a large bonfire. Probably the one the Tenders had built the night of Dougie's memorial that she wasn't able to find.

They played a game of Marco Polo until the steady beam of a flashlight came bobbing towards her. The instant Rowan reached her she literally fell into his arms, drinking in his minty scent like a glass of spring water.

CHAPTER 14

The night was every bit as dark as it had been moments before. Yet with Rowan blazing the way with his flashlight down some old logging road through the burned forest, all the terror had been wiped from the landscape like dish soap through pan grease. Relaxed now, Orna's story of getting lost in the woods came out more as comedy than the thriller it felt like at the time.

"I still don't know what that thing was," Orna laughed at herself.

"Probably a coyote." He pronounced it *kai-oat*. "Nosy but harmless."

As the road took them into the green forest again, she slipped her forearm into the crook of Rowan's elbow, his bicep taut as a tree burl. Clearly too shy to make the first move himself, she might as well ease things along.

"So," she said casually, "what was it you wanted to talk to me about?"

"I've got some bad news," he said glumly.

She let go of his arm, not liking where this was going.

"Senator Palmer isn't sponsoring the bill," he said.

"What?!" She feigned outrage though, based on how poorly the field trip had gone, she wasn't exactly surprised. "How come?"

"Kathy told me they can't come out in favor of logging." He sniffed. Surely, he wasn't crying? Probably not—hopefully not—his face a shapeless blur in the dark. "Said it would piss off too many constituents."

Based on the pushback at Orna's university talk, Palmer was probably right. "Maybe someone in the House?"

Rowan sighed. "I don't see why that'd be any different."

"Not even a Republican?" A longtime liberal, Orna couldn't believe she was suggesting it.

"We need a Democrat to get the environmentalists on board." Rowan was walking quickly, and, tired as she was, it was hard to keep up.

Shoot. If the Tenders fell apart, would Ray blame Orna and rat her out? She found herself sweating again. The only way to stay out of jail was to keep things going. "You're not giving up, are you?"

"It feels so hopeless."

She'd never seen Rowan like this before, so sad and mopey. There had to be an answer, or it'd be all over for them. And for her. As they reached the outskirts of the meadow, a two-thirds full moon floated up like a lopsided balloon over the spiky treetops.

She took his hand and pulled him to a stop. "What if we're looking at it wrong?"

Another sigh from Rowan, the flashlight beam pointing at the ground.

"This is about the climate, right?" she asked.

"Mmmhmm." He sounded bored, his hand limp in hers.

"How about instead of forests, we focus on that?"

"As in?"

Making it up as she went along, she hadn't figured out that part yet, so said the first thing that came to mind, "Greenhouse gases…"

"Wait." He squeezed her hand. "The carbon neutral piece?"

Say yes, Orna. "Yes."

"You mean, if Congress recognized biogenic emissions as carbon neutral…" Rowan's voice was full of energy again. He'd used the term "biogenic" before, something to do with tree carbon being different than fossil fuels carbon, though she wasn't quite sure how. "…federal renewable energy subsidies would pay for a bunch of new biomass plants?"

"And once they're built, they're not gonna let them sit idle," Orna chimed in, as if it had been her idea all along. "So, the obvious thing would be to—"

"Open national forests to restoration!" they said in unison.

"It's brilliant. Freaking brilliant." Rowan grabbed her shoulders and shook gently. "Why hadn't I thought of this before?"

"I'm sure you would've figured it out."

"See, this is *exactly* why we brought you on board. Fresh eyes." He pulled her in for a quick hug.

Caught up in the excitement, Orna leaned in and kissed him hard on the lips. But instead of kissing back, he broke away, the flashlight falling to the ground with a tiny smash and blinking out.

"I'm sorry," she squeaked, in shock from having made the first move—something she'd never done before—and the rejection—the reason *why* she hadn't. An impulse to dash off into the woods and let whatever was out there rip her to shreds.

"It's okay, it's okay," Rowan said, as if trying to convince himself. "I'm flattered, but…"

"No big deal. My mistake." Her face felt hot, like she

had a bad case of sunburn. "Just forget about it."

"No problem." He cleared his throat. "Anyway, as I was saying..." As she trailed along behind him, he babbled on about how, once biomass was officially declared carbon neutral, state incentives would also follow. He was a few feet ahead of her now, walking through the meadow. Normal, run-of-the-mill smoke—no imaginary ghost—poured from the boiler to mingle with the plume from the chimney jutting out of the cedar-shake roof, the lodge windows dark.

But Orna was barely listening. "It's Kathy Phauda, isn't it?" she blurted.

"What?" He slowed down so she could catch up. "Seriously? No."

"Isabel?" It was silly, but she had to ask.

"We had a thing once," he said to her surprise. "But that was a long time ago. Trust me, she and Ray were made for each other."

"It's me, then!" She kicked at the grass. Childish as she was acting, she didn't care. How come the few guys she actually wanted were the only ones *not* into her?

"Oh, Orna, nothing's wrong with you. Not a thing."

"Yeah, whatever," she groused, picking up the pace, walking ahead of him. "'It's not you, it's me,' am I right?"

Rowan caught up in a few strides. "As beautiful and smart and funny as you are—and you *are* all those things—I can't give you what you want right now."

"I get it." Of course, she didn't, and couldn't wait to get in her car and escape into the darkness where she belonged. She was done with men. Absolutely done.

"I'm not saying things can't ever work out between us," he offered. Which stung even more. The only thing worse than being told no—at least *then* she could get on with her life—was dangling a maybe in front of her.

Halfway across the meadow, she broke into a jog.

"But as it stands now." He paced her with ease. "I'm afraid it's not in the cards for us."

"It's fine, really." It wasn't. She was basically sprinting, burning up the last of her energy for no reason at all.

"You mean a lot to us—to me." His voice shook from his footfalls. "And I'd hate for this to stand between us."

She got to the Subaru and dug into her pocket for the fob. "I gotta go," she panted, out of breath, hoping Abba would be asleep by the time she got home.

"This doesn't have to be weird, you know," Rowan said.

"I'm not being weird." She beeped the car unlocked.

"You're being a little weird."

She opened the door, and the light went on. "I'm just tired. It was scary out there."

"I know it was. But I'd never let anything happen to you. Wait." Rowan's forehead was all worry lines. "You're not thinking of quitting, are you?"

"I dunno," she bluffed, as if she had a choice.

"Cuz we need you now more than ever."

"Uh-huh."

"Talk tomorrow?"

"I guess."

"Drive safe." He grinned and leaned in for a hug.

But this time she turned away, slid into the seat, and slammed the door in his stupid, smiling face.

CHAPTER 15

When Orna got back to the condo, Abba's door was half open, the light on. Quietly, she tiptoed upstairs and shut the door of her tiny bedroom, the faint scent of lavender from the unused candle on her dresser. Lying fully clothed on top of the blankets in bed, the scene of Rowan snubbing her kiss looped over and over in her mind.

While her body was beat from running around the woods like an idiot, her racing mind meant sleep wasn't an option. So, she grabbed the phone, pulled up her contacts, and scrolled down to JESSY B.

Best friends since meeting at college in their Jewish sorority, they'd both stayed in Burlington and were seeing each other at least once a week. Until three years ago Jessy married some hipster who owned a brewery and had a kid less than a year later. While they still hung out, it was usually only once a month, and instead of bar hopping they played board games at Jessy's house as she nursed little Jerry. Even after Orna moved and the pandemic hit, Jessy had become her daily lifeline via phone and video chat. Though since it had waned, they'd only spoken a few times.

Orna's phone read 8:57, almost eleven back east. She should wait until tomorrow. But if friends weren't there when you needed them most, what was the point? She pushed CALL.

Jessy picked up on the second ring. "Hey chica!"

"I didn't wake you, did I?"

"The boys are asleep, but I can't stop watching this Ted Bundy doc."

"The serial killer from the eighties?" Orna enjoyed the occasional horror movie but only because they were so fake. Unlike several women she knew, true crime wasn't something she liked thinking about, much less binge-watching shows on. And definitely not since her life had basically become an episode of its own.

"Late seventies," Jessy said. "Confessed to raping and killing thirty women—some think it was a lot more—and not necessarily in that order."

"Psychopath." Skin crawling, Orna got out of bed and peered through the window at the unlit strip of grass between her condo cluster and the next. No one there, of course. Who did she expect to see, Ray?

"For sure. Still kinda cute."

"Really?" Orna typed "Ted Bundy" into her phone's search engine and pulled up a photo of some moon-faced creeper with a unibrow. "C'mon, Jess."

"Dude got hundreds—and I mean, *hundreds*—of love letters in prison," Jessy said. "Even married one of them…when he was on trial for raping and killing a twelve-year-old girl."

"The fuck." Orna paced her room. What was it about a monster like Bundy that those women were drawn to? Did they want to save him? Or was it something darker? "He's dead, right?"

"Electric chair in eighty-nine." Orna could hear the smile in Jessy's voice. While no fan of the death penalty, Orna figured if anyone qualified it was that guy. "Guess where he was born?"

Orna froze, hand to throat. "Not Burlington."

"Right off Shelburne. At some home for unwed mothers."

"Jesus." Orna felt icky, like she needed to wash her hands. "The place still there?"

"Knocked down before we were born. It's an office building now." Jessy sounded disappointed, though it was welcome news to Orna. "So, what's up?"

"Oh, not much." All of a sudden Orna felt shy. Jessy was married with children, totally over this teenage drama nonsense. Hot in her sweater, she went into her closet to change. As she turned on the light, one of the bulbs flickered and exploded. She let out a yip.

"Everything okay?" Jessy asked.

"Yeah, yeah." Her heart thumped as she yanked her sweater off and tossed it in the hamper. "Bulb blew."

"A little high-strung, are we?"

Orna scoffed. If only she knew the half of it.

"You called for a reason," Jessy said. "Now fess up."

Orna sighed. "There's this guy I met…"

"Figures. Go on."

Sitting on the edge of her bed, Orna gave her friend the *Cliff's Notes* version—leaving out the accident and blackmail, of course—and ending with Rowan rejecting her.

"Sounds like a dick," Jessy hissed.

"He's really not, though."

"Well, he's stringing you along like one."

Orna grabbed a pillow and set it on her lap. "What if he means it? That there's a chance?"

"Aw, hon, this isn't the first time—" High-pitched crying in the background. "One sec." Voice muffled, Jessy said, "What's wrong, Jer-Jer?" Mewling as if from a cat. "There's nothing in your closet. Remember what

I told you about imagining things that aren't there?"

Orna was annoyed and a little jealous at the interruption. Would she ever have a kid of her own to protect from the boogeyman? Not with her luck.

More of the toddler's whining, and then a big sigh from Jessy. "Orna, I hate to do this, but Jerry had a nightmare, and I need to put him back down. Can we pick this up again in the a.m.?"

"Sure," Orna said, sadly.

"Great. Talk then." The line went dead.

Orna chucked the phone onto her bureau, and it fell to the floor. Afraid she'd broken it, she knelt down and picked it up. As if her day hadn't been bad enough, she'd cracked the frigging screen. Biting the inside of her cheek against the rage—mostly at herself—she set the phone down gently next to the Tree of Life jewelry box Abba had given her.

Though she'd meant to, she still hadn't transferred Eemah's jewelry over. She tugged open the bureau's top drawer, took out the old leather jewelry box, and popped it open. Necklaces, bracelets, earrings, and rings in every slot, most of it really nice stuff. She brought both boxes to her bed and sat down.

She picked up a sterling silver cable chain necklace and coiled it like a snake into the largest compartment of the new box. Next, she filled most of the remaining spaces with a gold bracelet, a few pewter rings, and a dozen earrings, from precious jade to what was probably cheap glass.

The old box empty, she closed it. Then opened it back up to double-check something. Sure enough, in the upper left corner the fabric lining wasn't quite flush. She pinched it and pulled back. In the hollow space underneath, a silver ring gleamed.

In the center of its midnight-black enamel face, a

white *Magen David*, Star of David. At the points of the upper part of the star, three Hebrew letters from right to left: ש ד י.

"*Shaddai*?" Orna said out loud. Though she'd forgotten a lot of her Hebrew over the years, she was pretty sure she'd never heard the word before. Excited to solve the mystery, she picked up her phone and typed in the English transliteration. Instead of something cool, *Wikipedia* told her it was just another name for God.

Boooooring.

But the silver was pretty, so she tried to slip it on her ring finger. It wouldn't fit. Even her pinky was too fat for it to go past the second knuckle. Eemah had been a small, almost elfin woman, but her hands hadn't been that tiny. Still, the fact that it had belonged to her mother made Orna want to keep it close.

Plucking the silver necklace from the box, she looped and knotted it through the ring and dropped it around her neck and under her shirt, the chunk of silver against her bare chest. Picturing Eemah's smiling face, Orna started to cry.

God, she missed her. The way her eyes lit up whenever Orna came into the room. Her bone-breaking hugs. The hint of fresh onion from all the time she spent in the kitchen. Even the things that used to bug Orna, she now saw in a new light. Like whenever she was going on a trip, Eemah would list a bunch of random things Orna could never imagine needing, anything from an umbrella to a banana to a pencil sharpener. And how, more often than not, if she brought it, the item would actually come in handy.

If it weren't for the cancer—pesticides? radiation? air pollution? genetics?—Orna would've still had a mother. But there was no bringing back the dead. Why hadn't she been told as a kid that life only got harder as you went along?

A knock at the door. Orna swiped the tears from her cheeks and cleared her phlegmy throat. "Come in."

Abba poked in his head, hair combed for a change under his *kippah*, beard neatly trimmed. "Got my ticket for the first. Figured the Thanksgiving rush will be over by—hey, what's wrong, *bubala*?"

"I'm just really tired." Of everything.

Dressed in T-shirt and tennis shorts, he limped into the room and sat on the bed. He'd taken his bandage off, that leg ghostly pale, the bite healing but still raw looking. "Aren't you supposed to cover it for another week?"

"I'm letting it breathe," he said in a monotone that meant it wasn't up for discussion. "Finally making use of my gift, I see."

"I guess you bought her most of this?"

He smiled. "The rest from your Bubby Ilana." All Orna's grandparents had passed away before her teens, but Bubby Ilana—Eemah's *eemah*—was the only one who'd died before she was born. All Orna knew about her was she was religious and a bit eccentric. "The necklace looks nice on you."

She started to pull on the chain to show him the ring but stopped and let it dangle back between her breasts. What if Eemah had hidden it for a reason? Like she'd gotten it from some old boyfriend? Or even...no, she couldn't picture Eemah cheating. Just the same, Orna decided to keep it to herself. "How's the book going?"

"Hate writing. Love having written."

"What's it about, exactly?" she asked. Something related to Judaism, though he hadn't let on any more than that.

He pursed his lips, eyes searching hers. "You

wouldn't be interested."

"You don't know that."

"Okay." He shrugged. "The *Kabbalah*."

"Huh." The only thing she knew about the *Kabbalah* was it was supposed to a type of ancient mysticism Jews weren't allowed to study until they were forty or something. And not at all if you were a woman; no surprise there, since the backwards Orthodox didn't even let women read the *Torah*. The excuse was that women were supposedly born holy, but that was only cover for a deep-seated misogyny.

She ran her fingers over the smooth, polished wood of the Tree of Life box. "Is that where this comes from?"

He nodded solemnly.

Trying to remember his previous lesson, she said, "If the triangle with the first three *Sephirot*—Crown, Wisdom, Understanding—are the cosmic energies…"

He nodded, a proud smile creeping in. "Also, the intellect."

"Then the others?"

As she traced the engraving with the pad of a finger, Abba explained in hushed tones how the middle triangle making up the next three spheres—*Geburah* or Strength, *Hesed* or Mercy, *Tiphareth* or Beauty—was about ethics and morality, or the soul. While the bottom triangle—*Hod* or Glory, *Netzach* or Victory, *Yesod* or Foundation—he called the Astral, and had to do with one's psychology or nature.

But one last sphere, מלכות, sat alone at the bottom. Orna rubbed it with a thumb. "And *Malkhut*?"

"The body. The senses." Abba tapped his good foot on the rug twice. "The Earth."

All her adult life, Orna had figured Judaism was like potato chips, comfort food that felt good to eat but did very little to nourish. Maybe she was wrong, and services and Hebrew school had only scratched the surface of its teachings. "Do the sides mean anything?"

Abba stroked a finger vertically down the right three spheres. "This is the masculine Pillar." Then the left. "The feminine." Then the center. "And balance."

"If this is the tree of good and evil," Orna began, checking to make sure Abba was nodding, "does that mean one side is good and the other evil?"

Abba yawned, one of his many fillings sparkling in the light. "That's enough for today." He kissed the top of her head, beard bristly against her scalp. "Sleep well, *bubala*." Up with a grunt, he limped out of the room and closed the door softly behind him.

Hungry for more, she was about to do an online search for *Kabbalah*, but the day had finally caught up with her, and her eyelids felt heavy. Without bothering to take off the rest of her clothes, she lay down on her pillow, Eemah's ring resting inches from her beating heart.

CHAPTER 16

Burlington, Vermont, 6 years earlier

Orna stood in the doorway to Eemah and Abba's purple bedroom, the smell of vanilla essential oil in the air, shades drawn to half-light. Eemah rested in her four-poster canopy bed, fluffy white comforter up to her chin, black kerchief around her head, lean face eggshell white in the reading lamp, a book of quotations open on her chest.

Orna had been pretty much living at home for the last couple of months, ever since Eemah started hospice care. The nurses who came in every day handled the delicate stuff, but she cooked and cleaned and chatted with her mother while losing to her at Mah Jong.

Steeling herself with a breath, Orna tiptoed into the room and sat on the antique velvet loveseat against the wall.

Eemah opened her eyes, which were glassy. "Good morning, *zeeskeit*," she said using the Yiddish word for "darling," something no one else in the world dared call her.

"It's the afternoon," Orna said.

Eemah smiled weakly and smoothed down the front of her nightie where her breasts used to be. "Hard to tell when you don't really sleep anymore."

"Thought they were giving you something for that?"

"They've got me on enough 'somethings' already, believe me." She rolled her eyes.

"You need your energy." Orna scratched the knee of her jeans with a fingernail, making a zipping sound.

"Death," Eemah said quietly, "is an act of HaShem."

"Again, with this?" Orna snapped, anger bursting through the sadness—or at least doing a decent job of masking it. "If I go on a shooting rampage downtown, that's an act of God?" She never said any of those things around Abba, of course, but Eemah never seemed to mind.

"I said dying, not killing. Killing is stealing a life that belongs to another."

"The Flood, Sodom and Gomorrah, the Ten Plagues," Orna snarled. "God supposedly killed people all the time."

Eemah shook her head, lips pursed. "He can't steal something that already belongs to Him."

Orna squeezed the arm of the loveseat. She had to get ahold of herself; the last thing she wanted to do was argue with her ailing mother.

"I have something for you." Eemah pointed at the dresser, and the sleeve of her nightie fell away from a bony forearm, papery skin almost translucent, blue veins running beneath. Oddly, it reminded Orna of the time they all went on a glass-bottomed boat off Martha's Vineyard, and she got creeped out by the seaweed waving in the murk below.

"I don't need anything," Orna said.

"Please."

Orna forced herself to her feet and slid open the top drawer. Inside was Eemah's leather jewelry case, which she'd borrowed earrings from countless times before. "But you're going to need it," Orna said, throat scratchy.

Eemah looked at her quaintly, as if Orna said she'd seen a fairy. "Your Bubby Ilana passed it down to me, and now I'm giving it to you."

Orna took out the box—like a small coffin—and set it on the dresser.

"It's your choice whether you observe or not." Eemah looked down at her hands. "And I know a lot of that comes down to our roles as Jewish women."

"Roles? They don't even let us sit with men at synagogue." Orna felt herself heating up again but couldn't help it. "It's like Jim Crow."

Eemah shrugged. "Maybe in some ways we're behind the times."

Orna was surprised. Her mother had never said anything like that before.

"But you're missing something." Eemah paused to catch her breath; just talking had become work for her. "Men pray to get closer to HaShem. We women are always by His side."

Orna grimaced. "Yeah, yeah, 'givers of life.' In other words, the babymakers."

"There are other ways." Eemah reached for a glass of water and took a tiny bird sip. "The real *mitzvah* is nurturing, healing, loving."

Orna cackled. More internalized misogyny.

"I know you feel like being a woman keeps you from things." Eemah shrugged. "And in many ways, it does, not just in our faith but in the secular world as well." Once again Eemah was being unusually frank. If her mother had always felt this way, why keep it buried for so long? "But the answer isn't becoming a parody of a man."

"Men run the world. It's time we take some of the

power back."

Eemah cocked her head. "What power is that?"

"Oh, I don't know." Orna paced the thick carpet. "How about the government? Our legal system? Pretty much every corporation?" Orna ticked off the points on her fingers. "You name it, they control it."

"There's certainly power in those positions. But let me ask you. How many hours a day does your Abba work?"

Orna didn't know what that had to do with anything. But it'd been the same since she was a little girl. Seven to five on weekdays, seven to noon on Sundays—taking Shabbat off, of course. "He's a workaholic. That's his choice."

Eemah smiled but with that patronizing squint Orna had seen so many times before.

"You took care of the house," Orna said. "And me. That's hard work, too."

"Yes, I did. And yes, it was. You were quite the little handful. Still are."

They both laughed.

"Growing up," Eemah went on in a more serious tone. "Do you think it was your Abba's dream to be an elder law attorney?"

Actually, Orna could picture her dad as a boy— oversized *kippah* on his curly little head—wanting exactly that.

"His dream was to be a poet." Eemah's eyes were far away. "The things he wrote me when we were courting and right after we married, you wouldn't believe." She smiled sadly. "But soon as he made partner…not a single line."

Abba read a ton, mostly philosophy and Jewish stuff, but up to that point Orna wouldn't have guessed he had a creative bone in his body. "How come he never talks about it if it was so important to him?"

"Because he's proud of his sacrifice. He gave up his dream so you could follow yours."

Orna stopped pacing, annoyed at the Jewish mother guilt-trip, and sat back down on the loveseat. "I've thanked him for every gift he's ever given me. Anyway, my *point* is that everything in this world revolves around men."

"You know where he lived before we married? A four-hundred square foot hole in the wall with a crooked table, two hard wooden chairs, metal cot, and a hotplate. Basically, a prison cell. And guess what? He *liked* it."

Orna smoothed back her hair in frustration. "You're really in denial, aren't you?" It wasn't a nice thing to say, but it was past time for her mother to shake off the chains.

"It's not the one-way street you think it is," Eemah replied matter-of-factly, unflappable as always. "We do for them, they do for us."

"Don't you get it? It's all about power."

Eemah squinted. "Remember *The Blob*?"

"What?"

"The old science fiction movie. With Steve McQueen."

Orna had no idea who Steve McQueen was but had watched the film as a teenager. "With the jellyfish thing?"

Eemah nodded. "What happened to anyone who attacked the Blob?"

"They'd get eaten." This was, hands down, the weirdest chat Orna had ever had with her mother. Maybe it was the morphine.

"And what would happen to the Blob?"

"It would get bigger."

Eemah waggled her eyebrows Groucho Marx style. "That's feminine power."

"The Blob."

"Masculinity is all about putting yourself out there, poking around in a hole, so to speak." Eemah grinned, showing her near-perfect teeth.

"Eemah!" Orna was taken aback. Never—never!—had the woman so much as *hinted* at sex before. For all Orna knew, her parents had done it a single time to conceive her, and that was that.

"Oh, grow up." Eemah chuckled. "Femininity is about opening yourself. Where the masculine forces itself into the world, the feminine takes the world in. Both are powerful depending on the circumstances, and both have the same goal: to become one with creation."

"That's the silliest justification of patriarchy I've ever heard."

"I don't expect you to understand right now." Without raising her voice one notch Eemah had taken on her no-nonsense tone again. "But I want you to tuck this away and turn it over from time to time."

Orna held up her hands and gave Eemah an exasperated look.

"You promise?" Eemah asked.

"If it's that important to you, then, yes, I promise."

"You're a good daughter. I see HaShem in you. Whether you do or not."

Orna's butt buzzed, and she pulled her cell out of her pocket. "If you say so." It was her date for that night, some stock-broker Jessy had fixed her up with. "I gotta take this." And left the room.

A little over a week later, Eemah was gone.

CHAPTER 17

A knock at Orna's bedroom door woke her from a sound sleep.

"What?" she croaked, pulling the blanket over her head.

"Someone here to see you," Abba said through the door.

"Who?" She peeked out her head, blinking at the morning light coming through the curtains.

"Says he's a work friend?"

She sat up with a gasp. *Oh my God. Rowan!* He'd thought over his rejection of her, realized he made a huge mistake, and wanted a second try. But did he deserve it?

Orna peeled back the covers. Depended on what he had to say. If he finally saw the light, who was she to fight it? Though she'd make him work for it—that was for darned sure.

Almost giddy, she leapt out of bed. "Be right down!"

She snatched a T-shirt and jeans from the dresser and yanked them on. Scurried into the bathroom—faced creased, hair mussed, but it would have to do—swished some mouthwash, spat, and wiped her mouth with the back of a wrist. Fixing a scowl on her face—smiling would look too desperate—she took her time going down the flight of stairs. She stopped halfway.

Silvio, hands in the pockets of his jeans, stood in the middle of her living room.

She checked to make sure Abba's bedroom door was closed and then stage-whispered, "What are *you* doing here?"

"I need to talk to you." His face was pinched, dark hollows under his eyes as if he hadn't slept for days.

"Did Rowan send you?"

Silvio shook his head.

Orna came the rest of the way downstairs and plopped on the couch. It was weird having her work and home life collide, but it wasn't like she had anything against the guy. "So, what's up?"

He looked down at his feet and licked chapped, cracked lips. "I was hoping you'd have quit by now."

"Gee, thanks." Orna yawned. For this she'd gotten out of bed?

"That's not what I mean. The Tenders..." His eyes were wide, crazy almost. "It's not about renewable energy. They don't give a *shit* about the climate."

She sniffed. "I know biomass has some problems—"

"That's *not* what I'm talking about," he hissed then took a deep breath as if to compose himself. "I mean, yeah, biomass is why I infiltrated the—"

"Infiltrated?" Orna was wide awake now.

"I'm a forest activist, and biomass is the biggest threat," he said with a trembling passion she'd never heard in the man's voice before.

Her mouth fell open as the truth dawned. "The wildfire bill. *You* stopped it."

He waved it away. "Doesn't matter anymore."

"You're a spy?" she whispered. All this time she'd thought of him as one of Rowan's lackeys. Apparently not. But while he might have a point about the flaws of biomass, no energy source was perfect, and he was clearly making a mountain out of a molehill. And, more important, if he was trying to take the Tenders down, she'd be the one paying the price.

"Rowan's not who he says he is," he said.

The fever in Silvio's eyes was something she'd seen before in men. He was jealous!

"This isn't about biomass at all, is it?" she said, acid creeping into her voice.

He nodded eagerly. "Right, it's just a cover."

"What I mean is, you found out what happened last night, and you're trying to make your move."

He cleared his throat. "I'm not gonna pretend I'm not into you." Cheeks pink, he cleared his throat. "But that's not why I'm here—"

"We both know why you're here." Silvio was like a hungry dog under the dinner table begging for his master's scraps. She needed to tell Rowan. She stood up.

"I just want you to be safe, Orna."

She scoffed. "From what?" Ray was the only one she needed to worry about, and Silvio couldn't help her there.

"I told you," he said through gritted teeth, his anger giving away the game. "From Rowan!"

She blew out her lips in disgust. Dude was just trying to get in her pants. As if she was that easy.

"The bonfire." A vein pulsed in his forehead.

"Yeah, what about it?"

"They only let me see so much." He peered out the window like a mental patient. "But on Halloween, after they thought I was asleep, they all went into the woods together."

The ash pit in the clearcut. "Who cares?"

"They're having another fire tomorrow night." He dry-swallowed. "And they invited me."

The door to the guest bedroom swung open, and Abba limped into the living room. "Sorry to interrupt, but we're late for our appointment."

Orna stared at Abba for a second before catching on. "Oh, yeah. We should probably go, then." She'd heard enough anyway.

Abba reached out his hand to Silvio, who shook it. "Very nice meeting you." The older man's hand on Silvio's back, he escorted him outside like a friendly bouncer. "Drive safe!" he said, before shutting the door in Silvio's hangdog face and locking it.

Abba turned to her. "Everything okay?"

"Yeah, yeah, fine." She wasn't shaken, just confused. Did Silvio actually have legit suspicions, or did he just have it out for Rowan? It wasn't like she could ask Rowan on the off chance it was about Ray. Maybe she should check it out herself. If there was evidence she could use against her blackmailer, it might be a way out of the mess. "Thanks."

"Don't mention it, *bubala*." He hobbled into the kitchen and opened the fridge. "How can I already be out?" He tipped a mostly empty jar of borscht, its insides coated with thick red beet juice.

Orna laughed. "Well, don't look at me. That stuff is nasty."

"I'll let it slide. This time." He wagged a finger. "But I've got my eye on you."

CHAPTER 18

The Subaru's headlights swept through the night and across the sign for the Silvercleft town limits. Cracks of light leaked out between drawn window shades on a few of the roadside cabins, stovepipes puffing smoke. Just past nine p.m. on a Wednesday, a lone pickup sat in the inn's parking lot, the building dark. Off season though it was, Orna had no idea how the place stayed in business.

Orna's email to Rowan that morning had been short and sweet, tipping him off about Silvio's undercover activism as well as his secret crush, wondering if the latter would make Rowan jealous. He hadn't responded yet. Of course, she hadn't said anything about the bonfire. Because she had to admit it *was* kind of odd to go a half-mile into the woods when they had the meadow right next to the lodge. On the night of the accident, she could see them wanting privacy for Dougie's memorial. But tonight, there'd be no reason for that.

She bucked along the ragged road past the closed general store and more cabins. Several of the driveways had trucks in them, but no one was out and about. Come to think of it, she never saw anyone in Silvercleft at all, whether doing yard work or walking their dog. Mountain folk were a strange bunch. She made the right turn and rumbled down the empty stretch of unlit road, swerving here and there to avoid potholes.

Her plan was simple. She'd sneak onto the property and scope out the meadow from afar. If it was simply another normal bonfire, then she could let the matter drop. If not…well, she'd cross that bridge if and when she came to it.

Instead of steering into Charwood's driveway, she kept going. Maybe an eighth of a mile around a bend the road petered out into an ATV trail, as the map app said it would, and she pulled over. As she killed the ignition, the glow from the dashboard faded, and night closed around her like a fist.

Slipping her headlamp on, she picked up the can of dog spray from the passenger seat in case that a-hole coyote, or whatever it was, came back, and stuck it in her back pocket. Dead quiet outside and still way too warm for fall in the Rockies, much less the week before Thanksgiving. Would it ever snow again in Colorado?

The dark was so smothering she wanted to switch on the light, but if she was going to stay unseen that wasn't an option. Thankfully, she was able to follow the road by keeping an eye on the moonlit gap of sky overhead, a river of midnight blue flowing between the black trees. She stumbled a few times and almost turned her ankle on a pothole but reached the driveway without any cars coming.

Toe-heel, toe-heel, she paced along the chewed-up dirt track pretending she was some Arapaho tracker. Finally, through the pines, orange flames like a rip in the night. She stopped. *See, Orna, just another boring fire.*

Then a yucky feeling squirmed in her belly. Why the heck hadn't Rowan invited her? Dumb as it was, she pictured him sitting on a log next to Kathy Phauda in her silk coat, the two of them feverishly making out. No longer worried about getting caught, she decided to keep going, the only sound a lone bird cawing from the trees. Who knows, if it was a party, maybe she'd crash the thing!

Right before the driveway broke into the meadow, she passed a stump which sprouted into a small tree. She squeaked in fright. Grabbing the dog spray, finger on trigger, she flipped on her light and got ready to fire.

Silvio in a hoodie smoking a cigar.

"You scared the heck out of me," Orna whispered, her heart a hummingbird. Clearly, Rowan hadn't spoken to him yet.

She aimed the beam at his face. And for a half second before he turned away a trick of the light made his eyes shine yellow. But what made her gasp was how most of the left side of his handsome face—from chin to cheekbone—was now covered in hideous blisters, like a human slice of pizza.

"What happened?" Orna asked, Eemah's ring cold against her ribcage.

He held up a hand to block the light. "You cannot be here."

She flicked off the lamp. "You get burned or something?"

For a few beats Silvio stood in silence, a dark cutout in the night, the sweet cigar smoke curling into Orna's nostrils, almost making her sneeze. "Yes."

"Oh my God! Have you been to the hospital?"

"You need to leave." While Silvio had been all amped up at the condo yesterday, now he sounded sleepy. Painkillers, probably; burns were supposed to hurt a lot.

Ray. Isabel. And now Silvio. She knew the Tenders built a lot of fires, but they were still, hands down, the clumsiest people she'd ever met. *Unless it's not a coincidence.* Orna shooed the anxious thought away like a buzzing fly. "What about the bonfire?"

"Nothing to see."

"Then there's no harm in me taking a look." She'd barely taken a step when Silvio clamped a hand on her elbow.

"What are you doing?" She tried to wiggle away, but his grip was iron.

"You must not."

"Why not?" The skin of his palm was hot as if he'd just come out of a bath. His breath stunk of smoke and rotten meat. "Is it Ray?"

He let go of her arm.

"You know about him, don't you?" she asked, holding her breath.

"Yes."

"And how I was the one who…"

"Yes."

Her throat was dry. "Did you tell Rowan?"

"No."

"Anyone else?"

"No."

She let out the breath. *Whew.*

Except now another person was in on it. Silvio couldn't do anything to help, but if she didn't make nice with him, there was a good chance he'd rat her out. If only she hadn't given him away to Rowan. Unless she could convince the head Tender to keep him around, the whole "keep your enemies close" thing.

"Rowan here?"

"He went to sleep."

Well, that solved that. There was no way she was running the risk of bumping into Ray at the fire.

"Go." Silvio gave her a push on the shoulder.

"All right, all right." Now that the guy knew he had no chance with her, he was being a total bitch.

As she walked back down the driveway to the road, Silvio's footsteps followed a stone's throw away. Though when she headed down the road towards her car, all was quiet.

Driving past the driveway again, Silvio stood at its threshold, hood drawn low over his face, cigar tip glowing cherry red.

CHAPTER 19

Feeling drained, Orna puttered along the dark road to Silvercleft. Soon as she got into cell range, she had to call Rowan to make sure he didn't fire Silvio, so the latter would keep her secret about Dougie. Then, to sidetrack his spying, she could start feeding him fake info about the Tenders' next campaign.

She cut left and cruised down Main Street, kicking up a dust plume as she rolled past the general store. Instead of things getting easier, they were only turning out to be more and more complicated. And exhausting. What were the chances she'd make it through the next year without going completely bonkers?

As she passed the inn, wonder of wonders, the downstairs windows were lit up. A little curious and a lot in need of a drink, she rolled into the lot. Out of the car, she clomped up the wooden boardwalk and lugged open the heavy door.

A wave of dry heat washed over her. Inside was a large room with low ceilings, scuffed dancefloor, and rough plank walls, the one by the door filled with row upon row of black and white framed group portraits. A giant moose head that had seen better days hung over the woodstove next to a wooden crate stacked with cordwood. The Allman Brothers' "Whipping Post" played softly from speakers propped in the corner.

At the bar, two blue collar guys in work clothes and boots—one in his late sixties and clean-shaven with a trucker hat on, the other maybe in his mid-twenties with a thick beard and wool cap—perched on the stools, glasses of light beer in front of them. Orna recognized each of their faces from the "climate action" bonfire on the night of the accident. After a quick look in Orna's direction both men stared straight ahead.

Orna let out a spiteful laugh. With this kind of welcome, no wonder the place was always empty. Still, she wasn't leaving without getting her damn drink.

As she stepped up to the bar, the older man whispered, "Shut up," to the younger one.

"This place even open?" Orna ticked a fingernail on the sticky bartop.

"Need something?" Old Townie asked coldly, almost but not quite making eye contact.

"Beer would be nice," she said pleasantly as she could.

Young Townie tapped the toe of his boot on the metal rail.

"What is it with this town?" Orna burst out, patience gone.

"People keep to themselves, is all," Old Townie said.

"You're friends with Rowan," she said, and both men shifted in their stools. "I saw you at the party."

Young Townie took a long swig from his beer, leaving foam in his moustache.

"They're a little strange, aren't they?" Orna poked, testing the waters.

"Never said nothing like that."

"It's okay." Orna flashed her best smile. "I work for them, and I still think they're weirdos."

"They take care of us," Young Townie said.

"What?" Orna took the stool at the end of the bar,

three empty ones between them.

He pointed at the stack of cordwood by the ticking woodstove.

Then it dawned on her. "You make that moonshine, don't you?"

The two men looked at each other.

Aha! That's why they were so antsy. Technically, moonshine was illegal. "Don't worry, your secret's safe with me." She winked, feeling stupid soon as she did it. "So, what do you do for work?"

"Contractors," Young Townie said.

"Oh, what kind?"

Young Townie opened his mouth to answer, but Old Townie kicked his boot, and he shut it again.

"We're grateful for everything you're doing for us, you know." Old Townie looked her steady in the eyes. "You'll tell Rowan that, won't you?"

"Why didn't you tell him yourself? Weren't you at the party tonight?" Orna threw it out to see if it'd stick. Silvercleft being such a small town, they probably knew more about Rowan's social life than she did.

A sinewy Granma Joad type in flannel shirt and jeans, long grey hair up in a bun, barged into the room, doors swinging shut behind her. "Sorry, Miss, but we're closed."

"This early?"

Frowning, the older woman picked up a rag and ran it over the bar.

"Just one drink?" Orna tried.

Bartender shot her a glare. "What do you want?"

There were a few taps, none of them labeled. "Maybe a red ale? Or a lambic? Nothing too hoppy. Just so long as it's local."

Bartender bent down, opened a small fridge, fished out a bottle, and slammed it on the bar. Coors Light.

Orna wrinkled her nose. "Take it to go," Bartender said.

"Can a bar do that?" Orna asked.

Bartender blinked at her.

"Well, what do I owe you?" Orna reached into her pocket for her wallet.

"On the house," Bartender said without a hint of friendliness and made a beeline to the front door. "Really got to close up now."

"Uh, thanks." Orna picked up the cold Coors, which was better than nothing. She turned to the guys still nursing half-full glasses. "Have a good night."

Both men nodded.

Bottle in hand, Orna strolled over to where Bartender stood by the open door, hands on hips. But instead of leaving, Orna crouched down to study the leftmost framed photo on the bottom row, hundreds of grim and dirty miner types gathered in front of this very inn, 1863 scribbled in pencil on top.

Bartender cleared her throat, which Orna ignored as she strolled along the wall. Each black and white group portrait took place the following year, the number of townsfolk shrinking after the mining boom had busted, women and children popping up, clothes getting more modern. 1923, the men in suits and bowler hats, women in stiff black dresses. 1968, everyone longhaired and smiling in flowy shirts, fringed vests, or bellbottoms. 1987, men in collared shirts and sweaters, women in blouses and high-waisted jeans.

"Miss!" Bartender said.

Orna pretended not to hear. The last photo on the top left was from 2005, with about fifty men, half as many women, and no children, nearly every face serious as the miners' had been.

"Where are the rest?" Orna asked.

"Out of my bar." Bartender stomped a workboot, nostrils on her button nose flaring. "Now."

"If you hate people this much, maybe you're in the wrong business," Orna griped as she went out the door. Then turned back, holding out her beer. "Can you at least open my—"

The door slammed shut in Orna's face, then the slide and click of a lock.

"You just lost a customer!" Orna yelled at the door.

Livid, she bit the inside of her cheek. She knew so-called "native" Coloradans hated city transplants, but this was ridiculous. Now she really needed a buzz. Angling the bottlecap against the wooden rail of the boardwalk, she punched down with the side of her fist, a trick she'd learned from Jessy in college. As always, the cap popped off, but she also shattered the lip of the bottle, and a froth spouted over her hand and dripped onto the planks.

"Screw this place!" Seeing red, she reached back and chucked the bottle across the road into the dark. A satisfying smash. But then she felt bad; she was no litterbug.

Headlamp out of her pocket, she put it on and crossed the empty street. A screen of trees hid a white picket fence with a gate, behind that a hundred or so gravestones.

Upset at having desecrated a cemetery, she opened the gate and walked along the mown yellow grass between chipped and weathered wooden crosses and worn slate and marble headstones, trying to find the broken bottle. Soon, her light glinted off shards in front of a newer-looking, polished stone reading, HENRY ROLSTON, DEDICATED HUSBAND AND FATHER, 1964-2005, as well as HOLLIE ROLSTON, BELOVED WIFE AND MOTHER, 1967-2005.

She knelt down to pick up the glass, some of which sparkled in the grass in front of the next grave, JOY GRAHAM, 1971-2005. Three deaths in the same year. Maybe they got in a car accident?

On a hunch, Orna kept strolling. JEFFREY PATTERSON, R.I.P., 1951-2005. What the heck was going on?

Orna counted eleven men and three women, from their mid-twenties to early sixties, all dying in 2005. The same year as the last town portrait at the inn. She racked her brain for what could've happened. Her first thought, thanks to COVID, was an epidemic. But H1N1 had been in 2009. Another fire, maybe? She needed to to do some research.

A sharp sting in her palm, she dropped the glass. "Shit!" Blood welled up from a small gash, which luckily didn't look that deep. Kneeling down to gather the pieces again, a few drops of blood dripped onto the grass in front of OUR PRECIOUS DAUGHTER, DESIREE HAMMERSLY, 1975-2005.

No longer wanting to be in that place, she hurried off to her car for the long drive home.

CHAPTER 20

As the smeary orange sun dipped below the peaks on the outskirts of Meadbury, Orna fit the thick white candles into Eemah's silver candlesticks.

Abba stroking his beard from the head of the table, she tore a paper match from the matchbook, lit both candles, waved out the match, and stuck the matchbook in the front pocket of her jeans. For a split second what looked like a tiny ghost—a mini version of what she'd hallucinated in the boiler plume at Charwood—danced in the wispy smoke from the snuffed match. But when she blinked it was gone.

Making a mental note to schedule an eye appointment, Orna lifted her hands and drew them towards her in a circular motion three times. It was part of the ritual, bringing the light to her, her family, her community. She wasn't coming back to the fold or anything, but with all the recent nuttiness she craved the normalcy of tradition. Besides, lighting the Shabbat candles—a task reserved for women alone—was one of the few things she still liked about Judaism.

She'd chosen not to practice the *bracha* in advance, curious to see how much she remembered. A breath in and she began, "Baruch atah Adonai, Eloheinu Melech haolam, asher kid'shanu b'mitzvotav, v'tzivanu l'hadlik ner shel Shabbat." The words rolled off her tongue, the meaning of the prayer basically, "God, you're the boss, so when you tell us to light candles, we do it."

"Shabbat Shalom," Abba said.

Orna stared at the candles, two trees ablaze in a forest fire. "Shabbat Shalom."

Back into the kitchen to take the supermarket challah out of its paper bag, set the knotty bread on a cutting board, get the knife out of the drawer, and bring it all to the table. Whereas only women lit the candles, men always cut the bread—at least in Orna's family. Like carving the Thanksgiving turkey, did it trace back to hunter-gatherer days when men got to tear off the first hunk from the carcass they'd dragged back to the cave?

Abba tested the blade with a fingertip and sliced into the crusty loaf. "Baruch atah Adonai, Eloheinu Melech haolam, hamotzi lechem min ha'aretz." Or, "God, you're super awesome, thanks for the bread."

"Amen," they said in unison.

He passed her a fat slice, the inside yellow and porous. She bit into the spongy sweetness; nothing like the yummy handmade loaves Eemah used to bake. Orna would use the rest to make French toast.

After finishing her piece, she went into the kitchen, put on mitts, and opened the oven. Hot air and the sharp, savory aroma of baked fish. She'd finished cooking the salmon, sweet potatoes, and green beans before sundown and left them in the off but still warm oven, per Shabbat rules. She took the glassware dishes out, set them on the counter, divided everything up onto two plates, and brought them to the table.

Abba popped a sweet potato into his mouth and moaned, "Delicious."

"I'm glad." Orna had barely sunk her fork into the flaky breaded fillet when her cell buzzed from the counter. Without looking she knew it was Rowan returning her message from earlier about Silvio. Instinctively, she moved to get up and then stopped herself. Not only was it dinner, it was Shabbat. While she didn't care a lick for the superstitions, the least she could do was honor the night around her father. A two-state solution in the condo: Israel downstairs, upstairs Palestine.

Three more buzzes—Abba calmly chewing as if he hadn't heard—and her phone quieted down. When another call came a minute later, he let out a breath through his nose but didn't say anything. She had to hand it to him. Since the snake bite he'd been pretty darned pleasant, as if he was following some version of, "If you can't say something nice, don't say anything at all."

Thirty seconds later, a single buzz; a text. The fact that Rowan kept trying to reach her meant he was taking the Silvio thing seriously. She really needed to get back to him but refused to rush the meal. And maybe a part of her wanted him to wait.

Only after setting the dirty dishes and empty pans to soak in the sink, already filled with hot water, did she excuse herself, grab her phone, and head upstairs. Indeed, Rowan had called twice, leaving a message the second time, and then texting, "Please call when u get this. I'll stay in range next hour."

Instead of bothering with the message, she perched on the edge of her bed and hit CALL.

Rowan picked right up and blurted out, "Why in the world would we keep him?"

She was more than ready for the question. "Now that we know what he's up to, we can stay a step ahead."

"High risk, low reward. Don't you think?"

"Not really." She fiddled with Eemah's ring through her shirt. "I can pretend I'm on his side and find out who he's working for."

"I dunno." His voice didn't sound as firm.

"What is it they always say in sports? The best defense is a good offense?"

A pause. "You'd really do this?"

She lay back on the bed. While she wasn't happy about piling on the lies, she'd come too far to turn back. "Absolutely."

"You're the best," Rowan said, and Orna hated how good it felt to hear. "I'll have a draft of the bill in the morning for you to look at, okay?"

"Sure." A bizarre way to make a living, but the fat check she'd cashed at the bank earlier that day helped.

"Talk to you tomorrow?"

"Hold on a sec." It had been gnawing at her since the night before, and she had to ask. She plumped her pillow and made herself comfortable. "What happened in Silvercleft in two-thousand-five?"

"Two-thousand-five?"

"Bunch of people died. I was at the cemetery."

"Gas main exploded. Fucking fossil fuels," he growled.

How awful. She rolled on her side and gazed at the floor vent. Gas and her people did not get along, to say the least. "So, that's why everyone burns wood in town?"

"Yep. Anything else before I let you go?"

She, of course, had plenty to say. That he was an idiot to reject her. That they had great chemistry. That you only had so many shots in life to find the right person. But she wouldn't give him the satisfaction. "That's all I got."

"Then I should probably get back to the bill."

"Sounds good." She almost hung up but didn't.

Neither did he.

Finally, he whispered, "Don't give up on me, Orna." And the line went dead.

CHAPTER 21

The woods were a little cooler today, though temperatures still hovered around an unseasonable sixty, and it wasn't even noon yet. Less than a mile in on the Meadbury trail—not the steep, snaky one where Abba had gotten bitten but a flatter one under tree cover smelling of dill—Orna's back had already sweat through her spandex top. Never a huge fan of winter, now she longed for the cold.

She would've asked Abba to come along, but his limp had gotten worse. He wouldn't show her his leg—had taken to wearing long pants around the condo—and refused to see a doctor, insisting everything was fine. She'd give him until next Friday morning, the day after Thanksgiving, and if it wasn't better by then, she'd make him go.

Per usual with Meadbury trails, she passed a bunch of people in the first mile but had the woods to herself after that. Stopping next to a house-sized boulder, she shrugged off her backpack and took out a small spiral notebook with a pen jammed inside. She opened to the first page where she'd written BIOMASS NOTES across the top.

Rowan had emailed her early that morning about a meeting he set up with Senator Palmer for Tuesday. No mention of what he'd said the night before about not giving up on him, she was bummed to find, only asking for feedback on his latest draft of the carbon neutral bill. From what she could tell, it looked pretty good if a bit jargony, packed with terms like "feedstocks," "stationary sources," and "biogenic emissions." To make it look like she was earning her keep, she tweaked a few sentences and sent it back to him.

A squeaking from above. Sitting on a branch a few feet overhead, a black squirrel with tufts on its ears scolded her, clutching a pinecone in its tiny arms. Orna chuckled.

Rowan's main ask was for her to come up with a "narrative," a story about carbon neutral biomass that the senator could easily digest, get across to colleagues on the Senate floor, and share with constituents.

So far, she'd sketched out a few talking points:

1. Fossil fuels carbon takes millions of years to form underground, stays there unless dug up and burned.
2. Tree carbon always being released from dying trees and sucked up by new ones, aka "biogenic" carbon cycle.
3. Replanting dead and dying forests with young trees sucks up carbon faster.

This was the most important thing Rowan had ever asked her to do, and unlike the field trip, she could *not* screw this up. She hadn't spoken to Ray since the pig roast but knew her future as a free woman was riding on this. Back on the trail again, notebook in hand, she practiced her pitch.

But one thing confused her, and after a few minutes she halted under the branches of a towering ponderosa pine to puzzle it out. One of the only studies Rowan had footnoted in the bill said that while some forms of biomass might be carbon neutral compared to fossil fuels, that was only over a forty-year time span for coal and ninety years for natural gas.

She ran her fingers over the rough orange plate bark of the thick trunk, not unlike a dinosaur leg. If this tree was cut and burned for biomass the carbon would hang out in the atmosphere for several decades. Which wouldn't be a big deal if they weren't already at 421 parts per million CO_2—the safe number supposedly being 350—with pretty much all climate scientists saying we had to cut emissions *immediately*. Of course, she was no Ph.D.—not even in the ballpark—so all this was best left for more educated minds. If Palmer brought it up at the meeting, she'd let Rowan do the talking.

Maybe a half-mile later, the grumble and grind of heavy machinery. No roads out there, so it couldn't be cars. And since this was Meadbury County Open Space, not a housing development either. After another hundred yards the trail was blocked by a plastic sandwich board reading DANGER in a red circle, then underneath:

NO ENTRY

RESTORATION IN PROGRESS

Interesting. Walking around the sign—public lands belonged to everyone, after all—she kept following the trail, the roar and whine getting louder, and then the quick buzz of a chainsaw. She was excited to see some of what she was advocating for in action.

To her left about a hundred feet away the forest floor rose and then dipped into a hollow. Just over the lip, the fluffy crown of a small ponderosa shook and disappeared out of sight, a crash an instant later. Heading off trail into the woods, she angled up the rise—a safe distance from any falling trees—so she could look down into the hollow.

A fifty-acre clearcut opened below her, dozens of piles

of logs—including some fat ones that had to be almost three feet in diameter—stacked human-high every few hundred feet around the edge of the brown, lifeless wasteland. The racket came from a huge bright-yellow machine that looked like a bulldozer—tank treads and all—but instead of a blade it had a mechanical arm with a claw at the end. A man sat in the cab behind glass panels.

As Orna stood there, the claw opened sideways like the jaw of some giant beetle and bit into the trunk of a tall pine a foot above the ground. In three seconds flat, the built-in saw blade hummed through the trunk, and the claw plucked the tree clear off the stump as if it were a dandelion. With a whine, the arm swung around a hundred and eighty degrees, the claw tilted, and dropped the tree with a crunch onto a pile of several just like it.

Orna was awestruck with the thing's power, the same gut flutters she got when a military jet thundered overhead. A mix of wonder at the triumphs of technology and wariness at the damage it could do— *had* done—in the wrong hands.

It was funny. All this time Orna had been picturing cartoon lumberjacks in flannels and suspenders, miniature Paul Bunyans with chainsaws instead of axes. Instead, there was one guy in one machine doing the work of dozens.

She strolled down the hill, keeping to the trees at the edge of the ugly cut. Though she searched for the telltale orange needles of beetle-kill in the canopy, it was a sea of green. And while a few trees here and there were naked and dead, the rest were alive and well. So, why were they cutting? Only one way to find out.

As she broke out of the sheltering tree cover into the naked clearcut, the temperature rose by at least ten degrees, the warm sun beating down on her face. Sauna dry compared to the forest, she crunched over wood chips that looked like shredded wheat giving off the antiseptic stink of sap.

She walked to within a stone's throw of the machine—its roar so loud she wanted to cover her ears—waved her hands and yelled, "Hey!"

The metal claw grabbed, sliced, and lifted another tree to drop in the pile then lurched forward on its treads towards the next in line, tearing and compacting the soil underneath. The operator obviously not seeing her, Orna bent over, picked up a small wood chip, and flung it at the cab's side window. It smacked the glass, and the man inside whipped his head towards her.

She waved in a friendly way, and a few seconds later he cut the engine, the silence like a library by contrast. That's when she realized she was out there alone in the woods with this logger.

Just as she considered bolting, he opened the door. Probably in his late forties, the man wore a grimy baseball cap, sweat-soaked T-shirt stretched across an enormous belly, and worn pants over work boots. "Hey lady, you're not supposed to be here!" he yelled.

Orna's fear fizzled as she realized the big guy couldn't catch her if he tried. "Can I ask you a few questions?"

His eyes ran up and down her body and then back to her face. "What about?"

"I'm thinking of getting into forestry," she said, which was sort of true. "And I'm curious about what you're doing out here."

He gazed at the clearcut and then his watch. "Hell, I was about to knock off for lunch soon, anyway."

Cooler in hand, he climbed down from the cab onto the treads and sat his huge butt down. He was even bigger than she'd realized, probably over three hundred pounds.

"What's your name?" he asked.

"Orna." She took a few steps forward but kept some space between them, just in case.

"Nice to meet you, I'm Buster." He flipped open the cooler and took out a strip of beef jerky. He tore open the plastic with his teeth and snapped off half of it in one bite. "So, what do you want to know?" he asked through a mouthful.

"This is a restoration project, right?"

He stopped chewing. "You're not one of them tree huggers from the college, are you?"

She flashed her best smile. "Do I look like I'm in college?"

He shrugged and eyed her up and down again. She had to force herself not to take a step back. "Fuel break."

"The whole thing?" She pointed at the depressing cut.

"Yup." He crammed the rest of the beef into his mouth and fished a can of root beer from the cooler.

"This would stop wildfires?" Playing dumb always got you the best answers.

He swallowed the jerky and popped the root beer. "The smaller ones."

"I thought the woods were overgrown because we don't let the small fires burn."

"That's all fine in the backcountry. But this is too close to people."

"Isn't that pretty much everywhere in Colorado these days?"

"Guess so." He took a long pull from the can. "Best thing people can do is take care of their property. Mow the grass and rake the needles. Make sure no trees or woodpiles are up against any structures. Metal roofs, screened vents. That sorta thing."

"And what about the big fires?"

"They go where they want." He burped into a fist. "Shit, a few years ago I seen one blow straight through a two-hundred-acre regen."

There it was again: regenerative harvest, logger speak for clearcut.

"What do you think the chance is of a small fire in this exact spot?" she asked.

He rooted around the cooler and pulled out a paper-wrapped sub sandwich about the size of his meaty forearm. "Slim to none."

"Then what's the point?"

He unwrapped the sandwich, all pink cold cuts, no lettuce or tomato between the bread. "You do enough of them across the landscape…" He chomped into the sandwich.

In a sense, Buster was right. If they cut down every tree in the forest, no more wildfires. But that would be as ridiculous as draining a swimming pool so no one could drown.

"Where's the wood going?"

"High-grade logs to the mill in Plunkett. Everything else to Hawk Valley."

The biomass plant. Orna had a sick feeling in the pit of her stomach. This hadn't been beetle kill but a healthy, living forest. Was this a one-off or the kind of logging actually fueling the biomass boom?

"Hey, so what're you doing later tonight?" Buster grinned, a smudge of mayo on the corner of his lip.

She had three different feelings all at once. The first was offended, that a guy like this would think for even a minute that he had a chance with her. The second was flattered, since her confidence had taken a hit from the whole Rowan situation. And the third was pity, that this poor *schlub* was about to be shot down.

In this case, number one came out on top. Not because Orna thought she was so amazing but the opposite—that little voice inside her head telling her she and Buster might be in the same league, and *that* was why Rowan was so hard to pin down.

"Sorry, I don't date loggers." Orna spun on her heels and stalked off across the clearcut without a look back.

CHAPTER 22

Woken by the gentle yet irritating chimes of her cell phone alarm, Orna groaned and pried open itchy, sleep-deprived eyes.

Right before she'd gone to bed, she'd gotten a call from a restricted number. Normally, she'd have let it go to voice mail, but this time she answered.

"If the bill goes through, this can all be over," Ray said and then the line went dead.

After hours of tossing and turning, Orna had finally fallen asleep. And now it was already time to get up.

The morning sun seeped through the curtains a lot brighter than she'd have thought for 6:30. Groggy, she reached over to the nightstand and picked up her cell. It read—no—8:01! She'd slept through her freaking alarm!

Instantly awake, she launched out of bed. She was supposed to meet Rowan outside Senator Palmer's Denver office at 8:45 for their 9 a.m. appointment. Without traffic, Denver was a thirty-minute drive, so if she hauled butt, she might be able to make it. She *had* to make it!

She grabbed yesterday's bra from the chair and yanked it on. Then the white blouse and black skirt hanging in her closet. Splash of water on her face, swipe of deodorant. Snatched the notecards from her dresser and booked it downstairs.

Abba sat at the kitchen table munching a bagel, glass of orange juice in front of him. "How did you—"

"No time!" She scurried past, scooped up her pumps from the shoe rack, took her purse from the hook, and ran out the door. "Back later!"

Already 8:07 by the time she got in the car. She kept to the idiotically slow twenty-five mile per hour speed limit through her neighborhood and beat the light across busy Main Street. Soon as she spilled out onto Route 77—luckily, traffic was thin since most people had off for Thanksgiving—she veered into the empty toll-only express lane and stomped the gas until she hit seventy-five.

8:12. She rubbed her bleary, scratchy eyes. What she wouldn't have given for a strong cup of black tea. No one ahead of her, phone in hand, she pulled up the text thread with Rowan, and dictated, "Might be a little late." She hit SEND. She buzzed down the window halfway, wind slapping her awake, and edged up to eighty. Amazingly, for the next fifteen miles she didn't pass a single cop.

At 8:39 she took the offramp into Denver, high rises sprouting in the near distance like mushrooms after a rain. Into a flowing stream of vehicles on the three-lane road heading downtown. *Gogogogogogo!*

She'd driven past the federal building a few times, but not wanting to take any chances she typed DENVER FEDERAL BUILDING into her map app, jerking back into her clogged lane as a cyclist whizzed by inches away, shaking his fist. She followed the directions, taking a right on a side street bordered by townhomes. Then a left at the green light onto busy 11th past fast food restaurants and rent-a-cars. And right again down a narrow one-way with empty parking lots to either side.

A block away from the destination, she found an open parking spot on the street and slipped in, scraping the curb with her front wheel. She turned off the ignition. No time to put money in the meter. 8:48. *Hurry up!*

Pumps in hand, purse banging against her ribs, she jogged down the sidewalk barefoot, sidestepping dark stains and wads of chewing gum and leaping over a tiny orange cylinder that might've been a syringe cap.

A minute later, the grey mausoleum-like federal building loomed. Shockingly dapper in an immaculate grey suit, ponytail slicked back, beard trimmed and gleaming with oil, Rowan sat on the bottom step of a long flight of stairs leading up to the glass front doors. Orna was torn. If the bill passed, she'd be free. But she'd also probably never see Rowan again.

"So sorry I'm late," she panted and sprung past him up the steps.

He caught up before she got inside. "Everything okay?" He sounded more worried than upset as she heaved open the door.

"Yeah, just overslept." She peeked at her phone. 8:52, still time. In the lobby, she came to a stop inches from banging into the chest of a tall, clean-shaven man in white shirt and black cap. Stupid Homeland Security!

Rowan dropped his wallet and keys in a plastic bin on the conveyor belt, and she did the same with her purse and phone in another. The belt slid forward, drawing their stuff into the metal detector as a stocky, short-haired blonde woman in uniform squinted at a screen.

Orna knelt down to kick on her pumps, and as she followed Rowan through the gate, an earsplitting beep. A third guard, a wiry young black man, held up a palm and wanded her, starting at her feet. That, too, beeped as it got to her chest. Her underwire? She patted herself and felt Eemah's ring.

Ring and chain in a second bin, this time the wand was quiet. Orna picked up her stuff and slipped the ring back around her neck and under her shirt. When she caught Rowan staring at her chest, he quickly looked away. Typical dude.

They hustled to the elevator. She smacked the UP button and found UNITED STATES SENATOR REGINA PALMER - FLOOR 3, SUITE 38 on the wall plaque. The elevator dinged open, they got in, she poked 3, and the doors slid shut behind them at 8:57.

Orna let out a huge breath. "Let's rock this," she said, and Rowan gave her an awkward high five. Even in that brief touch she felt the electricity between them. *Focus, Orna, focus!*

Down a narrow hallway, doors to either side, they found Suite 38. Rowan led the way into a small waiting room with a few chairs, a young Asian man at reception in front of two closed doors. Orna's mood soured as Kathy Phauda sashayed out of the nearer door and shut it behind her, runway-model gorgeous with flawless lipstick and eyeshadow, silky locks spilling over the shoulders of a form-fitting blouse. Orna had to stop herself from smoothing down her own frizzy curls.

Phauda waved them over, and they all went behind the front desk through the other door. It was a small office, and Senator Palmer stood up from her shiny wooden desk cluttered with stacks of paper. Short and slim in a navy blue powersuit, with a striking resemblance to the actress Halle Berry, the senator flashed a dazzling smile and came over to shake their hands with a firm grip.

"Welcome, welcome." Palmer motioned towards two padded chairs and sat back down in her big leather one. "Please have a seat."

Orna and Rowan did so.

"Nice seeing you two." Phauda smiled, and, to Orna's delight, left the room.

"So, what've you got for me?" the senator asked.

"We know you're not keen on a logging bill," Orna began, and the senator nodded gravely. "But declaring biomass carbon neutral is a win-win across the board. I assume you've read our bill?"

"Not yet." Palmer picked up a few pieces of stapled paper and shook them. "Gimme the bare bones."

Orna turned to Rowan, whose Adam's apple bobbed as he dry-swallowed. Wow. Here he was actually freezing up, his social anxiety on full display. It was all up to her.

"Well, to start with…" Orna drew a blank. She'd practiced her pitch for days but couldn't remember the first point? The room telescoped in and out. God, she was tired. Her only hope was to stall until it came back to her. "It's a real opportunity for bipartnership. Bipartisanship."

Get it together, girl! Then the gears clicked into place. Start with the problem. Orna cleared her throat. "Fossil fuels take millions of years to form. And when we extract and burn coal, oil, or natural gas, that locked up carbon goes straight into the atmosphere. Right, Rowan?"

"Yup," Rowan said enthusiastically.

"But biomass carbon is a cycle," Orna went on, her mojo rising. "When we release it, it's reabsorbed by the forest."

The senator raised a perfectly sculpted eyebrow. "That carbon doesn't go into the atmosphere?"

Rowan rubbed his hand on the leg of his slacks, of no use to anyone.

"Well, yes," Orna said. "But it's not the same kind of carbon dioxide. It's biogenic."

"As in, a different form of the molecule?" Palmer tented her fingers under her chin, nails a shiny mauve.

"I don't think so. But it's...biogenic." Orna licked dry lips, already out of her depth. "Always cycling back and forth between trees and the atmosphere."

"Sorry, I'm having a hard time understanding." The senator leaned back in her chair. "Other than the redwoods and some patches of old-growth, primarily on the Pacific coast, the vast majority U.S. forests were cut over the last hundred years, correct?"

Clueless, Orna looked to Rowan.

"Y-yes," he stuttered.

Palmer nodded. "And we've been burning fossil fuels since the seventeen-hundreds, no?"

"Sure," Rowan said.

"And that's why our carbon dioxide levels are so high, eh?"

"Uh-huh," Rowan said.

"So, doesn't that mean a lot of the carbon absorbed by trees nowadays is actually fossil fuels carbon?"

Rowan's cheeks were red; it was the first time Orna had seen him blush.

"Which means that when you burn a tree for biomass," Palmer pinned Orna with intense amber eyes, "it's not that different than burning coal, emissions-wise. Or am I missing something?"

Oh no. "It's biogenic." Orna peeped, out of answers. A falling sensation that was her freedom—her life— crumbling beneath her feet.

"You keep saying that, but I'm not sure it means anything," Palmer said quietly.

"The thing about b-biogenic c-carbon—"

"Let me ask you this, Ms. Tannenbaum." Palmer stared Orna down. "If we didn't burn those trees for biomass, wouldn't they be taking up more carbon?"

Here was Orna's window. Now or never to turn this thing around. "Actually," Orna sat up straight, "not only do trees absorb less carbon as they age, at a certain point they start emitting it."

Frowning, Palmer sifted through a short stack of printouts, plucked out a single page, and slid it across the desk. "Will you read the headline, please?"

Orna picked it up. It was the abstract from a study in *Nature*, the world's most prestigious scientific journal. She read out loud, "Rate of tree carbon accumulation increases continuously with tree size." That didn't sound right.

"And now," Palmer said, "in highlighter."

Sweat beading on her upper lip, Orna scanned down to the line run through with fluorescent yellow. "Thus, large, old trees do not act simply as sene—senescent…" She wasn't sure how to pronounce that one, and kept going, "…carbon reservoirs but actively fix large amounts of carbon compared to smaller trees." The opposite of what Rowan had been telling her.

"We're not talking about logging healthy old-growth trees," Rowan said finally with a shaking voice, "just dead and dying ones."

Orna thought about the Meadbury clearcut and wasn't so sure. But even if this *was* all a scam, what did she care? She had her *life* to think about! What was the point of protecting trees if she was in a prison cell?

"You look conflicted, Ms. Tannenbaum." Palmer cocked her head, studying Orna as if the younger woman were an interesting bug.

"It's nothing." Orna tittered.

Palmer pursed her lips before speaking. "We women have overcome far too much to censor ourselves now, honey. If you've got something to say, I want to hear it."

"I don't." Orna's mouth went dry. Why hadn't she brought water?

"You sure?"

"Yes ma'am. Congressma'am."

Palmer had seen right through her. It was all over. Might as well have stayed in bed. Orna felt like puking.

After gazing at Orna for another few uncomfortable seconds, the senator clapped her hands and got to her feet. "This has been very instructional. But I have other appointments. If you'll excuse me." And she motioned toward the door.

Rowan was glum and silent as they rode the elevator to the lobby. Orna kept waiting for him to say something—anything—but he didn't. She'd definitely messed up, but with the half-truths he'd fed her, how could she have done otherwise?

Only once they'd gotten outside again and were walking down the stairs, did he speak. "I don't know if we can come back from this."

Orna was mad about the lying but even madder at him for wanting to throw in the towel. This was her future he was messing with. "There are other senators."

"It took years to get in with Palmer." He hung his head. "Years."

"Maybe we don't need Congress," she said just to say something as they got to the bottom of the steps.

He almost perked up. "Another idea?"

She shook her head, not going to bluff her way out of this one. But he *had* asked her not to give up on him. "Where there's a will, there's a way," she said lamely then wished she hadn't. "We'll think of something, I promise." She'd comb the internet for answers the minute she got home. She just hoped Ray would take this as the temporary setback it was and give her another chance.

Rubbing his beard, Rowan stared off into the distance, eyes pits of sadness.

"Talk tomorrow?" Orna chirped.

Faking an unconvincing smile, Rowan gave her arm a squeeze and turned away.

Orna moped back to the car, promising herself a long, hot bath and a glass of wine—or three—when she got home. Maybe it'd still turn out okay. Always darkest before the dawn…though that wasn't even technically true.

A yellow piece of paper was under the Subaru's wiper. Ticket. Screeching, Orna grabbed it, crumpled it into a ball, chucked it on the sidewalk, and got in the car. Then—not wanting to have her name on some scofflaw database—got out again, picked it up, and jammed it in the glove compartment.

As she reached for the ignition, her chest tightened like an invisible man had her in a bear hug. She tried to inhale, but it was like breathing through a layer of plastic. As if caught in a rushing river, all she could do was sit back and let it happen.

Wait, Rowan's breathing trick! An oar to guide her downstream.

She blew out all her air.

Pinched a nostril and inhaled.

Then the other and exhaled.

Eyes unfocused, she gazed up into the bright blue sky, clouds bunching and stretching and breaking into vapor.

And after a few more bumpy breaths, Orna drifted gratefully back to shore.

165

CHAPTER 23

Orna speared a shred of turkey breast from her plate, expecting the worst. But, no, it was tender and only a little dry, much better than she would've guessed from a pre-cooked supermarket bird. Abba gave her a thumbs up from across the table, white coleslaw juice dripping down his beard.

Knocked down a notch from her latest panic attack—not nearly as bad this time thanks to Rowan's technique—Orna had decided not to cook Thanksgiving dinner herself and instead picked up food from the Compleat Chow deli, the natural foods chain with kosher options. She'd taken the dishes—turkey, mashed potatoes, squash, green beans, and stuffing—out of their plastic containers and dumped them into glassware, plates, and bowls, and reheated everything in the oven. At least it smelled like Thanksgiving. Fresh from the can, the ribbed cylinder of cranberry sauce quivered in its bowl like a giant grub.

"Tried the stuffing yet?" Abba dabbed his mouth with a napkin.

"Not yet." She took a bite. Spongey but savory; it was edible.

"I like it. Nothing like your Eemah's, of course."

Orna grunted, her mind elsewhere. The mental strain from flubbing the meeting with the senator was tearing her apart, and she had a sinking feeling she'd blown her last chance to escape the Tenders anytime soon. If ever.

She washed down the stuffing—and the thought—with a sip of room temperature water.

That morning, Rowan had sent Orna an email inviting her on a trip out to Hawk Valley to tour the biomass plant. She had zero interest in seeing it but leapt at the chance to spend a few hours alone with him. Grey as things had gotten, Rowan was the silver lining. Would he finally make his move or wimp out again?

"Pass the squash?" Abba asked.

She handed over the warm bowl.

"Where'd you find that?" Abba pointed at her torso.

She looked down. Eemah's ring had slipped out of her shirt and dangled from its chain. The cat was out of the bag. "Eemah's jewelry case."

He frowned. "That wasn't hers."

Oh, no. Had her instinct been right, that it was some gift from a secret lover? She clenched the ring in a fist. "It wasn't?"

He shook his head. "Belonged to your Bubby Ilana."

Orna silently scolded herself for even *doubting* Eemah. But Abba still didn't look happy. "And that's a problem?"

"Your Bubby—how to put this." He clinked his fork down on the plate with an embarrassed smile. "Didn't quite fit the mold."

"As in…"

"A bit of a *meshugana*."

"Like, clinically?" Which would certainly explain a lot about Orna's genetics.

"Let's just say she saw life in a way most of us do not."

Eemah had told her a few stories, how Bubby Ilana

had been a respected leader of Vermont's Jewish community and sadly dropped dead of a heart attack while getting things ready for what was supposed to be her last fundraiser. But nothing like this. "What kind of way?"

"Doesn't matter." He popped a forkful of dark meat into his mouth.

"I wanna know."

Empty fork in hand, he looked down at his plate. "*Mazzikim*."

"*Matzah* what?"

"*Mazzikim*." Then he mumbled, "You'd call them demons."

Orna scoffed. "Like little red guys with horns and tails?"

Abba shrugged.

She tried the green beans, which were oily and overcooked. "And the ring?"

Abba rolled his eyes. "Do you really care about all this?"

"No," she sniped. "I'm not at all interested in the fact that my dead grandmother believed in monsters."

"Good." He grabbed a roll.

"Abba!"

Sighing, he split the roll with a knife. "Your Bubby said it came from the old country, passed down the generations as protection from those…creatures."

"What is this, *Lord of the Rings*?"

Abba rolled his eyes. "A far older tale than that. King Solomon's Seal?"

Vaguely, it rang a bell, some silliness about cutting a baby in half and controlling spirits. Orna fingered the cold circle, the simple white on black Hebrew taking on new meaning. "Why Shaddai and not Adonai?"

"Comes from the word *shadayim*, which means…?" He cocked an eyebrow.

"Breasts."

He nodded. "Mentioned in the Bible almost fifty times, Shaddai is an androgynous manifestation of HaShem, an acknowledgment of how both men and women were made in the Creator's image."

One of the main pieces that had turned Orna away from Judaism was the idea of God as some old man with a long flowing beard, an angry Santa Claus in the sky keeping a list and checking it twice. But this…this was intriguing.

"The letters, too, mean something." Setting down the roll on his plate, Abba was in full scholar mode now. "What does *Shin* look like to you?"

Orna traced the ש with a thumb. "Lit candles?"

"Wow, very good, Orna." Abba fluttered his fingers. "The three pillars of the Tree of Life reaching high like flames, purifying and transforming our lives, aligning us with creation."

Orna's life had sure as heck transformed over the last few weeks. But certainly not for the better. She rotated the ring a few degrees to ד. "*Dallet* means door…"

"Right. And the image?"

"Hmmm. A right angle?"

"Picture it as a person." Abba tented fingers under his bushy chin.

"Someone bending over?"

"You're good at this," Abba said. Never much of a student in her girlhood, it was nice to hear for once. "Humble like an old person or someone *davening*, *Dallet* is the state of selflessness needed to pass through to the mystery of being."

While Orna rarely thought of herself as better than

everyone else—the opposite, in fact—selflessness was never her strong suit, either.

She went on to י. Basically, the tip of ש. "*Yod* is a flame?"

Abba clapped his hands together way too loudly. "The Divine spark which causes everything to be. *Adonai ehad*. One God." He picked up his roll and took a bite.

Orna had to know more. "Bubby was so scared of demons, of all things, she wore a ring to keep them away?"

Abba threw back his head to chortle, and almost choked on the bread, needing to take a sip of water to clear his throat. "Your Bubby wasn't scared of anything. Difficult woman, but she had guts."

"Wish I did, too," Orna murmured, heavy all of a sudden like someone had tossed a soggy blanket over her. Then covered her face with her hands and started to cry.

"What's wrong, *bubala*?" Abba cooed.

More than anything, she wanted to tell him. About getting drunk and running over Dougie. About taking Ray up on his offer to hide the accident from police. About him secretly burying the body. About her thing for Rowan. But it would crush him. Just crush him.

Still, she had to talk to someone or she'd burst. And if she didn't give away too much... "My new job. It's stressing me out." She dabbed her eyes with the napkin.

"Then go back to journalism."

"I can't. It's—it's hard to explain."

He worked his jaw, his face stone. "Is it that Silvio *momzer* I had to throw out of here?"

"No."

"If it's the money—"

"It's *not* the money," she cut him off before he could

go down that road.

"If it's not a good fit, find something that is." He shrugged, as if it was the easiest thing in the world.

"That's not what *you* did!" she snapped, more angry at herself than him. "Eemah said you wanted to be a poet."

"Poet's not a real job," he said and grinned, a fleck of green bean stuck between his front teeth. "But even if it was, I did it so you could have the choices I never did."

Heart melting, Orna took a sip of water so she wouldn't start crying again. He didn't know the details of what was going on with her, but what if he was right?

What if she turned herself in? Whether she'd been drinking or not, no court in the world would've expected her to see someone lying under her back tire in the dark. No longer hungry, she smushed a potato chunk with a fork.

Taking weeks to come clean was definitely a crime—the worst mistake of her life—but it was the first time she'd ever done anything like that. And she could honestly testify that she had nothing to do with moving the body.

She swirled the mashed potatoes around her plate. What if…what if they didn't send her to prison at all and just gave her probation? And even if she did get some time, wasn't temporarily being locked up with a clean conscience better than a lifetime of crushing guilt? And maybe it wouldn't even be so bad. She could meditate, write, do yoga, treat it like a monastery and come out a new person on the other side.

It was as if a fresh wind had blown away the smog. On tomorrow's trip with Rowan to the biomass plant she'd tell him the truth—if he truly cared about her, he'd understand; if not, it was never meant to be. And then Abba…the hardest part. But he loved her, and, she had no doubt, would forgive her. And *then* police.

Almost getting her appetite back, she took a bite of the potatoes. If she could survive a freaking pandemic, she could get through this.

Abba, however, had stopped eating and stared at his plate with glassy eyes.

"Something wrong with the food?" she asked.

He shook his head, sweat trickling down pale cheeks.

"You're not sick, are you?" Her first thought was COVID. Yet another variant was going around, and certain counties in Colorado still had some of the highest case counts in the country.

Orna went to his side and felt his damp forehead with the back of a hand. Yikes, he was burning up! On a hunch, she bent over and yanked up his pantleg.

Abba shoved her hand away. But not before she caught a glimpse of the pus-filled, infected wound on the back of his calf.

CHAPTER 24

Rowan, in Rockies cap and sunglasses, gunned the pickup over the rise heading west on I-70. From the passenger seat, the landscape opened in front of Orna into a jaw-dropping view of storybook snowcap peaks and rocky ridges. Window halfway open, the wind blew back her hair, but lost in the wastelands of her mind, she took no pleasure in the scenery.

After Thanksgiving dinner she'd driven a mostly compliant Abba to the hospital where he was diagnosed with sepsis, his infected snakebite spreading through his bloodstream. They hooked him up to an IV to pump him full of antimicrobials and said they needed to keep him for the next few days.

Groggy and pretty much out of it, Abba had been conscious enough to listen to Orna to read him news from her phone until he fell asleep around midnight. Then she headed back to the condo to get some rest before the morning's trip.

Rowan, to his credit, seemed to sense something was going on and did her the favor of keeping quiet. Another point in his column. Instead, they'd been listening to a Bob Dylan CD for the last forty minutes, some album she'd never heard before, full of way-too-long songs with dozens of nonsense verses.

The pickup swooped downhill. Below, a vast quarry had been hacked out of the grey bedrock in a staircase made for a giant. When the highway flattened out again Rowan hit the turn signal, glanced over his shoulder, and drifted into the left lane to pass a slow-moving RV. An extremely cautious driver, Orna hadn't caught him going more than five miles over the limit even once.

She opened her mouth to tell him the truth about the accident and Ray's blackmail but couldn't find the words. Best to put it off until the drive back, anyway—a half-hour outside of Meadbury would keep the awkwardness to a minimum. Instead, she picked up her phone from the seat and texted Abba, "How you feeling :)"

They whizzed by the exit for BLACK ROCK CASINO, a ridiculous place she'd never been and never would. Who takes a trip into the beautiful wild Rockies to gamble and eat buffet dinners indoors? Past the mining-turned-tourist town of Omaha Springs with its plunging waterfall and rotting wooden mill wheel, Dylan droning on about a "sad-eyed lady of the lowlands."

Traveling onwards and upwards, her ears popped. At that elevation, the lodgepole pine forest hemming them in on both sides turned to spruce.

"Those all the same species?" Orna shouted over the music so he'd know her moody silence had nothing to do with him.

Rowan turned the stereo down long enough to say, "Engelman and Colorado blue," and cranked the volume back up again.

As they kept climbing, finally a couple of inches of dirty melting snow mounded the side of the road and lined the forest floor, the air cool enough to make Orna close her window. Then a sign:

EISENHOWER –
EDWIN C. JOHNSON
MEMORIAL TUNNEL
ELEV 11,013 FT

They entered the tunnel punched into the mountainside. Lit by a string of lights, the passage was tight and narrow, icicles dripping from the cement ceiling not ten feet overhead. Orna wondered if there'd ever been any cave-ins, whether she could hold it together if they got stuck, and how good Rowan would be in an emergency. A minute later they were spat out on the other side into the blinding daylight.

"Continental Divide, baby!" Rowan shouted.

From there on out, every river flowed west. Orna, too, hoped her life would soon start going in the opposite direction.

"Did you talk to Silvio?" It didn't really matter anymore now that she was about to come clean. But she had been the one who set it in motion.

Rowan nodded, sun glinting off his shades. "Got him right where we want him."

She wasn't sure what would happen once she quit the Tenders, but Silvio was a big boy and could take care of himself.

Fifteen minutes later a blue reservoir spread out below them, its edges frozen white. Then more sprucy mountains. Downhill along a block of tall, ritzy hotels, the slopes of Vail ski resort hacked out of the forest, layered like a cake in fake snow with rainbow sprinkles of skiers in parkas. Quickly as it came, the snow disappeared, and bushy spruce gave way again to tall skinny lodgepole.

Her phone buzzed. A text from Abba, "Dear Orna, I

am doing OK, but I am still under observation. Abba."

Stable at least, thank God. She texted back, "Keep me posted. c u later tonight."

"Don't worry about it. I will see you tomorrow," he replied.

"What are you talking" she started to write, but then again, it *would* be late by the time she got back. And after the long day it might be best to get a full night's sleep and see him first thing. She deleted the text, wrote, "K," and set down her phone.

The minute Abba got home from the hospital she'd tell him everything. She could already picture his face falling, pinching the bridge of his nose in sorrow and shame.

Head overloaded and body lulled by the rhythmic rumble of rubber over asphalt, she soon found herself getting sleepy and nodded off.

Orna woke with a snort and rubbed the sharp crick in the back of her neck. She couldn't have been out long, but the landscape had changed yet again. Short, droopy junipers and some kind of wide-branching pine sprouted here and there on dusty hills the color of menstrual blood. Rock outcroppings jutted into the deep blue sky, boulders like fossilized turds down below. For all she knew she could be in New Mexico or Arizona, everything was that dry, jagged, and raw.

She wet her throat with a sip from her water bottle. "How much further?"

"Half-hour," Rowan said, never taking his eyes off the road.

From out of nowhere, a twenty-foot-wide sparkling river began carving its way along the foot of cinnamon cliffs not far off the highway.

Rowan jerked his thumb. "The Hawk."

Thanks to the drought, the water ran low through the rocky channel, but Orna did her best to enjoy the sight while she still had her freedom. Soothing as the river was, Dylan was getting on her nerves. For the third frigging time "Leopard Skin Pill Box Hat"—the folksinger's worst song—chunked from the speakers into her eardrums. She smacked the eject button, snatched the CD, and flung it on the dashboard.

She glared at Rowan, daring him to say something. But he kept nodding his head in time to a music that no longer played. Very unlike her ex, Seth, who would've gone off at her and checked the disc for scratches.

Orna wanting to say something but not knowing what, they ended up sitting in silence for a while. To the left, the river wandered through brushy banks, and to the right, pale yellow-brown hills like crumpled animal hide.

"Thar she blows!" Rowan called.

Across the river, perched on a small rise, was an ugly factory with a tall silo beside an even taller smokestack spouting vapor. The Hawk Valley Clean Energy Center. Piled next to the facility was a mound of wood chips the size of a ski resort bunny hill.

One hundred thousand tons of wood per year to power ten thousand homes. Seemed like a lot of electricity until you realized you'd need five hundred plants to cover Colorado's population of six million and growing—and that didn't count the lion's share of energy use, heating and transportation. With the hit on forests, the carbon emissions, and the air pollution, the more she looked into biomass, the less it seemed to pencil out. *Whatever. Let someone else worry about it. Got enough on my plate as is.*

Rowan took the exit for the town of Hawk, curved along the roundabout by a gas station, then past a couple dozen rundown bungalows into a nothing of a town. Just one plaza with a supermarket, bank, pizza place, and a few other depressing businesses like a dollar store and storage center.

Directly across the road from the plant sat a rectangular cement building with hardly any windows—a weathered sign read, HAWK VALLEY HIGH—its athletic field patchy and muddy. Rowan left the empty road for a dirt drive, bumped over a railroad track, and parked at the edge of a small lot next to a dozen other pickups. A front-end loader heaved a shovelful of woodchips from the massive pile.

"A beaut, ain't she?" Rowan said like a proud father.

"I killed Dougie." Orna's confession came out like an unexpected burp.

He looked at her with a bland smile, clearly not understanding.

"I was the one who ran him over," she explained. "Not Ray." Terrifying as it was to share her secret, it was such a relief to finally get it out, like removing a stray eyelash caught in an eye.

"Oh, I know." Rowan patted her hand.

Orna almost choked on her spit. "What do you mean, you know?"

"I knew the whole time."

It didn't make sense. And then it did, and a tide of hate welled up in her heart. "The blackmail...it was *you.*"

His smile was gone. "We needed you. Still do."

All the guilt. All the self-loathing. He was in on it.

And she'd thought the scumbag might've been the one… She clenched a fist and punched his shoulder, hard. Then again. And again. He sat there taking the blows, until after a few more jabs she ran out of juice.

"The anxiety? You faked that, too?" Orna growled.

He shook his head. "And for what it's worth, I never would've turned you in."

"So what?! You're a liar! And a sociopath!" Orna might've taken some solace in the fact that she no longer had a reason to go to police, that she'd be getting her life back. But there was only white-hot rage.

"Dougie was already dead, and I couldn't let that go to waste." He tried to draw her in with his sad baby-blue eyes, but this time she wasn't falling for it. "I'm very sorry it had to be that way. But this is bigger than the both of us."

"You're a hundred percent full of shit!" Orna tore at her hair, strands coming off in her shaking hands. "And we're not even helping the fucking environment!"

Rowan took a deep breath and let it out. "From the second I saw you, I knew you were one of us," he said. "Do you want to know the real truth?"

An icy blast of fear like she'd fallen into an arctic lake. *Run!* She unbuckled her seatbelt and fumbled for the door handle, knowing that when she pulled, the door wouldn't budge. But it swung right open.

"I know what you saw in the smoke," Rowan whispered. "Back at Charwood, during your panic attack."

She stopped halfway out of the seat. "I didn't see anything."

"Yes, you did."

Something in her throat made it hard to talk. "A hallucination. From the weed."

"I saw it, too."

She didn't know what his angle was this time, but clearly nothing that came out of the guy's mouth was true. How could she have been so dumb? Better a life alone than messing around with rats like him.

"I wanna go home." She flopped back in the seat and folded her arms below her breasts. "Drive me back. *Now.*"

"I will, Orna, I promise. But I'd like to show you something first."

For a second, she had the crazy thought he was going to pull out his dick. Instead, he took off his sunglasses and pointed at the smokestack puffing a stream of white fluff into the berry-blue sky. "What do you see?"

"Water vapor." Contrary to popular belief, it wasn't exactly smoke—didn't mean there wasn't any pollution, just that the particles were too small to see.

"What else?"

"It's a plume," she growled between her teeth. She didn't even know why she was still talking to the a-hole. "Of vapor."

"Remember those *Magic Eye* books from when we were kids?" He squinted at the smokestack, his crow's feet deepening.

She sniffed.

He went on, "You were supposed to stare at the pattern until you saw a three-D shape."

"Who gives a crap?" She had to find another way home. The front-end loader was back scooping more fuel for the fire. She wondered if that guy, or any of the other employees, lived near Meadbury and could give her a ride. Otherwise, a cab it was. She got out her phone.

"Were you able to see the shapes? As a kid?" he

asked.

He was still going on about the *Magic Eye* baloney? "Yeah, so what?"

"Do the same thing now with the vapor, the way you did during your panic attack."

She shot mental death arrows at his greying temples.

"Two minutes." He wouldn't give up. "That's all I'm asking. Then I'll take you home."

Humor the piece of garbage one last time, assume he wouldn't run them off the road on the drive back, and she'd never have to see him again. Now that she wasn't going to jail, she could start settling into her spinsterhood. Already well on her way, only thing missing was a house full of smelly old cats. "Promise?"

"Scout's honor." He held up two fingers, and she could actually picture the dumbass in full Boy Scout uniform, neck kerchief and all.

"*One* minute." She set her phone on her leg and looked at the vapor. "Starting now."

A few seconds passed. "You're not gonna shoot me, are you?"

The truth was, despite all his b.s., Rowan didn't feel dangerous. A liar, yes. Heartless, obviously. But murderer? Not so much. And even if she was wrong—again—they were in broad daylight with the front-end loader guy within earshot.

The plume swirled. "Thirty seconds," she said. It had to be some weird power trip, where he was trying to hypnotize her into—and then she saw it.

Or more accurately, them. Five sparkling white figures, blurry triangles for faces, bodies tall and thin as totem poles stretching like taffy, whirling and gliding like a school of giant fish on wide-open wings.

"What the…" She squeezed her eyes shut, sure it was

all a mirage. Had Rowan slipped LSD into her water bottle while she was sleeping?

When she opened her eyes, they were gone. Just churning clouds. But when she let her gaze go slack again, the flowing ghosts came back. "Am I insane right now?"

He laughed. "Not in the least."

She had no mental tools to make sense of it. All she could do was watch the billowy creatures dip and dive and melt into one another as they swam up and down the plume. Strange and otherwordly as the swooping things were, they were also beautiful. A sense of peace, of lightness, of *cleanness*, came over Orna. A feeling she hadn't had since she was a little girl, that everything in the world was okay, that it always had been and always would.

"Are they what I think they are?" she whispered.

"Which is…?"

"Angels." Like Isabel's Christmas ornaments in the forest. Like the masks and jack-o-lanterns at the Halloween party.

She laughed and laughed, couldn't stop laughing. "They're angels."

CHAPTER 25

It was hard to say how long they sat in the pickup, Orna unable to peel her eyes from the glowing angels swishing around the smokestack vapor plume. Their weird triangle faces without any features, the edges of their lean, supple bodies breaking apart like clouds in the wind and then reforming. She didn't feel high or drunk but a crystal-clear euphoria, at long last her mind tapped into something pure and good.

And then they were gone. Color bleeding out of her world, she tried the eye thing again, but it didn't work.

"Where'd they go?" She grabbed Rowan's elbow and squeezed.

"They're free now."

"Free?" She missed them so badly it ached.

He opened his door. "Let's go for a walk."

Side by side they strolled along the parking lot to the mound of chips. With the wind off the river, it was almost cool enough for a jacket. Rowan waved at the man in the loader who waved back.

"Does he know?" Orna asked, still in a kind of stupor.

Rowan shook his head, ponytail bobbing. It was like seeing the head Tender again for the first time. Everything he and Ray had done—the lying, the blackmail—had been about this. Not that she was going to let him off the hook that easy.

"Who else?"

"Ray, Isabel," he said. "Dougie saw them, too."

Wow. Turned out, Silvio had been right about there being more to the Tenders than met the eye. If only he knew the whole truth. Unless… "What about Silvio?"

Rowan smiled. "Now, he can."

So that's why Silvio had been so weird the other night at Charwood when she showed up unannounced. He'd seen them, too, but couldn't tell her.

"Are they really angels?" she asked, expecting him to say no. That they were an undiscovered species made up of ultraviolet light, mostly unknown but something science could identify and classify. Something like that.

"What else could they be?" he said.

They stopped at the edge of the mound which stunk of musty sawdust and soil.

"Like from the Bible?" Orna asked.

This couldn't be real. Born into the Jewish faith, she'd believed every word of the Torah until her mid-teens. Then for her entire adult life religion was nothing but superstition and oppression. But if angels existed, what else was true? The Garden of Eden? The Tower of Babel? The Ten Plagues, for crying out loud? It was too much.

Legs wobbly, Orna plopped down on the pile. Heat rose from somewhere deep inside the mound, warming her backside.

Rowan picked up a chip like a jagged whole wheat cracker. "'Then the angel of the Lord came and sat under the oak.'"

"What's that from?"

"*Judges* Six Eleven."

Could that really be what the verse meant, though?

An eighteen-wheeler rumbled down the drive towards the plant.

"Stop me if you've heard this one." Rowan threw back his head. "'Then God said, Let Us make man in Our image, after Our likeness, to rule over the fish of the sea and the birds of the air, over the livestock, and over all the Earth itself and every creature that crawls upon it.'"

Easy one. "*Genesis*. And?"

"God created man, but before that He made the angels to carry out His divine will." Rowan bobbled the woodchip in his palm. "And when the angels heard about God's plan, there was rejoicing. But not all were pleased."

Holy crap. Rowan, turning the chip over and over in his hand, was a Jew after all. Or *was* he?

"The unhappy ones—the jealous ones," Rowan went on, "tried to unite the angels to demand that God give up on creating man, that it would only bring chaos. When they failed to come together, they declared war on one another. Outnumbered, the jealous angels were driven deep into the Earth. And man was born."

The tractor trailer beeped as it backed onto a metal platform at the edge of the mound, rails to either side. The driver killed the engine and got out as a plant worker in coveralls opened the back. Both men stepped clear, and with a loud mechanical whine the whole platform tilted upwards, the truck with it. As it lifted, woodchips spilled out the rear onto the mound.

Rowan went on. "But before the jealous angels were chased away, they got in one last blow, imprisoning God's loyal angels the only way they could." He snapped the woodchip between his fingers and held up the pieces, eyebrows arched.

"Inside trees?" Orna asked, a hundred percent

confused now.

He nodded and flicked the broken chip into the pile.

"Why trees?" she asked. "And how?"

"What do you know about plant cells?"

"Not much." She'd gotten a C in AP biology in high school.

"Animals cells have permeable membranes." Rowan spread the fingers of his left hand and slid those of his right between them. "But plants have cell walls, making them virtually impenetrable." Rowan made two fists and bumped them together.

"You're telling me angels, literal *angels,* are stuck inside trees?"

He nodded.

It didn't seem likely. Scratch that, it wasn't possible. He had to be putting her on. But then what had she seen in the plume? "What about parts of trees, like branches and needles?"

"Anything that's wood," he answered, fiddling with his cap.

It reminded her of the Orthodox Jewish tradition of needing to bury the entire body to be whole. Which is why they weren't supposed to get tattoos, and why, after suicide bombings in Israel, rabbis gathered up every piece of flesh.

"Trees but not bushes or other plants?" she asked.

"Just wood," he said definitively.

It was like learning a new subject in school that she hadn't even known existed. "What happens when a tree dies of natural causes? Doesn't the angel go free?"

He shook his head. "They get trapped in another tree. Burning's the only way out."

Sounded a lot like reincarnation. Another thing she

didn't believe in. "How are you so sure about all this?"

"It's been passed down for ages." Rowan gave her a serious look, not a hint of doubt in his eyes. "We're dealing with the metaphysical here, so we can't know all the details, of course. But that's where faith comes in. You should try it sometime." He winked.

Every culture she'd heard of had myths or folktales about tree spirits, but instead of angels they called them fairies, *devas*, *kami*, or whatever. But those were just kids' stories.

Orna scooped a few of the rough, dry chunks of wood and crunched them in her hand. Still…the biggest lesson Orna had learned during the pandemic was that what you thought was real could change in the blink of an eye. If a virus could turn the whole world halfway into a zombie apocalypse B-movie, was it really that much of a stretch to believe in angels trapped in trees?

Yes, it was. She gritted her teeth. In fact, it had to be madness. Rowan and the Tenders were nutcases.

But she'd *seen* them! Unless it was a case of mass psychosis. She sifted the chips through her fingers, wondering if any could be caught inside. She shook her head. Impossible!

Because if angels were real, so was God. Which meant Abba had been right all along. And what did that say about life after death? The Jewish tradition was a little hazy on the afterlife. *Shamayim* was kind of a heaven, but nothing she'd been taught said it looked anything like the Christian version. And there was *Sheol*—The Pit—a kind of a hell, but no rabbi had ever told her she'd burn there for an eternity if she misbehaved. Frankly, since Eemah's passing it had been too painful to think about it at all.

"Does that mean there's a heaven?" Orna asked, hopeful, voice hushed.

Rowan stuck his hands in his pockets. "I dunno."

"But what do you think?"

"I wish I knew, but I don't."

Disappointed, she turned her hand over and let the chips fall into the pile. "If these are God's angels, why doesn't *He* do something about them?"

Rowan shrugged. "Why are there crib deaths? Wars? Genocide?"

There was no denying that if there was a God, He hadn't done much to stop six million of his "Chosen People" from being rounded up, packed into cattle cars, and dumped in camps to be gassed and burned like kindling in a woodstove.

Orna knew what he was going to say next before he opened his mouth, "God works in mysterious ways."

A cop out, as always. "Angels or not, why is it so important to get them out of the trees?" she asked.

Rowan frowned down at her like she was a naughty child. "How would *you* like it?"

After weeks of picturing herself inside a jail cell, she knew she would not. And if those things were real, she supposed setting them free was the right thing to do.

"Should we go inside?" Rowan reached out his hand.

Orna took it, and he pulled her to her feet. That look in his eyes—wild but sad—made sense now. This man didn't think of himself as an environmental activist but a spiritual leader. Yet instead of saving human souls, it was…angels? As David After Dentist, the young boy coming down from anesthesia in the old viral YouTube video famously said, *Is this real life?*

They skirted the mound on their way to the plant as the front-end loader dumped chips onto a conveyor belt angling up into the big silo, a second belt going from the silo to the plant itself. How many angels can dance on the head of a pin? How many on a woodchip?

"Why can we see them, and everyone else can't?" Orna was still on the fence about the whole angel thing. But whatever they were, burning trees did seem to make them appear.

"Runs in the family, in my experience. But I think a lot more people can see than admit it, except that when they speak out, they're called crazy. Some probably even teach themselves not to see."

It was almost like they were mediums, but the spirits they were in touch with weren't dead. Could it be that the Bible stories were true? Moses seeing the angel in the burning bush? Impossible, right? "Can they talk?"

"Nah." They reached the front door of the plant, HAWK VALLEY CLEAN ENERGY CENTER painted in big block letters overhead on the corrugated metal.

"How far back does this go?" Orna's mind was spinning, and the questions kept coming.

"Probably caveman times, some tree hit by lightning." Rowan looked off into the hills as if searching for it. "And they brought embers back to the cave so they could keep seeing them."

"Or maybe just to stay warm." She wasn't trying to be a Doubting Thomas, but there were a lot of weak links in the theory.

"God's plan either way," Rowan said casually. "Even if most of them couldn't see, fire cooked their food and kept away the saber-tooths. Which meant burning wood was here to stay."

Rowan lugged open the door, and they went inside to a typical office space: drop ceilings, fake plants, and a half-dozen men and women in business attire behind computer desks.

"Hey, Rowan!" A plump middle-aged lady at the

nearest desk waved an arm. "What're you doing here?"

"Hoping to take my friend on a little tour. That okay?"

"Just wear protection." She pointed to a rack of plastic yellow hardhats on the wall.

Rowan picked one up, turned his ballcap backwards, set it on his head, and handed a second one to Orna. She put hers on, though it was a bit loose.

He led her through another door, up a couple of flights of stairs, then one last door into a control room full of panels of dials and switches like film footage of NASA from the sixties. A slim greybeard in a headset sat in a desk chair in front of a dozen monitors, one of the mound outside, a few with chips sliding along conveyor belts, and a couple of the screens showing nothing but flames. A giant map of Colorado hung on the wall in front of him, a clock above it. To the left, a big picture window looked out over scrubby hills and forested peaks beyond. To the right, a red metal door, a throbbing hum that Orna could feel in her legs coming from the other side.

The worker was muttering a series of numbers, possibly delivery times, into his headset, "Twelve-twenty-six, one-fourteen, two-forty-three." He nodded at Rowan without missing a beat.

"Then what happened?" Orna asked, eager to hear the next part of the story, unsure whether it was fact, fiction, or a bit of both.

"Where were we?" Rowan rubbed his chin and squinted up at the ceiling. "Ah, yes. For hundreds of thousands of years all was well. Burning wood helped humanity survive and evolve, setting countless angels free in the process, whether we knew it or not. But then we found fossil fuels."

Rowan ran his fingers along the switchboard, a

blinking half-rainbow of lights from red to yellow to green. "Just a blip on the radar at first. The Chinese dabbling in natural gas around the first millennium, some coal burning in Europe in the fifteen-hundreds, but wood was still king. Then in the mid-eighteenth century, coal, natural gas, and oil—for both heat and electricity—took over, and wood became mostly, if not entirely, obsolete in the so-called developed world."

Rowan turned a black knob left and right and flicked a switch. The worker kept staring at his monitors, seeming not to notice. They must've really trusted Rowan to let him have the run of the place like that.

"Around that time was the gold rush," Rowan went on narrating in a calm, slow voice, the whole thing like some Ken Burns docuseries. "And in eighteen-fifty-nine, my great-great grandfather Fraser took the boat from Scotland with his wife, son, and daughter—my great-grandmother Myrtle."

"From Ellis Island straight to Colorado on the brand-new railroad. But instead of gold Fraser got turned on to silver, and he staked out one of the first claims on the ridge that soon became Silvercleft. In a couple of years he had enough money to build a smelter and became a rich man. He bought up a huge chunk of land, built Charwood, and retired in his late forties to a life of leisure with his family—all documented at the historical society, if you're curious. Then around the age of sixty, for the first time in his life, he saw them."

Rowan waltzed over to the water cooler in the corner, pulled out one of the paper cones, filled it, and handed it to Orna. He poured a cup for himself, tossed it back like a shot, and got himself a second before going on.

"A changed man, Old Fraser started preaching about angels—not that odd a thing back then, actually—and attracted a small following, somewhere around twenty men and women who moved in to Charwood. It was one of the many Utopian communities springing up around the country at the time, kind of a cross between Christianity and old school Judaism. But instead of sacrificing bulls and goats, they burned wood in big bonfires, which had always been the point—God didn't need meat, just wanted us to set His angels free."

Fascinating. "What did the townies think about it?" Orna had been so caught up in the tale, she hadn't touched her water. She took a sip, and it was warm.

"Whether for heating, lumber, or charcoal for smelter blast furnaces," Rowan counted off on one hand, "*everyone* was cutting and burning trees. Hell, outside of the high peaks and some of the backcountry, most of Colorado was cut over. Bare hills far as the eye could see."

Orna glanced out the window and imagined all the green forested mountains in the distance stony and bare. Nature always came back in the end.

"Anyway, great-great-grandpappy Fraser passed it on to Great Grandma Myrtle, and she ran the place until she died in the nineteen-eighteen flu epidemic. My grandfather Arden took over and kept it going through the Depression and the war by selling firewood. In the sixties, my Mom was put in charge. She went on with the firewood business but dropped the Christian stuff for more of a hippie commune vibe, which is how she met Dad. Things were going great until eighty-two, when the good folk of Silvercleft hanged them both from a ponderosa pine."

Orna almost did a spit take. "What'd you say?"

Eyes hard, Rowan crumpled his cup and tossed it in the trash. Without another word, he stalked across the room and lugged open the red door. A roar filled the room until the door swung shut again.

Amazed at what she'd just heard—his parents had been *lynched?*—she darted across the room, waved at the guy in front of the monitors, who nodded, and used most of her strength to wrench open the heavy metal door.

A roaring, sweltering, dimly lit industrial cavern filled with looping metal tubes fitted with valves and gauges and gaskets all the way to a high ceiling crisscrossed with steel beams. M.C. Escher staircases led up to elevated metal grates while others went down into darkness. In the center of the massive space a steel boiler the size of a train car stood on end, putting out heat ripples she could actually see.

Leather work gloves on his hands, Rowan knelt next to the mega-boiler and waved her over. As she got closer, he opened a kind of woodstove door into the flaming orange pits of hell. The heart of the biomass plant. Her mouth fell open, and from ten feet away her saliva dried up. Afraid her eyelashes would singe, she turned her head away.

When she looked again the boiler door was closed, and Rowan was heading down a staircase. She hurried after, wanting nothing more than to get out of this screaming crematorium of trees.

CHAPTER 26

A flight of steps later, Orna pushed open a metal door and stepped out into the cool air. Squinting against the light, she remembered her hardhat and tossed it inside before the door clanged shut behind her, cutting off the roar of the boiler. The silence was startling.

Rowan had already crossed the parking lot into the tall grass above the river, hardhat still on.

With no choice but to follow if she wanted to hear more—and boy, did she ever—Orna caught up. "You're not seriously gonna leave me hanging?" She slapped a hand over her mouth, wishing she'd used a different word.

"Not an easy thing to talk about," Rowan said.

"My mother passed away six years ago. Nothing as bad as what happened to your parents, but I still find it hard."

A sad half-smile from Rowan as they crunched through the dead grass, the hill sloping down to the flowing Hawk. "Well, word got out about what was really going on behind the scenes at Charwood, and some of the locals didn't like it so much."

"So, they killed everyone?"

He shook his head. "Just my folks. The rest were scared off by the burning crosses—"

"The KKK?!" Orna felt her eyes bugging out of her

head.

Rowan shrugged. "Doubt it. Probably just the easiest way to get their point across."

Jew or not, if she'd been a Tender back then, that definitely would've been it for her. She sidestepped to avoid twisting her ankle on a prairie dog burrow. "How old were you?"

"Not even one. Lucky for me, the week before they saw which way the wind was blowing and sent me down to Denver to stay with my aunt Linda. She'd never been keen on Charwood but cared about us."

"When did you find out?" And Orna thought *she'd* had a tough life.

"I was ten when Linda told me she wasn't my real mother and my parents had died in some car crash."

The river hissed like a snake as they drew closer, water tumbling over boulders and eddying along sandy banks. Upstream, a grove of fat cottonwoods hung bare branches into the flow.

"But I was eighteen and ready to go off to Oregon for school when she told me everything." Rowan stuck out his lower lip. "Well, her take on it. That my parents had been leaders of some acid-dropping cult that saw visions in the clouds. She also showed me the will, and I found out I'd inherited a lodge on three thousand acres in the mountains, and a lot of cash, to boot."

Orna was amazed by his journey — which, of course, didn't absolve him of his lies but at least put them into context. "And that's when you took over Charwood?"

Rowan shook his head. "What was I gonna do with some rickety old lodge and all that land? I put the place up for sale and took the train out west."

At that age Orna probably would've done the same. "But something brought you back."

They reached the pebbly banks and a reek of algae and fish.

"Not a week into my first semester at U of O I went to some party in the woods. Took bong rips and saw them in the campfire. All the pieces came together like a jigsaw puzzle." Rowan smiled, and then it was gone. "Next day I quit school, headed back to Colorado, and took Charwood off the market. Used a good chunk of my savings to fix up the lodge and get the firewood business started again."

"And your aunt?"

"She wasn't happy about it but didn't say much. Died a few years later."

"Aw," Orna said. Rowan was officially an orphan. "What about the monsters who killed your parents? They went to prison, right?"

He knelt down and picked up a small rock. "We came to an arrangement."

Orna thought about the townies hanging around the party, and the guys at the inn saying how they got free firewood. She shuddered; she could've been sharing a beer with murderers! "You just let it slide?"

Rowan looked down at his boots. "The cycle had to end."

Didn't seem like a fair trade, but if Rowan had healed his wounds, she wasn't going to be the one to tear them open again. Though it did mean no more trips to the Silvercleft Inn. "You're not afraid of them coming back?"

He shook his head. "That's what I've got Ray for."

With what Orna knew about the burly biker, she didn't doubt him there. "When did Ray and Isabel show up?"

"Pretty much at the beginning. I was doing a bunch

of permaculture around the property at the time, and that brought in some new folks. But almost none of them could see, and everyone left before too long. Except those two."

"Ray stole her from me, you know," Rowan grinned and rolled his eyes.

"No way." He nodded.

She almost laughed but was able to catch herself. "She dumped *you* for *him*?"

He shrugged. "What could I do? They were made for each other."

Sure, Rowan was older than Orna, but his level of maturity was shocking. Orna couldn't stay Facebook friends with her exes, much less go on living with one.

Rowan fingered the rock's edges, turning it around in his hand. "Anyway, that's when I had my *Schindler's List* moment." He sidearmed the stone across a calm spot in the river, skipping once, twice, three times before it sunk with a plop.

"Your what?"

"You know the film?"

She scoffed. "It's illegal to be Jewish and not see *Schindler's List*."

"Oh, okay." Rowan bent down for another stone, obviously not getting the joke. "Well, you know the whole 'I didn't do enough' scene at the end, with all the people Schindler saved at his factory seeing him off?"

Orna nodded, confused as to where this could possibly be going.

Rowan went on. "And he leans on his car crying as he realizes he could've saved another ten Jews if he'd sold it?" With a grunt, Rowan flung the rock, skipping it four times across the surface of the water. "That's how I felt."

"Hmmm." The analogy felt a little cringey. Probably the Jew thing. She shrugged it off.

"So, I spent a year super-depressed, realizing that no matter how many trees we cut and sold for firewood, we'd barely be making a dent. It was a rough time." A few strands of hair hung over Rowan's eyes. As he went to smooth them back, he knocked off his hardhat, which fell on a rock with a smack. Shaking his head and laughing at himself, he picked it up. "But then one morning I read an article about the stimulus package: hundreds of millions of federal dollars for renewable energy—biomass included—and I knew I'd found the holy grail."

He held out his hand towards the plant, its smokestack still puffing away. "I joined up with some folks in the industry and helped them secure eighteen and a half-million for the marvel you see before you!"

Orna whistled. Now she understood why the plant staff let Rowan do whatever he wanted; he'd basically built the thing and gotten them jobs. She tried the eye trick again on the plume, but it was still just vapor. It hurt her heart how badly she wanted to see the angels—angels?...why not? Angels!—again.

"One plant can free more in a day than a year burning firewood." He pointed at the sky. "And twenty-four more plants were built across the country during the next several years. With this green energy focus for Charwood, we were able to recruit a few new folks, including Silvio and Dougie." He smiled wistfully and toed the sand.

This time, instead of the typical shock wave of guilt, Orna saw Dougie's death through a wider lens. If all that stuff was true—and, other than her usual cynicism, what evidence did she have it wasn't?—in a sense, the kid had given his life for the cause. And maybe someday she'd be worthy of his sacrifice. "And the funding?"

"Dried up, and that's why no new plants have been built." Rowan sighed. "And with all the money doled out to keep the economy afloat during the pandemic, it's unlikely there's gonna be more for biomass any time soon. The only silver bullet we've got left is your carbon neutral angle. Despite how the meeting went, I still think Senator Palmer might be on board."

If Rowan thought their bill still had a chance, she had no reason to doubt him. But would that be enough? "What about the rest of the world? A lot of trees out there."

"We're trailblazers. If biomass catches on for real in the States, it's gonna spread everywhere. We're already exporting wood to Europe and Asia for their facilities. Only a matter of time before they start cutting their own forests."

If he said so.

A blue heron swooped down from a naked cottonwood and landed gracefully on a sandy strip of beach. It stepped into the shallows, folded one stilt-like leg under its body, and stood like a statue staring into the current.

"Where do the angels go when they're free?" Orna asked.

"Back with God. Where else?"

There it was again, the G-word. "And how many do you think are left?"

He shrugged. "No idea, but they keep coming, so we've got a ways to go."

Orna wasn't sure what was going on but felt something shifting inside like the gears of an old clock. Back when she'd considered herself a real Jew, the lack of freedom was balanced by a world that made sense.

Indeed, ever since she'd turned away from her faith she felt lost—even though that wasn't something she'd have admitted to herself. For the first time since she was a teen, she had a chance for life to have meaning again.

A flash of insight lit her up like a lightning strike. "What if this is God testing us? To see if we're worthy?"

Rowan raised his eyebrows, his old goofy grin back where it belonged. "You may be on to something."

She wanted to reach out and hug him. "What if we set them all free?" What she didn't want to think about was how many trees they were going to have to burn to make it so.

"'The wolf and the lamb shall graze together!'" he cried out in a phony preacher's voice, southern twang and all. "'And the lion shall eat straw like the ox; and dust shall be the serpent's food!'" More Old Testament. The animals were symbols for people, obviously—Peace on Earth.

"And if we don't?"

Rowan closed his eyes, licked his lips, and in a quiet voice said, "'Then the Lord rained down fire and burning sulfur from the sky and destroyed them all.'"

A chilly wind blew up from the river. Orna shivered, and the heron spread its wings and flapped off over the cottonwoods.

CHAPTER 27

Orna scarfed down the last bite of a lox and cream cheese bagel on her way out of the condo. She'd slept like a log after coming back from yesterday's trip—the best she could remember sleeping since before the pandemic—and had awoken refreshed, her troubles blown away like dandelion fluff. She'd even forgiven Rowan for his lies, as it seemed a petty thing to cling to in this incredible new reality.

Her phone buzzed from the back pocket of her jeans. Abba's response from her text earlier that morning asking how he was feeling. "In the clear." Great news, but she always knew he'd pull out of it. God had been on their side all along.

On the sunny drive to the hospital, her eyes kept drifting to the roadside pines, wondering which of them might house an angel. One in ten trees? One in a hundred? A thousand? It was overwhelming the work that needed to be done, pushing biomass across the country so it could spread around the world. But not only was she up to the task, she was energized—never before did her life have such purpose. She finally understood her parents' faith; belief in a higher power wasn't smothering, it was freeing.

She pulled into the hospital parking garage and found a space. Much as she wanted to reveal everything she'd seen to Abba, there was just no way. This was something you had to see for yourself to believe. But surely their spiritual paths would cross somehow.

Orna signed in at the front desk, got Abba's room number, and went down the hospital hall for the second—and hopefully last—time that month. At the far end of his small private room, Abba sat up in bed looking out the window over the parking lot, blanket tucked up to his waist, blue gown a few shades lighter than his *kippah*. While his face was thin and lined, beard hanging off his chin like a movie prop, he had a lot more color than when she'd brought him in.

"What's the latest?" Orna sat in the chair next to the bed.

He shrugged, still staring outside.

"Well, how's the sepsis?"

"I seem to be on the mend," his voice was flat, and he wouldn't meet her eyes.

"Great!" She tried to balance his gloom with some extra cheer, of which she had more than enough to go around for a change. "When can we get you the heck out of here?"

"Tomorrow, they said." It irked her how blasé he sounded. The man had just cheated death for the second time. How he could he be so ungrateful?

"That's excellent! I was afraid I'd have to kidnap you." He didn't crack the slightest smile. Something was off. "What's wrong, Abba?"

He heaved a sigh. "They had to operate."

"Operate?" Her heart skipped a beat and did double time to catch up. "On what—your leg?"

He nodded.

"So, how'd it go?"

He didn't answer, only swallowed and rubbed a thumb in circles on his palm.

This silent treatment thing was getting on her nerves. "How did it *go*?!"

He closed his eyes like he'd grown tired of talking to her.

Enough was enough. She grabbed the edge of the sheet and pulled it down, bracing herself for all sorts of gross red puffiness and pus. But instead of the infected shin she expected to find, nothing but empty space where his right leg used to be. Above that, a bandaged stump. Whimpering, she dropped the sheet back over his legs—leg.

Abba finally looked at her, his eyes glazed and far away.

The room swimming, Orna sat down hard in the chair. How could this be happening? This was the man she used to play catch with before her softball games. Who'd run a half-marathon not that long ago. Who walked to *shul* every freaking Shabbat. "What—what happened?"

"It was either my leg or me."

Orna was crushed. But he needed her to be strong. *She* needed her to be strong.

A few days ago, she would've flown into a rage, screaming up and down the hallway demanding to see the surgeon, threatening him with malpractice or worse. But thanks to her awakening yesterday—it was the first time she thought of it that way, but wasn't that what it was?—she could accept this was how God wanted it to be. Together, they'd get through it and come out stronger on the other side. She could barely believe this was the new her, but it felt right, like trying on a pair of pants that finally fit.

She reached over, grabbed his limp hand, and squeezed. He screwed up his face and took a deep breath in through flaring nostrils. Then he squeezed back.

CHAPTER 28

Night had fallen by the time Orna made it up to Charwood, and she parked the Forester behind Rowan's pickup, Ray's motorcycle, and Silvio's Prius. Grabbing the printout from the passenger seat, she stepped out into fresh mountain air, a tiny nip to it that still felt more like late September than the first week of December. Yet one-third of the country still denied climate change? She rolled up the paper, shoved it in the back pocket of her jeans, and walked through the pale light of a rising three-quarters moon to knock on the lodge's front door.

The last two days she'd spent tending to Abba at the condo. Nimble as he was getting on his crutches, he mostly lay in bed in the guest room. Three times a day, she cooked fresh meals for him—including a batch of matzah ball soup—which he ate with her at the table, slack-faced and nearly silent.

Sad as she was about it, she knew better than to push him, giving Abba the time he needed to come to terms with the loss of his leg. He could stay with her as long as he liked. But tough as he was, she was worried if he'd ever be able to get on by himself.

Rowan answered the door with a shy smile and reached out for a hug. She stepped into his embrace, feeling like a rock wrapped in tree roots.

As always, it was stifling inside even with the windows open, probably close to eighty degrees. But now she understood why. Who knew which chunk of cordwood might house the next angel? No one in the living room except Lottie snoozing on her chair by the fire. The German Shepherd opened a bloodshot eye and closed it again.

"Where is everybody?" Orna was excited to wipe the slate clean with the rest of the Tenders. Now that they were all on the same page, they could finally be friends.

"Silvio's outside somewhere, and I think Ray and Isabel are upstairs."

Rowan walked into the kitchen and came back with what looked like the same mason jar of moonshine from last time, mostly empty now, and two glass tumblers.

"How about after?" She took the rolled paper out of her pocket and smacked her palm.

He raised an eyebrow. "What's that you got there?"

"Let's get started, and I'll show you," she teased, knowing how pleased he'd be when he found out.

Smiling, he set the jar and glasses down on the coffee table, and she followed him upstairs, both of them making footprints in the crunchy ash. She'd never seen that part of the lodge before, and the stairs were so steep it was like climbing into a treehouse. Then through a long, much cooler hallway past several closed doors to either side—some sections lit by naked bulbs in ceiling fixtures, the rest dark—dusty cobwebs hanging from the walls like Halloween decorations.

"What's in all these rooms?" Orna asked.

"Not much, these days."

"Mind if I take a peek?" She stopped at one on her right.

Rowan shrugged. "Knock yourself out."

She turned the knob into a coal-black chamber. Nervous all of a sudden, hairs on the back of her neck prickling, she fumbled along the wall for the switch and flipped on the light. Just an empty room, maybe fifteen by twenty, a thick layer of dust on the wood floor. She pictured some longhaired hippie Tender from the seventies sprawled out on a mattress on the floor, Jefferson Airplane coming from a record player, incense wafting. According to Rowan's history of the place, that might've been the last time anyone slept there. But what if she helped with recruitment? If Rowan had found *her*, surely she could bring in more folks who could see.

She shut the door and caught up with Rowan as he turned a corner down yet another hallway, Eemah's ring cold against the bare skin of her chest. More doors to either side, snarls and grunts from behind one of them, like a dog fight. "Is that—"

Rowan chuckled. "What can I say? They like it rough."

Ear cocked to the door, Orna tried to imagine what sort of kinky stuff might be going on between Ray and Isabel but couldn't. Then something slammed against the door and a piercing howl sent Orna scurrying to the end of the hallway, laughing. Rowan stood in front of the last door on the left, a rectangle of yellow light slanting out.

Orna, peeking over his shoulder, expected a filthy bachelor's pad with unmade futon, dirty clothes on the floor, and the stench of stale body odor. To her surprise, a neatly-made bed on an antique wooden frame next to a matching bureau and desk—the latter with state-of-the-art Mac and large flatscreen monitor. The bare wooden floors swept clean, Colorado mountain landscape paintings on the wall, blackout curtains covering the two windows, everything smelled faintly of sage, floor vents piping in heat from the boiler.

Rowan sat on an ergonomic office chair and woke his computer with a twitch of the mouse. He scrolled through some emails, and Orna made herself look away so she wouldn't be tempted to snoop.

She unrolled the printout and set it on his desk, the page curling at the edges. "I took the liberty of putting together a list of possible co-sponsors for Palmer's bill, and also our best bets for a companion bill in the House." She brimmed with pride.

Not seeming to hear her, Rowan leaned forward in the chair, craning his neck to peer at the monitor.

She went on in a louder voice. "Half Democrats, half Republicans, because without—"

"Noooo," Rowan groaned and collapsed back in his chair to stare at the ceiling.

"Bad news?" So much for her moment of glory.

He rubbed his forehead like he'd banged it against something. "Palmer's officially killing the bill."

"Oh, no." Orna squinted over his shoulder and read the email from Kathy Phauda.

Rowan,

Always hate to be the bearer of bad news, but we're going to pass on your bill. Unfortunately, too much on our plate right now to do it justice.

Sincerely,

Kathy Phauda

Orna wasn't exactly shocked; after all, she knew the meeting had been a bust. But at the biomass plant Rowan had convinced her they still had a chance. Finally understanding all that was at stake, it was a crushing blow.

"I'm so sorry I let you down." She almost put her hand on Rowan's shoulder but thought better of it.

"Stupid cunt was putting us on the whole time," he growled through his teeth.

Yikes. She got his frustration, of course, but that kind of language coming from his mouth was upsetting. She picked up her printout. "Palmer's not the only one in Congress." She shook it. "We've got a whole list of—"

Rowan snatched the paper, leaving her with a stinging papercut on the tip of her left pinky. He crumpled the list and chucked it against the wall. She stood there sucking on her finger; never having seen him angry before, she didn't know what to say.

"That ship has sailed. Bitch was our last fucking chance." He slammed the desk with a fist. And then again.

Orna wondered if she should leave—if only for her own safety—then cast the thought away with a shake of her head. The bill had been a big deal, and this was his way of venting. Now, more than ever, he needed her support, not judgment.

"We'll think of something," she peeped.

Standing up, he kicked the chair across the room and stalked out the bedroom door.

"Where you going?" Orna scurried after him, down the hallway, past Ray and Isabel's room—quiet now—all the way downstairs. Catching up to him in the den, she grabbed his elbow, and he came to a halt. "Rowan, talk to me!"

Lottie sat up in her chair and growled, and Orna immediately let go. Soon as she did, the dog lay back down and closed its eyes.

Once they were both outside, Rowan slipped through the moonlight towards the storage shed next to the smoky boiler. He slid open the huge rolling door and smacked on a light. Orna stood in the tall grass up to her knees. "What are you doing in there?"

Before he turned off the light, Orna saw him cradling a chainsaw, face blank as a poker player. She pushed back the instinct to run. He wasn't going to hurt her. Indeed, he blew past her on the way to his pickup.

"What's happening?" she whinnied, frozen in place, heart beating like she was climbing a fourteener as she pictured Rowan at Senator Palmer's front door.

Soon as he opened the driver's door, Orna knew she had to stop him. But by the time she rushed over, he'd already shut the door, flipped on his headlamp, and was stomping off across the meadow. Her pulse slowed. No Colorado Chainsaw Massacre, after all.

Not knowing what else to do, Orna trailed along calling his name, his headlamp beam a yellow spear in the dark. He ignored her, and at the edge of the woods, the rumbling putter of the chainsaw like an idling engine. Hell of a time to cut firewood.

He ambled up to a small ponderosa and bit into the trunk with a rev like a redlining sports car. She paused a safe distance away as he drove the saw down at a steep angle. Then around the other side of the trunk. One last slash and Rowan yanked the blade out of the tree. He stepped back a few paces as the crown shook and lurched. The tree keeled over, its butt end bucking ten feet in the air as it crashed to the ground in an explosion of branches, twigs, and needles, all in the eerie glow of his headlamp. Why this couldn't wait for morning, Orna had no idea.

Seconds later, he was cutting into the next-closest pine, saw slicing through the trunk like a hot knife through butter. He dropped that tree in a few minutes and went on to a third. It was amazing how quickly he took down something that had been growing for probably a century, all to free the strange and wonderful creatures that had changed the course of their lives. Plus, she couldn't pretend the way he handled the saw didn't turn on her a little bit.

He started on the second cut when the chainsaw sputtered to a stop. Rowan grunted as he tried to restart the thing, but it was no use.

Now was her chance. She went over and set her hand on his shoulder. "I wanna try."

He turned his head towards her, and she shut her eyes against the blinding light. She figured he'd say no. That she hadn't had the training. That it wasn't safe. That she was just a girl.

Instead, he told her calmly, "Out of gas."

"Well, let's fill 'er up," she said, cheerily. If she was going to be a full-on Tender, it was time to get her hands dirty.

They went to the shed, piled to the rafters with cordwood and logging equipment—including what looked like a stripped-down lawnmower, WOODSMAX SPLITTER decal on its side—and he filled the chainsaw's small tank from a metal gas can. From a shelf he took down an extra headlamp, two safety helmets with plastic face shields, two pairs of ear protectors, leather gloves, and thick orange pants with suspenders. They dressed in silence, Orna excited and a little nervous thanks to a factoid she'd come across in her research that logging was the most dangerous job in America. But Rowan—who'd saved her from a mugger and found her lost in the woods—would never let something bad happen to her.

Into the woods again, where Rowan—over his temper tantrum and back to his old mellow self again—gave her a five-minute crash course on saw operation, showing her the power switch, chain guard, choke, throttle, and safety throttle. Face shields in place, he started it and handed over the heavy, humming thing. It was like holding onto a jet engine, the vibrations throbbing deep into her flesh, muscle, and bone.

She stuck the blade into the cut Rowan had already made in the small pine and squeezed the throttle. Almost with a life of its own, the saw chewed through the trunk in a spray of fragrant, glittering sawdust. Her upper body throbbing, she'd never felt such power before, like a warrior hacking through her enemies.

As she got closer to Rowan's first diagonal cut, he tapped her shoulder, and she let go of the throttle, blade still sunk in the wood. She slid off an ear protector.

"When I say, 'Now,'" he yelled over the puttering saw, face shield up, "let go of the throttle, hit the chain guard, and follow me!"

"Okay!" she shouted, set her ear protector back in place, took a deep breath, and pulled the trigger. Another few seconds and the cuts met.

"Now!" Rowan yelled.

She let go of the throttle, smacked down the chain guard, slid the saw from the tree like King Arthur in "The Sword in the Stone," and together they scampered to safety behind the closest ponderosa.

Their headlamps spot-lit the groaning tree as it teetered and crashed into the grass. Ten times as satisfying as when she'd caught that two-foot pike in Lake Champlain as a kid; plus, this time, she might've been freeing an angel.

She took down her second tree, a two-foot diameter ponderosa, in under ten minutes—Rowan making her do a cut twice because it wasn't at a sharp enough angle. Her arms and core sore and tired, back sweaty, she felled one more—calling, "Tiiiiiiiimberrrrrrrr" like in the cartoons—hit the chainguard and flicked off the power switch.

She clunked the saw down on top of her most recent kill and stripped off her helmet, ear protectors, and gloves. Side by side, they admired the half-dozen trees lying zigzag in the smushed grass.

Rowan switched off his lamp. "It'll never be enough, this way," he muttered into his chest, his firey rage burned down to sad embers. "That bill was all we had left."

"Like I said, we'll think of something." She felt a rush of warmth for this man who'd done so much good for the world. For her.

"I used to believe that, but I don't know anymore."

"I do." She turned off her lamp, and the shadows tucked in around them.

Their bodies were close, almost but not quite touching. It felt like the most natural thing in the world when he took her hand and gently pulled her towards him.

He tasted like every kind of mint rolled into one, peppermint, spearmint, wintergreen, some yet-to-be-identified sweet leaves from a tropical rainforest. His beard tickled her face and she wanted more.

They fell to the crispy grass in the moonlight, and seconds later their clothes were off, a cool breeze raising goosebumps across her naked flesh.

His hands warm and greedy, wood chips and stray sticks poked her back, but she didn't care.

Caught up in the heat of the moment, she willed her boundaries to dissolve, for her cell wall to break down.

CHAPTER 29

Beth El Synagogue was small but beautiful. The dozen or so pews seated about twenty people that Saturday morning, the day before Hanukkah, upholstered in the same ocean blue as the plush carpet. The ark on the bimah was made of gleaming blonde wood, its curtain blood red.

Abba sat beside her in a black suit, *tallit* around his shoulders, nose buried in a *siddur*, right pant leg pinned up to his knee. Unable to walk the two miles to keep Shabbat, Orna had driven him and decided to stay for the service.

Overhead, the morning sun filtered through three panels of stained glass. The largest in the center had a gold Jewish star on a bed of twining green vines, שלום—hello, goodbye, peace, *shalom* being basically the Jewish *aloha*—in the center. To the right, a bearded and robed Moses cradling the two stone tablets of the Ten Commandments, behind him a black mountain knifing into a sky jagged with lightning. To the left, a thick-leafed tree with glowing orange fruit.

For the past hour, Orna had drifted in and out of paying attention to the fortysomething smooth-shaven rabbi leading the service from the podium in tan suit and matching *kippah*, rainbow *tallit* over his shoulders. Her eyes kept wandering to the stained-glass tree—none other than the Tree of Life. She thought about the angels but also the fallen ponderosa pines beside which she and Rowan had slept together the night before.

Compared to her four previous lovers, the lovemaking had been…okay. Rowan was intense and then gentle at all the right times, but she still had a hard time staying present. A lot of it had been worries about them not using protection—something she'd only done with a committed boyfriend—but it probably also had to do with being out of practice. Though the part where he'd sprinkled a handful of fresh sawdust over her belly was definitely beyond weird.

The real question was whether it would turn into an actual relationship, as she hoped, or if it had just been a one-time fling. She'd find out the next time she saw him.

"Mourner's *kaddish*," the rabbi said somberly, breaking Orna out of her fantasies.

Abba got to his feet on his own—he'd brushed away earlier attempts to help him stand—and hunched over his crutches, *siddur* in hand, *tallit* swaying, empty pantleg dangling where it had come unpinned.

Orna whispered the Hebrew words, pronouncing every syllable, resisting the temptation to look at the other page with the English transliteration. "Yitgadal v'yitkadash sh'mei raba."

She finished in less than a minute, saying her mother's name in the right spot, and peeked over at Abba. He was *davening*, bobbing up and down like a floating piece of wood in a stormy sea. Face serious, bushy eyebrows drawn together, as befit a widower mourning his wife. But the lost, hangdog look he'd sported all week was gone, replaced with one that seemed set with purpose. Finally, she was beginning to understand what the whole "faith keeps you strong" thing actually meant. Focusing on yourself made you suffer, but opening your heart to the world's deeper truths, *that* was the path to happiness.

She tried to focus on the Torah portion—something about the Pharoah asking Joseph to interpret some dream about cows—but her mind went to the angels. If the Tenders were going to make any more headway, they needed to do something big. The public education campaign had been a bust, and the legislative angle clearly didn't have legs either. So, what was left?

The answer came to her during the first rousing verse of "Aleinu." In fact, it was ridiculous she hadn't thought of it sooner. The one stone left unturned was the legal approach. And who better to make it happen than the retired attorney standing next to her, belting out the last prayer of the morning?

Not until they were halfway home, stopped at a light on busy Broadway, did Orna find the guts to bring it up. "Can I ask you a question about the law?"

"What did you do this time?" he joked.

It wasn't that funny—especially not with how close it almost came to the truth—but she faked a laugh because it was the first joke he'd cracked since the operation. "What do you know about the Environmental Protection Agency?"

"All in the name, isn't it?"

The light turned green, and they got moving again. "Do you think it would make sense to have a lawsuit about how they keep track of greenhouse gases?"

"You can file suit over anything. The question is whether it'll go anywhere."

Orna sped up to pass a slow-moving Subaru—a

beat up, early model version of her Forester, in fact—a whiff of pot smoke coming through Abba's half-open window. "Well, right now they count carbon emissions from wood the same as fossil fuels."

"And you're saying they shouldn't?"

"Yep."

No response. He wasn't interested. She veered back into the right lane. Figured, as Abba had never been one to—

"I'll take a look, if you want," he said.

"You will?" She turned onto her road and had to stop quickly to avoid running over a gaggle of teenagers moping across the crosswalk from the sports field.

"Got a colleague in Montpelier who's an environmental lawyer. I'll run it past him and see what he thinks."

"That would be so amazing."

She snuck a peek at Abba, his brow crimped in thought, and rode the good feeling all the way back to the condo. Not only could this free more angels and give the Tenders a much-needed boost, it might be a way to share some of her newfound joy with her father while giving him something to keep his mind busy, as she hadn't seen him working on the book as of late. A win-win-win-win.

They parked, and Orna made sure not to help Abba with his crutches. Truth was, he had taken to them quite well and kept right behind her as they walked the path to her condo.

A lot cooler this late morning, somewhere around forty, the tang of woodsmoke in the air. As they got her to deck, a translucent grey plume snaked up from her next-door neighbor's chimney. She stopped short. *Holy crap, another angel!*

Smaller than the fluffy giants at the plant, this one was the height of a child but a third its width, with the same blurry triangle face and flapping wings. A living vapor trail, it swished and fluttered and did loop-the-loops like a bird celebrating its escape from a cage. Orna stood there awestruck, eyes tearing, that warm sense of peace washing over and into her. *Shalom.*

Maybe thirty seconds of watching the flowy creature ride the smoke like a waterslide before Orna came back to herself. She spun around, about to blurt out some excuse to Abba about daydreaming. But he was staring at it, too, his frown an upside-down U, brown eyes flashing.

"Can you—can you see?" she whispered, hardly believing it.

Which broke the spell, and Abba's face went slack. "See what?" Indeed, there was no longer anything in the smoke. He lurched past her.

But no way was she going to fall for that. It had been there, they'd both seen it, and now it had been set free. She caught up and paced alongside him. "You saw. I know you saw."

"Trick of the light." He humped forward, trying to outcrutch her.

"Bullshit, Abba," she said, cursing in front of him for one of the first times. "Bullshit."

He stopped, back to her, slumping over his crutches like he'd run out of juice. "I prayed you couldn't see them."

She knew it! "Why?" She circled around to face him.

He shook his head, studying the cracks in the cement path.

"They're angels, Abba," she said.

Red-faced and trembling, he locked eyes with her

and hissed, "They. Are. No. Such. Thing."

"What're you talking about?" She wouldn't let him ruffle her calm. "We have to save them."

"Save them?" He gaped, eyes wide and horrified as if she'd denied the Holocaust.

"They're trapped inside trees, and burning wood gets them out," she explained proudly, glad to be the one teaching him something for a change.

"*Mazzikim,*" he whispered, eyes on the chimney smoke.

Bubby Ilana's demons? Orna patted the ring hanging around her neck. "What?!"

"Just because people called your Bubby a *meshugana,*" he mumbled so quietly she could barely hear him, "didn't mean she wasn't right."

Orna was stunned. "Bubby saw them, too?"

His eyes were fierce. "Before HaShem created man, when the Earth was fire and stone, He made *ha Yeladim Shel Choshech.*"

Children of Darkness? Biting her lip and clenching her fists, Orna decided to let the old man have his say before she tore into him.

"Like the harsh wastelands where they lived, they were hideous: serpents of horn and wing and fang." Abba stroked his beard as if to soothe himself. "And, because there was no other way to survive the blistering deserts, they became creatures of pure selfishness."

While the Torah had hinted at some of the lessons of the *Kabbalah,* Orna had never even heard a whisper of this one.

"Because of the evil they could not help but unleash, HaShem banished *ha Yeladim* into Sheol." Abba closed his eyes and bowed his head. "Baruch HaShem."

Orna let her fists go loose. It *did* have some overlap

with Rowan's history of the jealous angels exiled inside the Earth. "But the good angels, Abba. *They're* the ones we're setting free."

"Foolish girl!" Abba's face was a purple mask of hate. "Angels are already free!"

Like a candle in the wind, Orna's faith wavered. She stared into the empty chimney smoke, trying to find the truth.

What if Abba was right, that the angels were really—but then she remembered what she'd learned in a religious studies class in college. How the Christians had turned Pan, the goat god of pasture and field—make believe but harmless—into the devil, the symbol of evil itself, to force everyone into going full Jesus.

Abba's hands shook with self-righteous fury as he gripped his crutches. Anything that didn't fit into the man's neat little holy box—even freaking angels!—had to be evil.

Orna's flame grew steady again. "You've got it all wrong, Abba." She tried to have some compassion for the zealot but found she could only spread it thin.

"If you leave them alone, they'll leave you alone," he grunted.

Orna shook her head, as much at what Abba said as this new insight: It wasn't that Abba didn't *believe*, the man was *jealous* she knew something he didn't! And most of all, *resented* her connection to God that he could never have!

"If you need money, I'll get you money." Abba's chest rose and fell as if he'd just run a mile. "But I forbid you from hanging around those people."

Her goodwill gone, she laughed in his face. *As if.* How much of a bigot do you have to be to ignore something you can see with your own two eyes?

Now, for the first time in her life, Orna's every waking thought wasn't about her but also them: the angels, the

Children, not of darkness but of light. How dare Abba look away from their suffering! From *their* Holocaust!

An inferno raged inside of her, and instead of tamping the flames, she blew on them. "Now I know why the world hates us!" she spat. Then stormed up the stairs to her condo, slamming the door behind her like a thunderclap.

CHAPTER 30

Orna got her toiletries—including some old condoms—together along with enough clothes for a few days and shoved it all in her pack. If this was the way Abba was going to act, she wasn't about to spend another minute around him.

Pack on back, she stomped downstairs to the living room. Even with his leg, with more than enough food in the fridge and cabinets it wasn't like he couldn't be on his own for a few days. And if he ran out of something, then good. It was about time he paid the price of his small-mindedness. Maybe a little suffering would open him to another point of view, for a change.

Abba stood in front of the closed front door on his crutches. Orna scanned the kitchen counter for her car keys, but they weren't there. "You seen my keys?"

His glower said it all.

"You took them?" she asked. Now he was being silly.

"You're not in your right mind," Abba said.

Laughing, she waltzed into the kitchen and tugged open the junk drawer where she kept her extra set. But they, too, were gone.

"Not funny anymore." She strode up to him, their eyes level as he hunched over his crutches. "Give them to me."

He shook his head.

She didn't have time for games. Rowan would have

to come pick her up. "Out of my way, old man," she said, kind of as a joke but also not. Much as she loved Abba, this was bigger than him, bigger than anyone.

"You're my daughter, and I'll do everything in my power protect you." He dry-swallowed, a vein pulsing in his forehead. "Even from yourself."

"From what? The truth?" She hitched up her pack and buckled the hip belt. "That's why I'm so behind in life, because *you* treated me like a child the whole time."

He shook his head, cheeks wobbling. "One day you'll see how much of that was for your own good. Just like this."

"Whatever." She reached past him for the doorknob, but he grabbed her wrist. When Orna tried to break away, she couldn't; he was much stronger than she would've guessed. She turned sideways, nudging him with her pack, but he only clamped down tighter.

Orna's bubbling anger came to a boil, and she yanked her arm away. Abba's crutches slid out from under him and, losing his balance, he tumbled awkwardly to the floor on his side with an "oomph."

Orna felt an instant stab of remorse. But already grumbling and snatching up his crutches to get to his feet—foot—Abba seemed no worse for wear. She took the chance to crack open the door, slip out, and hurry down the path.

Grabbing her phone from her jeans pocket, she called Rowan. He didn't pick up—probably out of range—so she left a message and trudged down the sidewalk towards the street. A bit of a walk would do her good. And if she got tired, she could call a Lyft.

She was still a block away from Broadway and its hum of cars when her phone rang, Rowan's name on the screen a welcome sight.

"Come get me," Orna said.

"Everything okay?"

The sound of his voice made her smile. "Yeah, I just can't use my car right now."

"I'll send Ray down. Where are you?"

While she was hoping Rowan would pick her up himself, this *would* be a good time to clear the air with Ray. On the other side of the street on a patch of bright green grass were a few picnic tables and a swing set. "The little park off Broadway and 29th."

"He'll be there soon," he said. "Looking forward to seeing you."

"Me, too." She waited a few seconds to see if he'd hang up first. He didn't, so she did. *Please let this be real.* She wasn't sure if she could take another heartbreak.

Instead of walking any further, Orna sat on a bench to eat a power bar and watch a woman about her age push a little girl in pigtails on the swing.

Half an hour later Ray rolled up on his grumbling bike, lit cigarette in mouth, scuffed black leather from head to toe like a Hell's Angel: cap, jacket, chaps, boots, gloves, and all. Orna was nervous and didn't know what to say, whether to offer an apology or demand one for herself.

But when he plucked the cigarette from his mouth to wave and smile sheepishly, baring his gap teeth, she knew that not only was everything cool between them, they'd been on the same team the whole time.

"This for me?" A helmet was bungeed onto the back seat, and she palmed its hard smoothness.

He nodded. "Keep you safe."

She unstrapped it and put it on, feeling like an astronaut on her first mission. Never once had she sat on a motorcycle, and she was a little scared. Eemah's—more like, Bubby's—ring freezing cold against her chest, she unzipped her fleece halfway, reached under her sweater, set the silver piece on top, and zipped back up.

Hopping onto the seat, she grabbed Ray's midsection, a layer of fat over a slab of bulging muscle. As she held on for dear life, Ray swung the bike around, waited for a gap in traffic, and rocketed towards Broadway. After the first few jolts of terror—like they were about to tip over any second—she squeezed the vibrating seat with her thighs. That made her feel more secure, the wind and cigarette smoke cutting against her helmet like the prow of a ship.

Things got bumpy on the way up the dirt road to Silvercleft, but Ray hit every turn perfectly, and the steep climb was nerve-wracking but uneventful—other than Orna having to hold her breath now and again from the biker's rotten egg farts. What were they eating up there?

Once on the ridge, while admiring the view of the treetops below, she accidentally yanked back on his jacket. A sickening patchwork of burnt black and pink skin on his thick neck, way worse than his hands. Why was every single Tender—except Rowan—burned like that? Was it just being around fires all the time, or had someone—*Orna!* she derailed the train of thought before it got too far down the track. *Stop with the negative thinking, already! You fishing for another panic attack?*

Eyes on the forest whipping past to either side, she let her murky thoughts settle and tried to enjoy the ride.

They pulled into Charwood's driveway safe and

sound, the sun high in the sky. Ray shut off the bike, and she got down, pacing around bowlegged to get rid of the stiffness.

The front door to the lodge opened, and Rowan came out. For a moment, as he walked towards her with his goofy smile, she was afraid the connection would be gone. That their moment of closeness had been only that, and he'd tell her how sorry he was for leading her on.

But when he took her hand and brought her in for a deep kiss, holding her against him like a life preserver, she knew better.

Up to his bedroom. And though there weren't exactly fireworks this time either, it was nowhere near as uncomfortable. Not only because his mattress was free of wood chips and sticks and she brought condoms, but the fear that she was being used had receded far enough into the background where she could pay more attention to her physical pleasure.

Afterwards, head on pillow, Orna stared up at the faces in the knots of wood on the ceiling. Then the thought sideswiped her. "What if we're still not doing this right?"

A pause. "If there's another way you'd like to—"

"Not that," she patted his lean, hairy chest and smiled. "I mean with biomass."

He sat up and leaned back against the headboard, long, messy, thinning hair hanging down to his shoulders. "What you got this time?" he said warily.

"Right now we're cutting trees, chipping them, and sending them halfway across the state to some plant." Her new idea energized her. "What if we get rid of the middleman?"

"The firewood business is slow going, Orna."

She shook her head and the blanket fell off her sweaty breasts, the ring tucked between them. Rowan wasn't afraid to stare, and, unashamed, she made no effort to hide. "Let's burn them where they stand."

"Huh?" Rowan gave her a dumb look.

She felt bad dumping her environmental ethics so quickly, but what were a handful of trees compared to freeing celestial beings of goodness and light? If God wanted the Tenders to make an angel omelet, they were going to have to break some forest eggs. "How many trees get cut in your average timber sale?"

He peered up at the ceiling to think. "Depends. Several hundred? Maybe more?"

"And how many burn in a wildfire?"

"I see where you're going with this." He plumped his pillow and lay back down. "The problem is, even with the really big fires, only some trees get killed. Most are barely singed, and the rest not at all."

"Okay, but that's still a lot, right?"

He shrugged his tanned, bony shoulders.

"And it's easier to bypass environmental laws to log a burned forest than a green one, no?"

"Sure."

"There's our answer." It was so simple; Occam's Razor for the win!

"What if people get hurt?" Not only didn't Rowan sound excited, he was being a total wet blanket.

"They evacuate the areas, right?"

He nodded.

"Well, there you go." As Rowan had pointed out on the field trip with Kathy Phauda, the game was rigged and playing fair meant they'd only keep losing.

"I dunno, Orna."

"During the pandemic, the U.S. could've saved hundreds of thousands of lives by having actual lockdowns, closing businesses that ignored public health mandates, ticketing anyone without a mask. But we didn't do anything like that because the powers that be wanted people to spend money and go to work." She spoke slowly to keep her rising temper at bay. Rowan should be on her side for this, not making her justify it to him. "And guess what? Other than some half-ass, almost never enforced suggestions in a few spots around the country, hardly anyone did a thing about it. If that many lives were intentionally shrugged off in the name of commerce, the *possibility* of a handful of deaths to save thousands of angels at a time is a no-brainer. Not only isn't it unethical to do this, it'd be unethical not to."

"Don't forget the firefighters," he said quietly.

"C'mon," Orna scoffed, wondering where the man's backbone went all of a sudden. "They're professionals, they know what they're doing."

He reached out and stroked her arm with a finger. "Let's sleep on it."

She brushed him away, no longer hiding her aggravation. "We're not sleeping on anything until we figure this out."

"I need to think about it," he groaned.

She rolled out of bed, the wood floor cool on the soles of her feet, grabbed her panties from the foot of the bed, and stepped into them. "I'll have Ray take me home so you can do that."

"Orna, don't." He tried to reel her back in with puppy-dog eyes.

"No, it's cool. You're not sure," she sniped, picking up her bra from the floor and snapping it on, unsure herself if she was bluffing or not. "I wouldn't want to rush your thought process."

A sigh. "Okay."

"Okay, what." She unhooked her sweater from the bedpost.

"We'll do it."

"You sure?"

He threw up his hands. "I don't like it, but what other choice do we have?" Frowning, he blinked at her. "We'll do it your way."

Orna hung the sweater back on the post. "Damn right," she whispered under her breath as she went to him.

CHAPTER 31

It was a warm, windy late Sunday afternoon by the time Orna and Rowan got back from the Meadbury hardware store. *Stores*, actually—five, in total; to keep from getting on anyone's radar they'd only bought two gas cans at a time. On the way back, they stopped at three different stations to fill the ten of them stashed in the back of Rowan's pickup under a bungeed-down tarp.

As they turned into Charwood driveway's, Orna made herself stop chewing the gummy inside of her cheek. If everything went right, she'd have done a real *mitzvah*, and the glory would be hers. But if it went wrong…

It *wasn't* going to go wrong. The plan was foolproof. All they had to do was drive two hours to the Bluff National Forest twenty miles outside Graniteville— the opposite side of the forest from their field trip with Kathy Phauda. A barely used dirt road would take them a dozen more miles into the forest, nowhere near a single house. They'd douse the undergrowth and some of the smaller trees, toss a match—the matchbook still in her pocket from a few Shabbats ago—and get the hell out of there.

They couldn't have picked better weather, what with the ongoing heat, drought, and high winds forecast for the next few days. Plus, the fact that it was the first day of Hanukkah—honoring how a day's worth of oil kept a lamp lit for eight—was a great sign.

Orna and Rowan hadn't gone far under the driveway's swaying canopy when he slammed on the brakes, Orna bucking against the seatbelt. An old, rusting Mercedes was parked in the way, RUNS ON VEGGIE OIL streaked across the back in sloppy red paint, greyish-white smoke pouring from the shuddering tailpipe.

Two hippie-types dressed in black, maybe mid to late twenties, stood to either side of the idling car. The driver sported long black dreadlocks down her back and wore a zipped-up hoodie and leggings. The passenger had blonde hair falling over his ears, a green bandanna around a skinny neck, and was in a T-shirt and black jeans.

The visitors swiveled their heads to glare at the pickup—the woman with high-cheekbones and of Asian, possibly Japanese descent, the guy pale, freckly, and fine-boned, almost delicate—before turning back to Silvio. The Tender, in a dirty grey sweatsuit, stood puffing a cigar in the middle of the road a few yards in front of the Mercedes, meaty arms crossed against his broad chest, legs planted wide. A horrible time for guests. Orna glanced back to make sure the tarp still hid the cans.

Rowan was already rolling down his window, and Orna got a whiff of French fries. He poked out his head and called in a friendly voice, "Can I help you folks?"

"What did you do to him?" Dreadlocks pointed at Silvio, her voice loud. "He on drugs or something?"

Orna opened the door and got out as Rowan switched off the ignition. "You know Silvio?" she asked.

The hippies nodded.

Fanning the tailpipe smoke—smelling like the inside of a fast-food restaurant—from her face, Orna realized who these people were. "You're forest activists."

The hippies' eyes met briefly over the hood of the Mercedes. "We just want our friend back," Bandanna said with a hint of a Southern accent.

"We've known about Silvio for a while," Orna said calmly, feeling in control of the situation for once. "And he's with *us* now."

"Listen, we haven't changed our minds on biomass or anything." Dreadlocks stuck her hands in her hoodie pouch. "We still think it's pretty much the worst thing you can do."

"But all we want is Silvio," Bandanna said.

"Well, why don't you ask him?" Rowan got out of the pickup.

"Ask him what?" The woman's dreadlocks quivered in the steady breeze like silent wind chimes.

"If he wants to go with you," Rowan said.

"What're you talking about?" Dreadlocks eyed Silvio.

"C'mon Sil," Bandanna motioned with a flip of his hair. "Let's get the fuck outta here."

Very slowly, Silvio shook his head back and forth.

Dreadlocks went over to Silvio. A few feet away she stopped and gasped. "What happened to your face, dude?"

The scuff of footsteps, and Ray and Isabel—in tight leather and flowing hemp, in turn—came striding around the bend from the lodge. Orna was glad to see them, but she had this. She held up a palm, and to her surprise, the two stopped.

"You've got your answer." Orna needed to end things before they went any further. And watch out for anyone trying to follow them to the national forest later. "Now, please leave."

The forest defenders looked at each other and seemed

to come to some wordless agreement, as Dreadlocks spun on her heels and marched back to the Mercedes.

Just then, a gust of wind swept down from the high peaks, whipping the tarp in the back of Rowan's pickup. Orna casually turned to check, and her stomach gave out as, sure enough, a corner had blown up to expose two of the gas cans. She jerked her head back, hoping—praying—their guests hadn't seen. Dreadlocks didn't seem to have noticed as she opened the driver's side door, but Bandanna, standing there on his heels, quickly looked away.

Shit. The second the hippies got out of there, they were totally going to call the cops and blow it. Orna had to do something. "Know what? I'm sorry for being rude," she said in a cheery voice. "Why don't you guys come in for a drink, and we can figure this out."

"Orna's right." To her pleasure, Rowan seemed to immediately catch on to the game. "Where are our manners? You've come all this way."

"We really need to be going." Bandanna opened the passenger door. "It's a bit of a drive back."

"Just one drink." Orna smiled like she was being photographed. "And then we can all take Silvio to the hospital to see what the klutz did to his face." She forced a chuckle.

"There's no way we're—" Dreadlocks started.

"Okay," Bandanna interrupted, catching Dreadlock's eye. "We'd be happy to." Dreadlocks wrinkled her nose but stopped talking.

"The lodge is just ahead." Orna pointed. "Drive up and park anywhere. We'll be right behind you."

The forest defenders got into the Mercedes and puttered forward in a blast of fragrant exhaust, Silvio standing to the side so they could pass. Ray and Isabel were already on their way back to the lodge.

Soon as the Mercedes slipped around the bend, Orna tucked the corner of the tarp back over the cans, the reek of gas sweet in her nose, and got into the pickup. Her stomach churned, and she felt a little nauseous. Why couldn't things go right, for once in her life?

"They saw," Orna said, as Rowan started up the ignition.

"It's just gas."

"Trust me, they know something's up. They're gonna rat us out."

"Well, what're we supposed to do, kill them?" Rowan laughed as he shifted into drive, and they headed up the driveway. Silvio was loping off into the woods, probably to take a whizz.

"We've either got to come up with some story, which I doubt they'll buy," Orna said, "or bribe them."

"Bribe them?" Rowan swung the wheel to dodge a pothole.

"Give 'em some money for protecting forests in exchange for keeping quiet."

"You think that'll work?"

Orna dropped the bucket into the well but came up dry. "It has to."

The forest defenders sat bolt upright on the living room couch between Orna and Rowan, everyone with a couple of shots of moonshine in their tumblers. Silvio was still off in the woods, Ray and Isabel weren't around—which was good as they'd only make things more tense—while Lottie lay on the floor by the front door. As always, the den way hotter than it needed to be, fireplace crammed full of burning logs, open windows barely making a dent in the swelter.

"To Silvio!" Rowan raised his glass.

"To Silvio!" Orna echoed.

Rowan and Orna took sips, though neither of the activists would touch their glasses.

"We never got your names," Orna chirped, doing her best to be friendly to the intruders.

"I'm Nolya." Dreadlocks tried on a smile and let it drop. "This is Dendron."

"I'm Orna, this is Rowan."

The head Tender took another sip.

An awkward silence Orna was all too familiar with; everyone pretending things were cool when they definitely were not. "Love your hair, by the way," she said to say something. "Silvio hasn't been in touch with you for a reason," Orna said, wanting to get things over with. "And if he wants to stay at Charwood, that's his choice. But we still want to make it up to you."

Sweat beaded on Nolya's forehead. "How so?"

"You guys do direct action. Treesits, road blockades, stuff like that, right?"

Not a peep from the two as Orna took another swig of moonshine.

"We're not trying to trick you." Orna patted the woman's thigh which was muscular as a gymnast's. "We're saying we *support* what you're doing. Believe it or not, we care about the forest as much as you do."

An eyelid twitch from Dendron was the only response.

"What if we made a contribution to your work?" Orna went on.

"How much?" Dendron said, earning a glare from Nolya.

Orna pulled a number out of thin air. "A thousand?"

"Multiply that by ten and you've got a deal," Dendron said. "Cash."

"Five thousand." Rowan drained his glass and clunked it on the table. "Would that square us?"

"Sure," Nolya said, flatly, after a pause. "Even Steven."

Orna's relief was like a cool breeze. Everyone had their price. Sure, there was a chance the two would still go to police, but Orna didn't think so; they looked like they needed the money. Besides, the Tenders had something on their side the forest defenders did not. God.

Rowan went upstairs, and, Orna forcing small talk with the two about the weather, came back a few minutes later with a thick roll of greenbacks in a rubber band, which he tossed to Dendron, who accidentally dropped it on the dusty wood floor. Orna had never seen that amount of cash in one place and wondered how much Rowan kept on hand. Nolya picked it up, slid off the rubber band, and everyone watched her count the bills on her lap until she gave a nod.

Orna held out her hand and Dendron shook it, his limp and sweaty. "Pleasure doing business with you," she said.

"Let me walk you out," Rowan said and led the way to the front door. Lottie stood up with a big yawn. As Nolya walked past, the woman leaned down to scratch the old pup on the forehead, and Lottie groaned in pleasure.

Rowan's arm around Orna, they waved as the forest defenders got back in the Mercedes. It was going to be okay. Tomorrow's trip would go as planned, and over the coming days—or even weeks, depending on how well the fire spread—hundreds, or possibly thousands, of freed angels would be flitting around the mountains on their way back to the source.

Rowan closed the door and gave her a big kiss. "You did it."

"Hey, it was your money." With the adrenalin gone, Orna felt sapped.

"Everyone knows Jewish American Princesses don't come cheap." Rowan lightly elbowed her in the ribs, and Orna gasped as if offended. She wasn't.

The Mercedes started up in a cloud of grease smoke and rolled down the driveway.

"I feel like I need a nap," Orna said, a bit dizzy from drinking her whisky too fast.

"You know what? Me, too." Rowan gave an exaggerated wink. "Just need to feed the boiler, and I'll be right up."

"K." Orna went upstairs to Rowan's bedroom, where she lay down on the comforter and closed her eyes.

CHAPTER 32

Orna woke with a groan, head swimmy, in Rowan's bed by herself. She hadn't meant to fall asleep, but the stress of her fight with Abba, then dealing with the forest defenders, plus the moonshine, had gotten the best of her. She got up and twitched away the blackout curtain, dusk settling from the sky onto meadow and forest. They needed to move if they were going to get in and out of the national forest before dawn.

No one in the living room, just Lottie snoozing on her chair by the glowing embers of the fireplace. Orna, most though not all her grogginess gone, checked the kitchen, but it was empty, too.

"Where is everybody, girl?" she asked the sleeping dog, who perked up an ear and let it fall without opening her eyes.

Orna went to the front door and swung it open. In the driveway Silvio's Prius in front of Ray's bike in front of Rowan's pickup. Not a Tender in sight, just the red sun sinking in a haze and a steady, refreshingly cool breeze. Snagging one of the headlamps from a coat hook by the wall, she put it on and went out to see if Rowan might be in the shed. Wind rippled the tall grass like the surface of a pond, the usual thick grey clouds chugging out of both boiler and Charwood's chimney, woodsmoke a prickly spice in the air.

Outside the shed dozens of split logs had been strewn across the grass, and she slid open the door.

Her headlamp shone on a car parked in the cleared-out space between the stacks of cordwood. The forest defenders' Mercedes.

Orna's stomach curdled. Another of Rowan's stunts, like lying to her about Dougie's accident or knocking down the tree in front of Kathy Phauda. Mean as those were, at least Rowan had a reason. But this one made no sense—unless he figured the bribe hadn't been enough. So, what was the dummy doing now?

She turned to face the night. Snaking over the jagged treetops into the navy-blue sky was a thin plume of smoke. It came from the direction of the clearcut she'd stumbled on the night she got lost.

Forest fire? She let her gaze go slack. Two huge angels swirled and spiraled in the smoke. Heart leaping, she hurried over to the logging road. Maybe Rowan was trying to find out if the forest defenders could see. Seemed risky, and if he'd bothered to ask, she'd have told him so.

Dreading whatever new mess he'd gotten them into this time, she picked up the pace to a jog. Then stumbled on her own feet, her balance off. Brain still fuzzy, it was almost as if she'd been drugged. But all she'd had was whisky. Unless Rowan…no. Just no. No, no, no, no, no!

Shutting off her mind and settling into a brisk hike, she went deeper into the trees.

After a few minutes the forest shed its needles, and she was in the burn, tree skeletons melding with the shadows, her muscles tense, mood dipping down into a minor key. For some reason she was afraid of what she might see out there, and almost turned around to go back to the lodge—or even Meadbury—to think things over. But then she heard Rowan's voice.

Dead ahead, the trees opened into the big clearcut hacked out of the black woods. There was smoke but no wildfire. Just three figures in those triangle Halloween masks, the tallest in a hobbit cloak holding a blue spruce branch—which she could tell by their clothes and build were Rowan, Ray, and Isabel—all standing around a good-sized campfire feeding it sticks. In the smoke above, the two angels danced and swooped.

She walked over, the heady scent of fresh pine rising up as her boots crushed the green needles carpeting the ground in a large circle around the campfire. "Is now really the best time to—" Orna started, and then her breath hitched.

A few yards outside the firelight, a massive pile of charred tree limbs and log rounds. Sprouting from its center were two skinny, branchless, eight-foot-tall trees, each with a figure bound to it—wrists overhead, ankles below—triangle masks over their faces, spruce boughs crowning their heads. The tips of dreadlocks dangled from under one of the masks, its owner in hoodie and leggings, the other in T-shirt and jeans. Nolya and Dendron.

Livid, Orna raced over to Rowan and got up in his face. She tore off his dead pine-needle mask—slits for eyes, dots for nostrils, gash for a mouth—and threw it on the ground. "The fuck is this?!" Flecks of spittle hit his cheek.

Rowan set the butt of the spruce branch on the ground and hung his head, looking sad and very tired. "We can't trust them."

"And you think kidnapping is gonna change their minds?" she stewed. "Now they've definitely *got* something to tell the cops!"

A masked and leathered Ray bent over to pick up a fat dead branch and toss it in the fire, the angels pirouetting in response. Behind him on the ground was a gas can next to a small bale of wire.

Orna's hot blood turned to frozen slush. "You're just trying to scare them, right?" Her knees weak from what had to have been a sleeping pill in her moonshine—Rowan had drugged her, after all!—she squatted in the soot. "Tell me you're only messing with them."

"You're the one who said it." Rowan picked up his mask from the ground. "That it was worth a handful of lives to save thousands of angels."

"But not on *purpose*!" Her world had blown apart. Again. Rowan was, had always been, and always would be a monster. How could she have been so blind? She rubbed her eyes with the heels of her hands to try to stop the spinning.

"It's the only way, Orna." Rowan nodded to Ray—that sick bastard—who snatched up the can and popped the cap from the nozzle. "The other option is the end. Of us. Of Charwood. Of everything."

Orna couldn't believe she even had to say it. Who *was* this lunatic she'd been sharing a bed with? "It's murder!"

"What do you want to do?" Rowan asked gently as Ray dribbled gas along the foundation of the stick pile. The pyre.

There had to be another way. There always was. "Isabel, you're not okay with this, are you?" Orna asked.

The Tender nodded her mask.

Silvio! Falling out or not, surely, he'd want to save his friends. Orna stabbed her beam around the clearcut. "Where's Silvio?"

"Keeping an eye on the lodge," Rowan said. "But he gave us his blessing."

What??? Orna's ring was an ice cube against her breastbone. She whirled around to the forest defenders wired to the saplings, a modern-day re-enactment of the Salem Witch Trials. "You guys won't tell anyone about this, will you?" she yelled at them.

Both hostages shook their masks furiously from side to side and said something in muffled voices Orna couldn't understand, as if they were gagged. But, of course, they'd say anything to get out of there. And, once free, Rowan was right that there was no way they'd keep quiet.

Unless…

"Can they see?" she asked Rowan, holding tight to that last straw of hope.

His head hung over his chest like a naughty boy caught stealing cookies. "I tried."

"But—"

"I'm sorry, Orna."

With that, Isabel yanked a branch out of the campfire, tip aflame.

Orna sprinted over to stop her, but the Tender, sprightly under her long gown, was too quick and chucked it into the pyre, a ring of flame wooshing up around its base.

The pyre's flames fed on the night's shadows, and Orna screamed.

CHAPTER 33

Orna's first instinct was to clamber up the pyre and set Nolya and Dendron free, and she lurched into the circle of pine needles. But the fire spread too quickly from the gas, so hot it singed the ends of Orna's hair with a sulfur stink. More horrified than she could remember being in her life, Orna could only stand there whimpering as orange and yellow flames licked the captives' feet.

"Stop this!" Orna shrieked. Killing people was crazy enough. But burning them alive? Pure evil.

Ignoring her, Rowan lifted his masked face to the night sky and shook the spruce branch in front of him, over a shoulder, to his right, his left, above his head, and then towards the ground. A horrible mockery of the *lulav* ceremony where, to honor the harvest festival of Sukkot, Jews shake a palm branch in all the directions of God.

Then the head Tender chanted out in near-perfect Hebrew, "Ha malachim m'hashamayim, yad yamin shel HaShem, ani kore lachem lishcon beguf hazeh." Or, in English, *Glorious angels from heaven, right hands of God, I call on you to inhabit this flesh.*

As the head Tender intoned his prayer to the heavens for the second time — the bonfire too far gone for anyone to save the forest defenders, even if they wanted to — Orna staggered on her feet, crying, "Why?" over and over again.

A gust of wind blew the thin smoke from the campfire into the pyre's thicker plume, and the angels surfed over, squirming through the air like translucent eels. Beneath them, Nolya and Dendron bawled in stifled voices, uselessly twisting and heaving their bodies against the wires holding them fast to their saplings, flames at their ankles. What a horrible way to die, baked in a bonfire. Or was it *bone*-fire?

Ray and Isabel faced the blaze, holding hands and swaying as fire crawled up the captives' legs and torsos, clothes smoking. Then Nolya and Dendron's masks and crowns caught, and they were human matchsticks.

Rowan yelled Hebrew words Orna had never heard before that sounded like Biblical names. The angels whipped around the smoke like sharks circling their prey, the stink of broiled pork chops in the air.

Orna collapsed on her knees and, clutching handfuls of sooty soil, puked.

Soon, Nolya and Dendron's saplings bloomed in flame. The angels spun faster and faster in a blurry cyclone, Rowan waving the branch and stomping like a madman as he shrieked out the Hebrew.

Dendron's body sagged. One of the angels shot down the smoke and disappeared into his fiery mask.

Rowan kept bellowing more names until Nolya, too, fell limp against her binds, and the second angel vanished inside her mask. He stopped chanting, tossed the spruce branch into the bonfire, and leaned over, hands on knees like a winded sprinter. The only sound the crackle and roar of the flames. Finally, the saplings snapped and crumbled, and the forest defenders' bodies fell mercifully into the fire.

Shaking with hatred at this brutal, cold-blooded murderer—a man Orna had somehow thought she was in *love* with—she scooped up a handful of dirt and flung it at Rowan, sprinkling the hem of his cloak.

Just as Orna was about to get to her feet to pummel him with bare fists, movement in the cherry red coals at the pulsing heart of the pyre.

Nolya's body tumbled from the blaze to fall facedown onto the green needles, smoking. Mask and crown gone, her handful of remaining dreadlocks scorched and shriveled down to the roots on her pink scalp. Clothes shreds and tatters, the skin of her back, rear end, and legs either melted like mozzarella or blackened like a well-done steak.

Then what was left of Dendron slid from the pile to flop on top of Nolya, only patches of his blond hair left, throat one big blister like a bullfrog's vocal sac, body a charred ruin.

Orna, on all fours, found herself blubbering to God, thanking him for finally ending their suffering.

Until Dendron opened his lashless eyes and pinned Orna with a bloodshot glare.

CHAPTER 34

It finally dawning that Orna, herself, was in danger, she sprang to her feet and booked it across the clearcut. She wasn't sure if she could outrun the Tenders, but she had to try to put as much ground between her and—whatever had just happened—as she could. She dug the toes of her boots into the dirt, pumping her arms like in her softball days when she'd hit an easy grounder straight to shortstop but had to run it out.

Halfway across the clearcut she risked a look back expecting to see one—if not all three of them—in hot pursuit. But Rowan, Ray, and Isabel just stood there, the silhouettes of the dead forest defenders sprawled on the ground.

Orna's lungs straining, she slowed to a jog at the edge of the forest. One last peek, and the Tenders still hadn't moved, the fires flaring in the middle of the dark clearcut like twin suns.

She pushed into the woods in the opposite direction from Charwood, the light of her headlamp weaker now. *Shit, batteries!* No undergrowth to trip her up, a branch smacked her in the face. Eye stinging and watering, blurry but otherwise okay, she made her way deeper into the burn.

Her best bet was to veer west towards Silvercleft and knock on someone's—anyone's—door for help. The townies might know who she was, of course, but soon as she told them what she'd seen, they'd have to take her in. Only problem was, she had no idea which way was west. And if she picked wrong, she'd go further into the forest. If only she had her cell—even if she couldn't get a signal, there was the compass app—but she'd left the fucking thing on Rowan's nightstand.

Nothing to do but keep running.

A cramp under her ribs like a hot branding iron. Gripping her guts, she had to stop. Switching off the headlamp, she listened to the night, dreading the crunch of sticks. Just the whistle of the rising wind in the bare branches.

Cramp or not, she made herself keep going. In a few minutes, the forest opened like a curtain, and she was in the tree plantation she'd found a few weeks before—though it felt so much longer than that, a different lifetime almost. The full moon peeked its pale face over the ragged tree canopy, gauzy behind a bank of streaming clouds.

Kneeling next to a shin-high baby pine, Orna took a breather, wiping her hurt eye with the back of one hand and rubbing her cramp with the other.

Turned out Rowan was *not* her cool new boyfriend but a full-blown psychopath who'd roasted two human beings alive in some fucked up ritual sacrifice for, what, the health of the forest or some crazy shit like that? And Ray and Isabel—not Silvio, though?—were happy to help.

But the killings were nothing compared to the other thing. Had the angels really gone *inside* the forest defenders, or did it just seem that way? And Dendron's eyes opening, that had been some sort of dead body reflex, right?

Maybe Abba had been right all along. Because whatever those creatures in the smoke were, they weren't angels. And whatever Rowan was, he wasn't husband material.

She laughed out loud and slapped a hand over her mouth to stop giggling, her mind like the thermos she'd dropped in the lunchroom as a kid, its protective glass layer shattered.

Doesn't matter now! Keep on truckin', girl!

Hurrying along the narrow rows of trees, she headed towards the big pile of dirt or sand; she could climb it and scan for houselights from the village. The soft pine branches brushed her knees and then waist as they grew taller.

Once at the pile the sand looked weird, grey and almost fluffy. She dipped a finger in, and it was soft like dust. Because it wasn't sand, it was ash.

Obviously, with all the woodfires, they had to dump the stuff somewhere. A thin layer had also been spread on the dirt; farmers used it as crop fertilizer, so it probably helped grow trees, too.

A few white chunks in the ash. Orna plucked out a piece the size of a half-dollar and studied it under her fading headlamp. Too heavy to be wood, it was off-white, maybe some kind of quartz. She tossed it back into the pile, next to where another thin piece jutted, and plucked that one out. It was about four inches long and curved, jagged at both ends. A rib, most likely from the pig roast. The chunks weren't rock but bone.

For some reason she held onto the rib with one hand and kept digging in the ash with the other. In up to her elbow, her fingers groped a rough, round stone. She palmed it and pulled it out.

A jawless human skull, cracked open on one side like a giant egg, each eye socket stuffed with a large pinecone. Yelping, she tossed it back on the pile. Furiously, she wiped her hands on her jeans, clearing her throat of the acid spewing up her gullet.

A grunt from behind her. She spun around, and where the beam of her headlamp faded into the dark, a very large pig stood—maybe two feet tall at the back, pointy ears perked up, mouth hanging open beneath a long, flat snout.

But this was no normal pig. It was burnt to a crisp, its skin a layer of charcoal over bulging muscle and fat. The creature lowered its huge head and scratched at the ground with a back hoof, kicking sparkling ash into the air.

Instinctively, Orna grasped the rib in her fist like a prison shank and got into a wide crouch. "Want some of this?!" she heard herself snarling, drunk with adrenalin.

The burnt hog snorted and weaved its head back and forth, yellow eyes aglow, back hunching as if about to charge.

A human figure stepped out from behind a small pine, walked over to the pig, and patted it on the head. Like a friendly dog, the animal—clearly the thing that had chased Orna the night she got lost—turned tail and trotted off under the trees.

Even though she couldn't see the person's face, it had to be Rowan. But wait, too short. Whoever it was had eyes that shone like a raccoon's and was dressed in a hoodie, shorts, and sandals. Slowly, he came towards her.

Though the hair and eyebrows were gone, most of the nose and lips burned away, the whole front of his babyface peeling grey skin, she knew who it was.

Dougie.

Heart jackhammering, ring cold against her tight chest, the air too thick to breathe, Orna swayed on her feet and thrust the broken rib out in front of her.

As Dougie inched closer, his fried face slack and stupid, Orna's eyes blurred. Legs no longer working, she teetered over backwards.

Fall broken by the ash pile, Bubby's ring freezing, her headlamp beamed up into the sky like a tiny lighthouse on a foggy night, flickered, and winked out.

CHAPTER 35

Orna came to flat on her back on something hard and uncomfortable—a piece of plastic, maybe—rope cutting into her wrists and ankles where they were tied down tight. For the first time, she'd passed out from one of her panic attacks. Yet, somehow, she was moving, headlamp gone, the moonlit, wind-whipped tree canopy sliding by overhead, Bubby/Eemah's ring achingly cold between her breasts, the silver somehow absorbing the rapidly cooling night air.

Dougie leaned into the rope he held across his chest, dragging her through the pine duff, bumping over roots and rocks and pinecones. Awful as his burned faced was, not only was Dougie alive, there didn't seem to be anything wrong with his head. Which could only mean one thing: She hadn't killed him.

Overjoyed as she was to see the kid still alive and her crime erased from the Book of Life, she reeled with the thought that it had all been another gruesome Tenders' trick! Though this one had been, by far, the cruelest. All the guilt and the tears, for what? So Rowan could get her to join his wacky cult?

And why the masks and chants and theater if what mattered was burning trees to free the—what did Abba call them? *Mazzikim*. Children of Darkness. Orna shivered. Was that what those things really were?

A thump on her back from a rock lit up her spine and

brought her back to the present.

If they were hiding Dougie, why let her see him now? Her whole body twitched. Unless they planned to kill her and dump her bones with whoever's was in the ash pile!

"Dougie," she squeaked in her friendliest voice. "So good to see you, man!"

He kept pulling like a draft horse. The scrape of plastic over the forest floor, the snap of a stick here and there.

Her hands tingling with pins and needles, she tried another tack. "You don't have to do this."

"Have to," he croaked in a voice dry as dead leaves.

At least he was talking. "I know he hurt you." It was obvious now that Rowan had burned each of the Tenders on purpose, possibly as some initiation. Or branding, like they were cattle. Or maybe just to keep them in line. "He hurt me, too. But we can get help. Together."

"No help."

She wasn't sure if he meant he didn't need help or there wasn't any. Both of which sounded like symptoms of mental trauma. Maybe Stockholm syndrome, where you side with your abusers. "There are doctors who can treat you. And we need to stop Rowan from hurting anyone else."

"No hurt."

"That's right, no more hurt." Orna's heart bounded like a jackrabbit. Could she really be winning him over? "But first you need to untie me."

The scratching of the dragged sled quieted to a hiss, and the night sky opened overhead. They were in the meadow, soon to be at the lodge. She only had a few minutes.

"Dougie, let me go."

The shush of grass.

"Please?" Orna whimpered.

Nothing. Holding back a sob, she strained at the ropes, but it was no use.

Bucked onto Charwood's driveway, the hard, packed dirt jarring her bones. Dougie stopped in front of the porch steps and bent over to untie her ankles, then one wrist. Close up, his face was even more of a disaster: loose, hanging flaps of flaky, rubbery skin stinking of rotten meat. What had they done to the poor kid?

Flexing her numb fingers and coiling every muscle in her body, Orna got ready to spring.

The instant the rope came off her other wrist, she rolled from the sled onto her elbows and scrambled to her feet to run. She hadn't gone a step before Dougie seized the back of her neck, grip like a monkey wrench.

"No more." His fingertips squeezed the sides of her throat like it was soft clay.

"I won't, I won't," she whined in agony, straining for air, black stars dancing, knowing if he went any harder he'd choke her out.

Thankfully, he let go to snatch her wrist and yank her towards the front door. Coughing and wrung out like a rag, Orna didn't have the energy to do anything but get pulled along. Once inside, Dougie slammed the door behind them and brought her through the roasting living room. Lottie watched them pass from her chair by the fire with a surly glare.

Then upstairs and down the hall, to Rowan's room, she assumed. Whatever was about to happen, she'd never let that scumbag touch her again.

Rounding the corner, Dougie flung open the first door on the left and flipped on the light. A large, plush bedroom, queen-sized bed with fluffy white comforter and throw pillows against one wall near a small couch and curtained window. An antique desk and chair were tucked into one corner, and in the other, a small table with electric kettle, a few plates, bowls, and glasses, and a stack of spoons. A shelf held bags of pasta, containers of soup and almond milk, and a bunch of canned goods. A few earth-tone throw rugs covered most of the shiny wood floor, a couple of framed photos of snowcapped mountains on the walls. A half-open door led to a bathroom with tile floor, modern sink, tub, and toilet.

Warm but not too hot, everything smelled like cinnamon toast.

"What's all this?" she asked, but Dougie was already leaving, pulling the door shut behind him.

"Wait!" But her only answer was the snick of a key in the lock. She was a prisoner, and this was her cell. Dread boiling up inside her, she shook the knob, but it wouldn't budge. "Don't freak, Orna," she mumbled to herself, pacing the room. "You'll find a way out."

Over to the window, she yanked the curtain aside. The meadow grass was probably fifteen feet below. Survivable, but if she hurt her legs—all too likely from that sort of drop—she wouldn't be able to get away at all. She glanced around the room, gaze landing on the bed. The sheets! She could tie them together and climb down! She darted over and stripped the comforter.

A knock on the door. *Fuck!* "Hold on, I'm changing!" She pulled the comforter into place, put the pillows back, and scurried over to the couch. "Okay!"

The click of the lock, and the door cracked open. "You decent?" It was Rowan.

Rage barely scratched the surface of how she felt about this living, breathing piece of shit. More than anything else, she wanted to beat him to a bloody pulp.

But without a weapon she didn't stand a chance. No, her best bet was to act like she'd come to her senses and was on his side again and wait for a chance to bolt.

"I am!" she called out cheerily.

The door opened more, and Rowan stood in the doorway in a fresh set of flannel and work pants, wet hair slicked back in a neat ponytail, beard oiled.

"Hey, hon," she said casually and chewed the inside of her cheek.

Hands in pockets, Rowan looked shy and confused. "You okay?"

"Still reeling from the Dougie thing," she said, honestly enough. "I ran over *something* that night, though."

"Jack-o-lantern," Rowan held back a smile, like telling a dirty joke in uncertain company.

Orna forced a laugh and hoped it sounded natural. "I get it."

"You do?" He'd yet to come into the room.

"Not all of it, but I'm sure you'll fill me in when you're ready. You always have." She smiled, making sure it reached her eyes. "Sorry I panicked like that." *Sorry I was caught.*

"I didn't want to kill them."

"I know." *Then why did you flambé them?*

"I was going to tell you. About the angels."

The bottom fell out of Orna's stomach. Much as she knew she needed to hear the truth, she wasn't sure she could take much more of it. "What about them?"

"You saw. How they went inside."

Even with the heat from the vent, Orna felt a chill. "Yeah, what was that all about?" she asked like it was no big deal.

He heaved a sigh. "It's how we make guardians."

"Guardians? What does that mean?"

Rowan turned his head towards the hall. "Okay, you can come in," he called in a loud voice.

"Who are you talking—" Orna cut herself off as slow, uneven footsteps came down the hall. Step, drag, thump. Step, drag, thump. Getting closer. Orna bit her cheek so hard she tasted blood.

Rowan came into the room and stepped aside. Though it wasn't possible, Nolya leaned unsteadily against the doorframe. Under a Rockies' cap her face was lobster red as if from a bad sunburn but otherwise okay. The long-sleeved cashmere sweater and flowing, Isabel-style hippie dress covered her body except for a pair of broiled pink hands.

The ring cold against her chest, Orna slumped back into the couch with a whimper.

CHAPTER 36

"How is she still…?" Orna whispered, peeking at Nolya from the corner of an eye, praying she didn't come any closer.

Rowan's mouth twisted in an embarrassed half-smile. "Well, technically…"

Orna had seen the poor woman literally get burned to a crisp. Okay, she survived, but how was she walking around? And what about Dendron?

"What—" Orna had to clear mucus from her throat to speak. "What are you saying?"

"The angels go inside before the body gives out."

"And that keeps her alive?" Dropping the girlfriend act, Orna scrunched even further back on the couch to get as far away from the two as possible.

Rowan tilted his hand side to side in a *sort of* gesture. "Somewhere in between."

This couldn't be real. There was no such thing as the living dead. "There's gotta be another explanation." Through her fleece and sweater she pinched the freezing ring away from her chest, no reason for it to be so cold. "Shock, maybe?"

"I assume you've heard of guardian angels," Rowan said.

Orna's insides twitched like she had to go the bathroom.

"If you say their names," Rowan nodded towards Nolya, whose blank expression made the forest defender look like she was on heavy downers. "They come to you."

"But why inside of *people*?" So many questions. So much insanity.

"It's the only way they can interact on the physical plane."

"You have to burn someone half to death for it to happen?" she snapped.

Rowan nodded sadly.

"Why do it, then?" Orna let out a slow breath to try to calm down. Barking at him wasn't going to help her.

"They protect us."

"From what?"

"Our enemies, Orna." Rowan shook his head like it was the most obvious thing in the world. "So we can keep doing the work."

"And after?"

Rowan squinted. "After what?"

"After it leaves. Will she get better?" Orna felt bad talking about Nolya when she was right there. But judging by the dull glaze in the woman's eyes, she didn't seem to be following much anyway.

"I've never seen them leave." He toed a spot on the floor. "But it's better than killing someone, right?"

Orna wasn't so sure. Was Nolya still in there, watching but unable to do a thing, like in some night terror? Or was it more of a blacked-out coma?

"Wait." Like a filmstrip across Orna's mind, images of Ray's burnt neck and hands. Isabel's scalp. Silvio and Dougie's faces. Lottie's patchy fur. "Who else?"

Rowan dropped his eyes.

"Who else???" Orna keened.

He shrugged a shoulder.

Oh my God. Oh my God, it's all of them.

Nolya farted, the stench of rotten eggs floating over. Just like Ray and Isabel always were.

Orna closed her eyes and slapped hands over her ears. "I can't deal, I can't deal, I can't deal," she whimpered to herself.

But she wasn't a toddler playing hide and seek. She was a grown woman, and this was happening. And if she was going to get out of it, she had no choice but to screw her head on tight and push through the fear.

Orna opened her eyes and pointed a finger at Rowan. "You, too?"

Rowan shook his head violently, as if offended by the idea.

"But you control them," she said.

"With their true names."

Orna sat up straight. No telling what scrap of info might be of use. "How do you even know that?"

"*The Key of Solomon.* Parents left me a copy, though I don't think they ever used it."

King Solomon from the Bible. "What if they're not angels?"

"What do you mean?" Rowan knit his brow.

Orna didn't want to say the D-word. "You're the one who told me there were good and—and not-so-good angels."

He sneered with naked disgust. "They're the good ones."

No point in arguing, but she was on team Abba for this. Not good angels or even bad ones here, but Children of Darkness. She felt her throat closing up but quickly reminded herself the sensation was all in her head—that, this time, she didn't have the luxury of passing out—and almost instantly the symptoms went away.

"You killed Silvio because he was on to you," she spat.

"First of all, I didn't *kill* him. He's just…occupied." Rowan crossed his arms like he was chilly. "Second, I wouldn't have done anything if you hadn't blown his cover."

Rowan stood maybe fifteen feet away, but it was like he'd slugged her in the gut. Sadly, he wasn't exactly wrong. If it hadn't been for her big mouth, Silvio would've still been alive. As would Nolya and Dendron.

She teared up but wouldn't give Rowan the satisfaction of wiping her eyes. "What about Ray and Isabel?"

"Three years. Three fucking years, and the slut cheats on me!" He clenched his fists. "At a damn biker bar!"

Orna closed her eyes so she wouldn't have to look at the scumbag. And to think she'd admired him for being mature enough to live with an ex and her lover, Ray. "Why Dougie?"

"He volunteered," Rowan said. "Like I told you at the plant, we needed you. Still do."

Okay, Orna, stay focused. She took a deep breath in through her nose and slow breath out through her mouth. *Just because he's killed—or whatever—everyone he knows, doesn't mean he'll do it to you. He* cares *for you. Otherwise, you'd already be dead. Or worse.*

Orna took a quick peek around the room. *Dude's gonna keep you here until he can trust you.* But one thought nagged like a splinter. Rowan had to know Abba would call the cops before very long. Which meant the head

Tender would be making his decision about her soon.

Back to Plan A. "I think I'm starting to understand." She eked out a smile.

"It'll take some processing." Rowan gave the smile back. "I gotta take care of something. If you want a shower, there are towels in the bathroom and clothes in the closet."

Rowan cocked his head, and Nolya lurched a few steps into the room, dragging an old hiking boot that looked several sizes too large. As much as Orna hated—hated!—that sorry excuse for a man, she didn't want to be left alone with that—that thing. "Don't go."

Rowan chuckled. "She's not gonna hurt you. She'll do anything you tell her to…give or take." He blew Orna a kiss, which made her want to puke. "Now get some sleep. We'll talk about next steps in the morning."

"Wait!" Orna felt like a kid scared of the dark asking for one more story at bedtime. "What next steps?"

He frowned. "Honestly, Orna? I don't know."

Then he slipped out of the room, shut the door, and locked it behind him, leaving Orna with the guardian.

CHAPTER 37

Nolya swayed like a drunk, reeking of burnt hair, bloodshot eyes staring a hundred miles away.

Unnerving as the creature was, Orna felt sorry for her and wondered if she was reachable at all. "How you feeling?"

Nolya stood there slack-jawed, drool leaking down her red chin.

So much for small talk. "That you, Nolya? Blink twice for yes."

No blinks.

Time to find out if what Rowan said was true, for a change. "Make me something to eat."

To Orna's surprise, Nolya limped over to the table, picked up a cup of noodles, and stripped off the lid. She got the electric kettle, staggered into the bathroom, and ran the sink.

Orna took the chance to dart to the bedroom door. Before she could test the knob, Nolya came barreling out of the bathroom and got hold of her shoulders. The guardian's crispy sausage fingers kneading Orna's muscles shot an oil slick through her guts, and she didn't resist.

"Let go," Orna demanded.

Nolya did as she was told. But the second Orna tried for the knob again, Nolya grabbed her, the thing's breath rotten worms.

"Just teasing," Orna said, the ring cold against her chest. What the hell was going on with that thing? And why did it happen every time she was next to a guardian? She needed some time alone to think. "I'm not hungry anymore. I'm gonna take a bath."

Nolya let go.

"Thank you." Orna strolled into the bathroom and hit the light.

The electric kettle was still on the sink, and Orna had an idea that set her heart on fast-forward. She closed the door, snatched the kettle, rushed to the far side of the tub, plugged it into the outlet, and set it on the floor out of sight. As she turned the gleaming faucet to hot, the door blew open and slammed back against the wall. Nolya loomed in the threshold, the same bland expression on her ruddy face under the baseball cap.

"Little privacy?" Orna asked.

Nolya didn't budge.

"Can you talk?"

"Yes." Nolya's new voice was high and creaky, like someone stepping on a loose floorboard. But it made the creature a little more human, a tiny bit less terrifying.

Bubby and Eemah's ring so cold it felt like it was burning a hole in Orna's flesh. She plucked it out and dropped it over her sweater, under her fleece, Nolya's eyes following her every move.

"What are you?" Orna asked.

A snorting, crackling sound in the back of Nolya's throat. At first, Orna thought the guardian was choking. But no, she was talking.

"English, please," Orna said as the water pooled at the bottom of the tub.

"Child of God."

Not saying much, as technically so was every living

creature on Earth.

"Where do you come from?"

"Below."

And Abba for the win. A real-life Child of Darkness.

Orna's hands shook, and she had to push back the instinct to run. The only way out was through. "And why are you here?"

"To help."

"With what?" Orna's voice trembled.

"The Great Shift."

Orna did not like the sound of that. "What shift?"

"How it was and soon will be."

Fascinating as this interview with a *mazzikim* was, the water was about a third of the way up the tub. Good enough. "What's your true name?"

A cow's dull, unblinking gaze; either too dumb to know or too smart to tell.

"Turn around," Orna commanded.

Blank stare.

"You heard me!"

Nolya didn't move a muscle.

So be it. Orna pulled her fleece and sweater over her head and tossed the dirty things on the bathmat on the floor.

Nolya's eyes flicked down to Orna's bra.

Orna pinched the ice-cold ring between her fingers. "This what you're looking at?" She moved it to the side as far as the chain could go, and Nolya's head turned to follow like a dog with a tennis ball. *I'll be damned.* The ring was, after all, supposed to protect from demons. Just how much, she'd have to find out.

Turning around, Orna unhooked her bra and threw it on the tile. Then untied her boots and kicked them off, pulled down her jeans and panties, and took off her socks, the tile cool on her feet.

Orna stepped into the tub, the hot water so soothing to her sore, tight back muscles she couldn't help but let out a groan. Ash and dirt flaked off her, clouding the water. Closing her eyes, for the next full minute she pictured what she was about to do. *You got this!*

She opened them again, and Nolya hadn't moved an inch. Orna reached out a hand. "Can you help me out?"

Like a loyal butler, Nolya reached forward and took Orna's hand with her horrible fried fingers. Orna got out of the tub, water dripping onto the tile. "Towel, please."

Nolya handed it over from the rack, and Orna dried herself and wrapped it around her body.

Deep breath in. Abs tensed. And Orna shoved Nolya hard in the mid-back, the guardian plunging face-first into the tub, knocking off her hat to uncover what was left of her melted web of dreadlocks.

As Nolya splashed around in her soaked sweater and dress, gripping the rim of the tub and trying to pull herself to standing, Orna bent over, picked up the plugged-in kettle, stood on her fleece and sweater on top of the bathmat, and tossed it into the bath.

Nolya jolted upright, eyes rolled back to veiny whites, body seizing as the lights over the sink flickered. A puff of smoke from the guardian's open mouth, then her whole body crumbled into ash, settling and clumping at the bottom of the tub in a grey-black muck.

Orna yelled and pumped her fist in victory. And the lights went out.

CHAPTER 38

It was dark. Can't see your hand in front of your face dark. But Nolya was dead, and whether the thing inside her was, too, Orna was pretty sure it couldn't hurt anyone now. Meaning all the guardians could be taken out, perhaps with the help of Bubby and Eemah's ring—however that worked—the silver room temperature again.

And thank God for that, because surely Rowan had noticed the power outage and was sending another one up after her.

Orna dropped to her knees and felt around the wet tile for her clothes. Not bothering with underwear or socks, she yanked on her jeans, sweater, and boots. Then crawled on hands and knees until tile turned to wood floor, and she got to her feet.

With the moonlight leaking through the window Orna could just make see the furniture and groped her way across the bedroom, hands out in front. At the window she pulled up on the sash, but it was stuck. She felt around for the clasp, undid it, and tried again. Still no dice. Running her fingertips across the sill, she felt the metal nail heads. *Shit. Only one way out now.*

Over to the bed, she tugged off the comforter and wrapped an edge around her fist like a boxing glove. She jabbed at the pane, but not hard enough to break it. Rearing back, she leaned into the punch with her shoulder. A satisfying smash and tinkle of glass. She knocked out the remaining shards from the window and swept them onto the floor.

Back to the bed to pull off the top sheet, which she knotted to a corner of the comforter. Then she stripped the fitted sheet and started tying that to the top sheet. All together, it should get her most—if not all—the way down from the window.

The rattle of a key in the lock.

Hurryhurryhurry! She fumbled with the knot, fingers sweaty.

A whoosh of warm air, footsteps pounding, and a shadow gliding towards her. The ring an icicle between Orna's breasts, she spread open the sheet, and soon as hands grabbed her waist, brought it down like a butterfly net. Whoever it was fell on top of her, knocking her onto the bed.

Orna struggled to keep the sheet over her attacker's head, but they got free, hot compost breath in her face. Desperate to keep their teeth away, she pulled the sheet taut and looped it around where their neck had to be. In doing so, her knuckles brushed against a mushy bubble of skin, and her gorge rose; from what she'd seen at the bonfire, it had to be Dendron and his throat blister.

As she joined the ends of the sheet together, Dendron clawed her forearms. Orna cried out in pain, blood trickling down her stinging arms, but held tight, using her greater bodyweight against the slender guardian.

Orna squeezing her fists together, Dendron gurgled, and she could vaguely see him in the moonlight scratching at his throat. She had the instinct to turn her face away and close her mouth. And not a second too soon, as Dendron's blister popped, the liquid rot spraying her cheek.

Eyes watering, stomach hitching, Orna's arms shook

with the effort as Dendron tried to slip his fingers under the sheet. With or without the help of the bitter cold ring, she couldn't hold him much longer. She kneed upwards, aiming for his crotch. It took a few tries until she hit paydirt, and he grunted and went limp. With a surge of strength Orna yanked him to the side, and he bowled off the edge of the bed, thudding to the floor. *That's right, motherfucker!*

Hoisting up on the sheet, Orna got to her knees and stood on the mattress, then heaved back like a cowboy on the reins of a bucking bronco. Dendron thrashed around, but she had leverage. A few more kicks, and he slumped to the floor and lay still.

Instead of letting go, Orna kept tugging until she heard a sickening snap. Then the sheet came free as Dendron sifted into a pile of ash.

The ring icy against Orna's sternum, she had to fish it out and lay it atop her sweater again. As a kid, she'd always wished she'd been born in Middle Earth so she could hike around the woods fighting orcs with Frodo and Strider and Gandalf. Now that she'd been cast in the starring role of this *Lord of the Rings* knockoff, she took it all back.

The distant blast of what sounded like a trumpet from low note to high. Orna held her breath to listen. Then again. And a third time. Though it had been years since she'd last heard it, Orna would recognize the sound anywhere. A *shofar*, the traditional ram's horn blown on the Jewish new year of Rosh Hashana.

Abba!

Orna's heart leapt like a deer over a fence and then crashed and burned. Unless the cops were with him—and no way they'd let Abba be there if they were—what could a one-legged old man do against a houseful of demons and their homicidal master?

She went over to the window, stepping through the pile of ash that had been Dendron, and leaned out. Fat yellow beams of light around the side of the lodge from the driveway. Now that the bedroom door was open, at least she didn't have to climb down from the window. But she still needed a weapon.

Into the closet to feel around. Just a bunch of hanging clothes. Then she knocked into something, and it fell to the ground with a smack. Kneeling, she ran her hands over prickly straw at the end of a long wooden handle. Broom. Not great, but it would have to do.

Back in the moonlit bedroom she snapped the broom over a knee and was left with a sharp, jagged stick. A quick test thrust, and she rushed out the bedroom door, feeling her way along the walls down the dark hallway. Then around the corner towards an orange glow seeping from the first floor. Standing at the top of the stairs, she peeked down into the den.

No one there. But Lottie's easy chair faced the guttering fireplace. From that angle, Orna couldn't tell if the chair was empty, if the dog was lying there fast asleep, or waiting, ready to rip out her throat.

Muttering a short snatch of prayer, "Baruch atah Adonai aloheinu Melech haolam," Orna tiptoed downstairs.

CHAPTER 39

Heading down the flight of stairs, Orna took the ring in a fist. Still warm. Standing on the bottom step, she slipped it back under her sweater.

Now or never! Broomstick in hand, Orna strode across the den watching Lottie's chair. But it was empty, thank God, and her eye fell on the hatchet sunk into the kindling stump. Figuring her arsenal could use an upgrade, she yanked it out and hurried across the room.

As she turned into the front hallway, the scrabbling of toenails over wood floors. Ring icy again, Orna spun around as Lottie careened out of the open kitchen door, heading straight for her. Planting her feet, Orna brandished the broken broomstick like a spear, gripping the hatchet in her other hand.

Lottie came to a skidding stop just outside of Orna's thrusting range. Eyes red, runny, and filled with loathing, the old German Shepherd bared yellow teeth and black gums.

"Good doggie," Orna cooed as she backed towards the door, knowing full well this was no more a dog than the things upstairs had been Nolya and Dendron. Lottie paced her but didn't get too close.

As Orna reached behind to grab the doorknob, Lottie let out a kind of half-growl, half-yawn. And then again, until Orna realized the dog had said, "You are all dead meat."

Blood curdling, Orna turned the handle, slipped outside, and slammed the door behind her a half-second before the dog thumped up against the wood.

It was finally cold out; not quite freezing but enough for Orna to see her breath, the wind a steady gale. Abba, in his suit and *tallit,* stood on one leg behind the open door of her Subaru balancing a shotgun on top of it, the car's headlights on. The firearm's muzzle was aimed at Silvio, who stood protectively in front of Rowan, Dougie and Isabel flanking the head Tender to either side.

Orna had never once heard Abba talk about guns, pro or con, but sighting down the barrel—square *teffilin* box strapped to his forehead, left arm wound in the black leather strap as if it were the High Holidays—he sure looked like he knew what he was doing. She was both proud of him and scared out of her mind.

If Orna had a plan—and she didn't, really—it was to beg Rowan to let Abba go and take her instead. But with all eyes on her father, she reared back and chucked the hatchet at Isabel—the nearest guardian—with all she had. It spun through the air, blade over shaft over blade. And missed the guardian entirely, smashing the windshield of Rowan's pickup instead.

Everyone turned to Orna as she made a break for her car. She'd only gone a half a dozen steps when Isabel loped after her like a mountain lion. Halfway to the car, Orna got tackled hard to the driveway, the guardian's bony knee grinding into her upper spine, face in the dirt.

The ring like liquid nitrogen against her ribcage, Orna shoved herself up to all fours, tossing Isabel off her back as if she were a child. No question, now: Not only did the ring warn Orna of guardians, it made her stronger.

But as Orna rose to her feet, her leg was swept out from behind, and she was eating dust again. One-on-one the ring gave her the upper hand against a guardian but clearly not against two. Orna bucked and spat as they pinned her to the ground, but it was pointless, and she stopped struggling.

Isabel held Orna's forearms together as Dougie tied off her wrists with climbing rope. Then, sitting on Orna's kicking legs, he did the same with her ankles. Once bound, Isabel yanked Orna's hands between her thighs, and Dougie knotted wrists to ankles.

Abba pointed the shotgun at the guardians, its sling blowing in the cold wind, but perhaps seeing he couldn't fire without possibly hitting Orna, swung it back to Silvio who hadn't left his spot in front of Rowan.

"Get outta here and call the cops!" Orna shrieked. The ropes were already cutting off the blood flow to her fingers and toes. It might be over for her, but with the only real weapon in the fray, Abba still had a chance.

Abba ignored her, fat clouds bunching in the sky above him.

"See, Mr. Tannenbaum!" Rowan called out. "I told you she was fine."

Abba growled, "If you hurt a single hair on her head—"

"I promise I'll keep her safe. Cross my heart and hope to die." Rowan scratched his fingertips over his flannel.

"You mean, keep her prisoner," Abba said.

Rowan's comeback was lightning fast, almost as if he had it planned. "What, like *you* did all those years?"

A low blow. With no truth to it…at least not much.

"If you don't let her go by the count of three," Abba

shouted, the wind whipping his *tallit,* "I'm going to end that thing and then you!"

For a moment, Rowan stared at the ground as if at a loss for words. Then he got his bluster back. "No, you won't."

"What makes you think that?" Abba said. "One."

"Exodus Twenty-Thirteen," Rowan said smugly. "'Thou shalt not kill.'"

"A mistranslation!" Abba roared, the only person in the world who'd debate scripture in the middle of a gunfight. "The original Hebrew says, 'Thou shalt not *murder*.' Two."

"Which is killing with malice aforethought. Isn't that why you brought the shotgun?" The Tender folded his arms across his chest as if to say, *Checkmate*.

Abba indeed seemed stumped for a few seconds. Then he set his cheek against the stock of the shotgun. "Ecclesiastes Three-Three: 'A time to kill.'"

Orna was torn. She wanted nothing more than for Abba to get away and call the cops, something he couldn't do without being in cell range. But she was pretty sure he wouldn't leave without her, and that meant killing Rowan. Yes, the bastard had lied to her—over and over and over again. Yes, he'd taken the lives of those closest to him. Yes, he'd brought those creatures into the world. All enough to put him behind bars for the rest of his life, to say the least. But did he deserve death?

The thing was, if *she'd* fallen for the whole angel shtick, who was to say Rowan hadn't, too? After all, much worse had been done over the ages in the name of God by well-meaning Christians, Muslims, and Jews alike.

"Three!" Abba yelled.

A shadow slipped out from under Rowan's pickup.

"Behind you!" Orna screamed.

Abba spun, cradling the shotgun, and fired. An orange-yellow flare and ear-splitting blast as Ray launched backwards into the air. The instant the guardian hit the driveway, he turned to dust, the wind strewing his ashes into the chilly night.

Meanwhile, Silvio bolted forward and stripped the shotgun from Abba with a single hand. Clamping onto the back of Abba's neck with the other, Silvio threw him face first onto the driveway, boot on neck, gun muzzle to his skull.

Orna closed her eyes, held her breath, and braced for the shot. Her only hope was that it would be quick.

"Put it down!" Rowan demanded.

Orna opened her eyes. Silvio hadn't budged.

"Naamah!" Rowan barked. "I said, put it down!"

Silvio's hands and forearms shook as if the shotgun weighed a hundred pounds, and the firearm dropped to the ground. The guardian turned his half-boiled face to Rowan with a twisted scowl of pure hatred.

CHAPTER 40

Moonlit clouds roiled above the swaying treetops as Orna got dragged along the logging road yet again, tied down on her side to the sled. But this time Isabel, in her pine-needle mask, did the hauling as they headed back towards the clearcut. A cloaked Rowan ambled in front of Isabel—shotgun slung over his shoulder, head bowed as if in thought, headlamp lighting a shifting patch of packed dirt—Lottie leading the way into the chilly darkness ahead.

Orna knew what would happen out there. She felt like crying but was out of tears.

Dougie, also in a mask, trudged along behind, Abba slumped motionless over his shoulder, wrists tied together.

"Is he okay?" Orna whimpered.

Rowan stopped and turned around, face a grey blur as he passed Orna, like his features had been wiped clean. Walking alongside Dougie, Rowan took Abba's wrist. "Pulse is strong," he said, then set his hand on Abba's back. "Breathing's good. Just got knocked out."

Thank God, Orna thought Sght. And then wondered if the alternative would've actually been a blessing.

But the death march went on, and Rowan caught up to her on the sled.

"They're not angels, you know," Orna tried, knowing it was her last chance.

"Yes, they are," Rowan snipped, keeping pace with

her and Isabel. "And if God didn't want me to set them free, He'd have stopped me a long time ago."

"What you're doing has nothing to do with God," Orna said, trying to keep the edge out of her voice. "But it's not too late to turn back."

"The only way out is through," he recited her saying in a voice so quiet and sad it almost made her feel sorry for him. Almost.But like an actress, she took that spark of feeling and blew it into a flame. "We can figure it out," she said, not sure if she was telling the truth or not.

"Charwood's over, Orna."

The dense overhead canopy thinned to bare branches as they entered the burn, the moon floating in the cloud cover like a rotten egg in dirty dishwater. "Then we run away," Orna said desperately. "Canada. Mexico. Wherever. So long as we're together."

"Oh, Orna."

"What? You don't love me?"

Rowan sighed. "Course I do. But you don't love me."

"Yes, I do." Like ashes in her mouth to say it.

"You really think you can forgive me?"

"Of course. Just let my dad go."

A long moment of scraping sled and roaring wind. The temperature had dipped below freezing, and Orna shivered in her ropes, waiting for Rowan to speak.

Finally, he did. "Remember the mugger in Meadbury?"

"You protected me." She was really getting into character now. "And that's when I starting falling for you." At least the last part was true.

He laughed spitefully, shifting the shotgun to his other shoulder. "It was Ray."

The fucker. After all the lies, it still felt like a slap to the face to know even that was a sham.

"And Dougie?" Rowan's voice was high and weird. "He didn't volunteer. I forced him."

Maybe it was the cold or lack of circulation from being tied down, but Orna's whole body went numb. Deep into the burn now, the gig was up. No one could ever be cool with what Rowan had done, and they all knew it.

"So, you're gonna burn us alive?!" she warbled, dropping the act. "Let those things inside?"

"Told you I needed you." Rowan was crying.

"It won't *be* me!"

"Sometimes," Rowan sniffed and wiped his nose with the sleeve of his flannel, "a man's gotta take what he can get." And then he tramped ahead to catch up with Lottie.

"Rowan!"

He wouldn't answer, and Orna saved her breath. Would he really go through with it? And, if so, would any part of her and Abba be left?

A campfire blazed when they reached the clearcut, a masked Silvio feeding sticks from a small pile. Overhead in the smoke, two Children of Darkness wriggled and writhed. Beside it, a heaping pyre of broken branches, two limbless saplings sprouting from the center.

CHAPTER 41

Orna lay on the sled next to the pyre, back muscles screaming, hands and feet numb from the ropes and the cold. Lottie sat eyeing her from a few feet away, drool dripping down her scarred muzzle. Isabel and Silvio—still masked—chucked branch after branch from the pile into the blazing campfire, while Rowan watched the Children churning overhead in the smoke.

Soon as Dougie set Abba down on his back on the carpet of green pine needles, the older man blinked himself awake.

"You okay?" Orna asked, saving the apologies for later. If such a time even came.

"Tov," he said—Hebrew for good—sitting up with a groan, testing his hands still tied behind his back.

Smart move, as she was pretty sure Rowan only knew a few snippets of the language. "*What do we do?*" she responded in Hebrew.

"*Your boyfriend,*" Abba said. Even now, he had to get in the dig. "*He called one of them by name.*"

"*You mean—*"

Abba shushed her, looking around, but everyone was busy with the fire. "*Still have the ring?*"

She nodded, the piece of silver nestled between her breasts like a giant snowflake.

Abba blinked long and hard a few times. Orna worried he might have a concussion. "*What about the others? Do you know their real names?"*

She shook her head.

"I'm going to say a few words, and when I'm done, I'll need you to repeat after me." Though her father's face was grim, he was strangely calm. She had to hand it to him, the man was good under pressure. And hopefully, he knew how to get them out of there, because she had nothing.

"'Surely,'" Abba muttered, "'he will save you from the fowler's snare and from the deadly pestilence.'" The verse rang a bell, some psalm. But why was he saying it in English? Unless he wanted Rowan to hear? But Abba's voice was too quiet, and besides, the head Tender only had eyes for his monsters in the smoke.

"'He will cover you with his feathers, and under his wings you will find refuge,'" Abba said, a bit louder. "'His faithfulness will be your shield and rampart.'"

The psalm had gotten Dougie and Isabel's attention, though, and they walked over. Together they lifted Abba under his armpits and carried him like some anti-war protester to the pyre and up the pile of sticks.

"'You will not fear the terror of night, nor the arrow that flies by day,'" Abba had his normal voice back, though he made no effort to stop Dougie from winding a length of wire around his midsection to the dead sapling and then twisting the ends together behind him. Propped on his right leg, Abba went on like a rabbi sermonizing his congregation. "'Nor the pestilence that stalks in the darkness, nor the plague that destroys at midday.'"

Isabel untied Abba's wrists from behind his back only to bring his hands together in front and tug them over his head. Abba winced as Dougie wired his arms to the sapling.

Orna could only watch in horror from the sled as

Isabel set a crown of spruce over Abba's head, covering his *kippah*.

"'If you say, The Lord is my refuge, and you make the Most High your dwelling,'" Abba called out, as Dougie and Isabel crunched down the pile towards Orna, "'no harm will overtake you, no disaster will come near your tent!'"

Unlike Rowan's ritual, whatever her father was doing was nothing but theater. Comfort food without any vitamins. Abba paused, as if also coming to terms with it.

Isabel untied the short length of climbing rope connecting Orna's hands to her feet, wrists and ankles still knotted tight. As they did with Abba, the two guardians carried her up the sticks. The frosty ring against Orna's skin and the brisk night winds scudding clouds across the sky sent a shiver down to her marrow.

Isabel slammed Orna's back against the sapling, pain a lightning strike down her spine. As the guardian grabbed her hands, Orna made a double fist and slugged Isabel right in her mask's slitted mouth, knocking it off.

"Whore!" Isabel snarled, and Orna was happy to see a thin trail of blood trickling down the guardian's pretty chin. Then Isabel spat in Orna's face, the warm wetness globbing on her cheek.

Abba picked up the psalm again but at a faster pace. "'For he will command his angels concerning you to guard you in all your ways.'"

Angels? Orna thought. *How about some actual ones, this time?*

Isabel roughly yanked the spruce crown over Orna's head, and Dougie pulled out a couple of bandannas from the pockets of his grimy shorts. He started to tie the first one around Abba's mouth as a gag.

"Let them finish their prayers," Rowan said glumly, face turned up to the smoke, mask on top of his head like a catcher between batters. Was the head Tender having second thoughts? If so, why didn't he stop the insanity?

"'They will lift you up in their hands so that you will not strike your foot against a stone!'" Abba shouted. "'You will tread on the lion and the cobra; you will trample the great lion and the serpent!'"

Pointless.

But seconds after the words left Abba's mouth, the twirling demons began to zigzag around the smoke like flies trapped in a glass. Faster and faster they spun, bumping against the edge of the plume as if trying to get out.

Then they faded to transparent, flickered, and were gone.

Holy shit, it worked! Orna and Abba might get out of this, after all!

Rowan jogged around to the other side of the fire, circling around and back again, fanning the smoke as if trying to find out where the Children might be hiding.

However, the psalm seemed to have had no effect on Dougie, Isabel, and Lottie, facing the campfire and swaying side to side. Nor Silvio as he snatched the end of a branch and drew it out of the blaze, tip burning. He walked towards the pyre, flame guttering in the wind.

A black thought flitted into Orna's mind like a bat to a cave. Being past midnight, it was officially the second day of Hanukkah...and this time she and Abba were going to be the candles.

"At first, I was not sure why I hated you so much," Silvio pointed at Orna with his free hand. "But now I know. You are the granddaughter of Ilana Kirschwald."

Orna's mouth went bone dry. The thing knew Bubby?

Abba spat into the air. "Ignore the beast and repeat after me!" He took a breath and began, "Adonai malech, Adonai ha'aretz!"

Orna said the Hebrew, *"Lord and King, Lord of the Earth!"*

A gust blew Silvio's torch clean out. He tossed the branch down and stomped it with the heel of a sneaker.

"Malkuth!" Abba yelled over the roaring, wintry wind, his breath a puff of white. Then, in Hebrew, *"The Tenth Sephirah: The Kingdom, The Glory of God, The Queen!"*

Orna tried the words from the *Kabbalah* but kept stumbling on them, until she finally got them right. If Abba's prayers could rid the smoke of the Children, surely it would do the same for the guardians.

Snickering under his mask, Silvio wandered back to the fire. "I was there in the candlelight when your mother died."

Orna turned to Abba, who seemed to read her thoughts. *Did this monster take Eemah?*

"Lies!" Abba snapped.

"Your father is an ignorant fool," Silvio fished around the fire for a new stick, "unable to keep his wife from rotting away and his daughter from becoming a God forsaken harlot. But he is correct: I just wanted to watch." He tugged out a long, gnarled branch, this one with a fatter flame at its end, and strolled back to the pyre.

Rowan stood dumb and useless as a scarecrow, eyes on Silvio's torch. He might not be helping Orna and her father escape, but at least he wasn't trying to silence them.

Abba craned his neck towards the streaming clouds

and bellowed more Hebrew, *"I call upon the four elements—air, water, fire, wind—to purge this foul creature: She who emerges to seduce us in our dreams!"*

She? As Orna mouthed the words, the wind bent the flame on Silvio's torch, though it held fast.

"This strangler of children!" Abba bawled. *"The Archdemon Naamah!"*

Orna's eyes stinging and tearing with windblown ash, ring searing her flesh with the chill of space, she, too, belted out the terrible name.

A few feet from the pyre, Silvio—like the features on his mask—froze. As if pushing against an invisible wall, he leaned forward and dug the toes of his sneakers into the ground but couldn't move an inch. The prayer had bound him!

"Leave this vessel, Naamah, begone!" Abba sung out, and Orna shouted in response.

Silvio arched backwards like a gymnast, and the torch dropped from his hand onto the edge of the pyre. Mercifully, the flame shrunk and went out, its tip glowing orange. Then the guardian's shoulders jerked like a short-circuited robot, arms flailing faster and faster and faster until they were a blur, mask falling to the ground.

Too soon to let up, Orna kept reciting the Hebrew, *"Leave this vessel, Naamah, begone!"* the freezing ring biting her flesh.

Silvio dropped to all fours and gagged, dry heaves racking his body, spine hunching like a caterpillar.

"Leave this vessel, Naamah, begone!" Orna shrieked again.

Silvio's mouth opened wide, wider—too wide— and he vomited out a thick cloud of white smoke and collapsed on his side.

The same long, thin, translucent winged form she'd seen so many times before, its triangle face blank, whisked over to the campfire and hovered in the smoke.

Ever so slightly, Silvio's arm shifted, and his legs stirred. Still alive! Though with the burns he'd suffered—probably smoke inhalation, too—he didn't stand a chance without serious medical attention, and soon.

Rowan, meanwhile, stood open-mouthed like a gawker at a car accident, Isabel, Dougie, and Lottie rooted to their spots.

An arctic draft swept across the clearcut and broke up the smoke. The billowy figure, tall as a basketball hoop, settled down into the campfire itself, turning from translucent to the thick white of a jet's contrail. Once within the flames the massive cloudy form went solid, a scaly layer of grey-green skin congealing over its coiled, snakelike body.

Black pinprick eyes empty as the void bored deep into a wrinkled triangle face above two pits for nostrils and a jagged pink slash of a mouth—not unlike the Tenders' masks. A pair of stubby, crooked, yellow horns corkscrewed from the top of the thing's tortoise-like skull. Balancing its thick, tubular upper body on a coiled tail, it spread and flapped enormous scabby wings, pleated like the neck frills of an exotic lizard, sharp talons spiking from their tips.

CHAPTER 42

Orna's eyes ached from staring at the thing in the campfire that was Naamah, Child of Darkness—basically, the face of a mummified tortoise with the body of the Greek snake-monster known as a Lamia—but she couldn't look away.

"Can she leave the fire?" Orna squeaked.

Abba shook his head uncertainly, which didn't make Orna feel any better.

Rowan, however, launched to his feet and stepped to the edge of the flames. "As the one who freed you," he aimed the shotgun at Naamah, "I command you to return to the trees!"

Naamah threw back her shriveled head in booming laughter, and a tremor like a small earthquake thrummed through the sapling at Orna's back.

"You humans never cease to amuse me." Naamah's voice made Orna queasy, a deep, syrupy tone overlaid with another several octaves higher and raspy like a cicada's chirrup.

"We have *never* been bound within your trees." Naamah bobbed and weaved in the fire like a snake charmer's cobra. "And you have no mastery over us once we shed our human disguise."

Rowan stumbled backwards. "But you're *angels*..." The head Tender waved a beckoning hand at the guardians who were left, and Dougie and Isabel—

masks off—along with Lottie, obediently crowded around him.

Silvio, meanwhile, groaned from his bed of needles, chest heaving. Orna had to do something if he—if any of them—were going to survive.

With everyone distracted, Orna tried to wriggle her wrists out from under the wire, but all she did was scrape off a layer of skin. "Abba, we need another prayer."

"Patience." Abba's eyes locked on the thing in the campfire as if entranced.

"You're angels!" Rowan shouted, lowering the shotgun. "*Aren't* you?"

"The handservants?" A purring of disgust from the back of Naamah's throat. Naamah swiveled her triangle head towards Orna and Abba, black beady eyes making Orna dizzy until she shut her own. "Though some have called us Nephilim, Grigori, the Watchers." Naamah turned to Dougie, Isabel, and Lottie. "We are the *true* Children of God! Is that not so, my brothers and sisters?"

"You promised I would sit at the feet of our Lord," Rowan whined like a little kid who'd had his ice cream cone stolen.

"And so you shall." Naamah spread wide its scaly wings as if about to dive into the campfire's embers. "Upon your death."

"Then why are you here?!" Rowan sniveled.

"Because Ashmodei—our king, my son—commanded it." Tucking wings against her body, Naamah turned back to face the Tender with a withering stare. "However, seeing as your bloodline has served us well, I will grant this request before attending to my next affair."

Orna's heart lurched as a wisp of smoke curled up from the edge of the pyre, the branch Naamah-as-Silvio had dropped still glowing orange at the tip. *Please, God, don't let it catch.*

"In the beginning..." Naamah, in her nauseating voice, hulking body ever-shifting in the campfire, began her tale. Though Orna knew the words were poison, she couldn't help but listen. The story, a cross between the Book of Genesis and Rowan's—and a tiny bit of Abba's—pre-history, went as follows.

...God made the Earth of fire and stone and peopled it with the Children, who lived for aeons among the flames. Until the rains fell, the blazes died, the molten rocks cooled and hardened, the planet chilled, and the Children retreated into the burning bowels.

From time to time, the Children peeked out through cinder cones to mourn the slime clotting the cold seas, which belched fumes that fed the greenery that clung to the ground-up stone. And in the brine, other creatures emerged and infested the decaying planet's oily sheen of life, from amphibian to reptile to mammal to ape to human.

Seething with envy, aching to know why God had chosen these miscreants as His new favorites, the Children haunted humanity in their dreams. Weaker than the fanged and clawed predators, slower than the hoofed grass-chewers and winged insect-eaters, humans had but one power: to have dominion over Earth.

And the envy of the Children turned to rejoicing as they knew this would be humanity's doom...and the Children's salvation. For they saw how fires spewed fumes that scorched the greenery and choked the skies. Fires that could someday shift the planet back to its ancient order of fire and stone.

So, the Children, in forms pleasing to the eye, came to humanity in the smoke of lightning strikes and wildfire, feigning imprisonment in the trees. And, as the Children planned, they were worshipped as spirits, and entire forests were burned to "free" them.

As humans became fond of fire—it warmed them, cooked their food, kept away the beasts—the Children no longer needed to appear in the smoke. Indeed, in the blink of an eye, humanity spread across the Earth incinerating trees, and in the modern era, the fossil plants of yesteryear.

As the planet heated, the Children of God exulted, for they knew the Great Shift was underway. That before long the greenery would shrivel, the soil blow away, the rivers and lakes vaporize, all yielding to the bleak beautiful wastes— the mountains of slag and oceans of flame—and the Children would regain their God-given mastery…

"Thank you all for your service," Naamah ended with a ghastly grin and mocking half-bow.

Half depressed, half defiant, Orna licked dry lips, not knowing what to believe. This couldn't be the story of life on Earth, of her species' place in the grand scheme. And certainly not their future. "Abba, is any of it true?"

Perhaps it was the rushing wind, but Abba didn't seem to hear and, indeed, wouldn't look away from Naamah. Was he falling under her spell? "Abba?" No response.

Rowan, too, had nothing to say, could only stand there shaking his head as his guardians clustered around him. And Silvio turned over onto his back and wheezed, surely not long for this world.

More urgently, the sticks at the edge of the pyre had finally caught fire. No gasoline had been used or it would've ignited already, but the wood was bone dry, and it was only a matter of time.

Orna opened her mouth to yell at Rowan to untie them, but he was leaning over to whisper something in

Isabel's ear. Knowing Rowan, the guy had some trick up his sleeve. Hoping for the best, Orna decided to draw Naamah's attention.

"If this Great Shift is already happening," Orna shouted, "then why bother with burning trees?"

Naamah swept her tail in the embers, orange sparks floating up and carried off by the wind.

"Because," Naamah hissed with a smirk that made Orna's spit go sour, "you humans are on the cusp of the impossible: using up your precious fossil fuels. For the Great Shift to be complete, you must torch the forest once more."

"Which is why we homed in on the last of our devotees," Naamah turned to Rowan, who cowered in fear, shame, or both. "And in your dreams inspired you to propagate the notion that burning trees not only wasn't a *bane* to so-called life on Earth but a *boon*."

The wind fanned the flames from the edge of the pyre towards Orna and Abba, smoke stinging Orna's eyes. Isabel, meanwhile, had snuck into the darkness beyond the campfire. Luckily, it appeared Rowan still had power over the guardians, and Orna had no other choice but to root for Isabel.

The head Tender had bent over to the point where he'd almost folded in on himself, as if finally accepting the reality of the dark forces he'd been catering to half his life.

"People are wising up, you know," Orna said, as Isabel silently emerged from the shadows behind Naamah. What was the guardian up to? Orna had to keep talking. "They're not buying the biomass stuff anymore."

"That may or may not be so," Naamah said. "But it is a moot point, as I have learned on my recent visit."

"What's moot?" Orna said, the flames now a

semicircle around the pyre. She wanted to scream at Rowan to untie them, but he was cradling the shotgun against his chest as if about to do something.

Naamah replied, "Enough trees have been burned as of late so that the Great Shift will soon pass the point of no return, what with—"

A flash and boom as Rowan fired straight at Naamah's belly.

CHAPTER 43

The shot passed straight through a seemingly indifferent Naamah as if she were a hologram, doing no more damage than a flashlight beam. Which Isabel seemed to take as a cue to dash into the campfire, leap onto Naamah's broad back, and climb her body like a tree.

The guardian clutched Naamah's horns and jerked her tortoise head backwards, Isabel sinking her teeth into the creature's saggy skin even as the hem of her dress caught fire.

Orna cheered as Isabel—still under Rowan's control or of her own volition—gained the upper hand, Naamah wriggling and coiling down to half her height in the flames. Until the demon rocketed up again, spreading her giant wings and bursting Isabel into chunks, the pieces turning to ash before they hit the ground.

Orna's heart sank into her stomach and fizzled. Even after all the guardian had done to try to hurt her—from blowing pot smoke in her face to hog-tying her—Orna felt a pang of pity, wondering if, had things been different, she and the real Isabel might've been friends. And, who knows, maybe even Ray, too.

"—the melting of the poles," standing tall again on coiled tail, Naamah went on as if she'd just swatted a fly. "But even if you stop the burning and power your civilization on the breath of butterflies, your kind will still find some way to complete the Great Shift."

"How do you know it'll get that bad?" Orna felt stupid for arguing, except it wasn't only her life she was fighting for but her sanity. What Naamah was saying was not—could not—be true. "The climate's a huge mess, for sure. But it's not like it's gonna toast the whole planet."

The slightest close-lipped smile from Naamah, whether of respect or scorn Orna could only guess. "It is all in the hands of God. But we have faith."

Orna hated to admit it, but she couldn't deny *everything* Naamah was saying. Whether the Earth was on its way to a literal hellscape or not, humans did seem to be on a suicide mission. And perhaps the ancient being had *some* wisdom that might be useful in terms of getting things back on track—assuming Orna got out of this alive. "I wanna know why."

Abba tried to shush her, eyes flashing with anger and fear, but Orna would not be silenced. Especially if she was about to die, she needed to learn the truth.

"Why?" Naamah drilled into Orna with those beetle-shell eyes.

Orna felt woozy but wouldn't look away. "Why!"

"Your hunger," Naamah jeered. "One taste leads to another, and soon all that matters is the next bite, which must be bigger, better than before. Unlike the rest of creation, you do not consume to live, you live to consume."

Orna stuck out her chin as if to shove the words—cliché as a bumper sticker—back at the demon, but of course it was a little true. After all, beavers might knock down trees to make a dam, but only humans erase entire forests.

As if sensing Orna's denial, Naamah grumbled, "Look at your men!" Naamah glared at Abba, who knit his brow but didn't wither under her gaze. "They take and take—from the land, from each other, from your future—in blind pursuit of power and riches, stepping on every neck in a desperate struggle to lead the pack, any pack."

Orna naturally agreed that men were the ones who started wars, led polluting corporations, and committed nearly all the crime. But Naamah was just talking about the worst handful of men and their shadow while completely ignoring the best—or even, the average—men and *their* light. After all, here was an elderly, one-legged Abba tied to a post in the middle of the winter woods, about to be burned alive because he thought nothing of trading his own life for his daughter's.

But Naamah wasn't done, and her voice took on the droning, superior tone of a college professor. "Have you ever asked yourself *why* your men are like this? Is it that they take *pleasure* in plunder and spoil, hurting and hoarding?"

Naamah scanned each of their faces—Orna, Abba, and Rowan—in turn, as if waiting for a reply. When none came, she barked, "No! Men do as they're told… by the *womb*-men." Naamah nodded her head towards Orna.

Absurd! As if Orna—or any woman Orna had ever known—were responsible for men's selfishness and cruelty. Textbook chauvinism.

"Is it not the men who scramble to the top of whatever petty heap you value, the ones you want the most?" Naamah said. "With never so much as a glance at the ones propping up that very pile from the bottom?"

It was nothing short of blatant and outrageous misogyny to blame the mass murders of Hitler, Stalin, and Mao, the greed of tech billionaires, the power grabs of sociopath politicians, on your typical woman doing her best to survive in a male-dominated world. Naamah might've been female, but her obvious disgust for womankind was more toxic than the nastiest incel spewing online hate from his parents' basement.

While Orna was debunking Naamah's warped worldview, Rowan, as if finally growing a conscience, stumbled over to kneel beside a dying Silvio, Lottie and Dougie following at arm's length. The head Tender set the shotgun down and took Silvio's hand.

"Now, the real question is…" Naamah let it hang a moment, "what is it that compels women such as yourself to reward brutes like him with your precious eggs?" The demon jerked her head towards Rowan.

Angry acid gurgled up in Orna's throat. It was a non-starter. Obviously, if she'd known the truth about him early on, she would've run away fast as her legs could've carried her.

"Surely," Naamah said, "it cannot be all about vanity and luxury. So, what is it?" This time, Naamah didn't wait for an answer. "Offspring! The loot your men pillage is not for them, nor is it ultimately for you, but to fatten your larvae as they pupate into blowflies."

"That's no sin!" Abba piped up in a thin voice. Pointless as the conversation was, Orna was cheered to hear him. "'Be fruitful and multiply, sayeth the Lord!'"

"Indeed, a species has a right to breed," Naamah hissed softly, even thoughtfully. "We Children, too, have our offspring."

Shuddering, Orna tried not to picture how any of that might work.

"Yet the great irony is that you humans do not flirt with extinction due to a *lack* of progeny but too many!" Naamah sneered. "So, again, I ask you, why?"

Orna, still raging over this bloated worm daring to blame her, of all people, for Rowan's mania, had nothing to say. But Naamah answered herself with a scoff. "Your delusion of death."

Now Orna understood. Naamah was neither misogynist nor man-hater but a misanthrope. In the demon's jealousy for God's grace, she hated all that was human. And while humanity did have its dark side, it also had its light. But the Children couldn't see that because they, themselves, had only dark.

With a third of the pyre burning, Orna had no more time to waste.

"Rowan!" she yelled. But the Tender, face in his hands beside a deathly still Silvio, was too busy feeling sorry for himself to even look at her.

Yet Naamah wouldn't—couldn't—shut up. "But even your meager sciences know that life is energy, something that cannot be destroyed. No, death is but another transformation, and it is *that* you fear. For, despite your miserable, suffering existence—with most of that pain brought upon yourselves—you thirst to remain stupid apes forever." Naamah shook her triangle head. "While compared to your pitiful span we Children seem immortal, everlasting life is not even for us, nor would we ever wish it so. The only unchanging form is that of our Creator."

Orna hacked as smoke billowed in her and Abba's faces. "Untie us!" Orna screeched to Rowan, but he only gave her that sad puppy dog look, as if it was all out of his hands.

"As of late," Naamah mused, twitching her tail restlessly, "I have begun wondering whether our meddling was even necessary, or if your kind would be on the same path regardless." She flapped her leathery wings once as if to shrug. "No matter. Our work here is done."

Abba spoke up again, "HaShem won't let you get away with this!"

"Is that so?" Naamah licked thin lips with a slimy

blue tongue.

Abba cleared his throat and shouted at the sky, where clouds hung low like bleached guts, "We call upon the order of Issim! The Souls of Flame! The Archangel Metatron!" Abba's eyes bulged, lips quivering in religious fervor like a Biblical prophet. "Banish this being back to Sheol!"

Naamah threw back her head and laughed, the inside of her mouth soft and pink and toothless, and again Orna felt a rumble in the sapling. "You, old man, cannot so much as summon a bowel movement much less an angel. As your superstitions claim, it is your women alone who are truly holy."

It was up to Orna, then? The heat of the fire warm on her shins, she cried out, "We call upon the order of Issim! The Souls of Flame! The Archangel Metatron! Banish this being back to Sheol!"

"The handservants hold no sway over us Children." Naamah bent over laughing like she'd played a great prank. "Much as I loathed your grandmother Ilana, she was a foe I could respect." Naamah cut off her laughter and stood ramrod straight. "But you. You are less than nothing."

The ring still cold against Orna's breast despite the flames licking inches away, she yearned to hold the silver in her hand. "Untie us, God dammit!" Orna screeched to Rowan. But only Lottie, perking up her ears, seemed to hear.

A gust fanned the fire close and hot on Orna's feet, and she gagged on the chemical stench of rubber as the soles of her boots began to melt.

"My parents *died* for you. I *killed* for you!" Rowan sobbed at Naamah and then turned his face to the sky. "God, are you testing me? The way you did with Job?"

In a lightning strike Naamah whipped her tail,

knocking Rowan's legs out from under him to send him face first into the pine needles.

For a few long seconds, Orna feared he might've been killed and with it her and Abba's only chance to escape the fire. But Rowan, with a shake of the head, pushed himself up to his knees.

"Cut 'em down!" Rowan yelled to Dougie, and the former frat boy scurried up the flameless side of the pyre. Orna almost squealed for joy as the guardian pulled a wire cutter from his pocket and snipped Abba's binds. *We're gonna live!*

Handing Abba the wire cutter, Dougie surfed down the unburnt slope of sticks and rushed back to Rowan's side. But Rowan, still on his knees, swatted the guardian away and then did the same to Lottie, each of whom stood loyally at arm's length.

Abba, meanwhile, wasted no time freeing Orna, and they leaned on each other as they skidded down the sticks to solid ground.

CHAPTER 44

Orna helped a sweaty but visibly unhurt Abba to a seat on the pine needles as flames snaked the rest of the way up the pyre to the dead saplings, where they'd stood minutes before.

Time running out, she went over to Silvio, the unburnt side of his face deathly pale. Hand on his chest, she was relieved to feel it rise and fall, if barely. With Rowan kneeling there staring at the ground, green cloak gathered around him as if he were a small bush, and Naamah watching from the campfire, Orna snatched up the sled.

Abba shook his head mournfully. "You have to banish her back."

Important as saving Silvio's life was, Abba was right. They couldn't let Naamah go to wreak more havoc across the world. "What do I do?" Orna asked.

"I'm not sure, *bubala*." Abba tugged his beard. "Just focus on the letters and make the ritual your own."

Orna, far enough away from Naamah where the demon couldn't hurt her, had no reason not to try. As if reacting to her decision, the ring warmed against her chest.

Sliding the silver chain from around her neck, Orna dropped the ring in her palm, the defrosting שדי beading with water.

Pad of her thumb on the ש, she said the words as

well as she could remember from Abba's lesson weeks ago, "Shin for fire and transformation." Her throat was dry, and it came out as a hoarse whisper.

Naamah, swaying in the campfire flames, tilted her head as if in idle curiosity.

Orna's thumb on the ד, she said, "Dallet to pass through the door to the mystery of being."

Other than a squint of mild annoyance, Naamah's expression barely changed. Orna had to try harder.

' "Yod. The single point from which all creation emerges!" Orna's raw voice rasped in and out. "The unity within the many. The foundation of all foundations. The divine spark which causes everything to be."

Orna had said the right words, yet Naamah only stood there smirking.

"Abba," she whispered, "what am I doing wrong?"

Naamah answered for him. "You do not believe. And I am no longer entertained. I will see you on your deathbed." A lewd wink from an empty eye, and the demon fanned her wings.

On instinct, Orna jammed the tiny ring around the first knuckle of her pinky far down as it could go. "Stop, Naamah!"

For a wonder, Naamah froze, the faintest wrinkle of doubt on her brow.

A tingling surged through Orna's blood, the ring no longer warm but hot, and she closed her eyes.

Picturing a giant glowing ש, Orna mouthed quietly to herself, "Transformation." And thought about how, in a matter of weeks, she'd gone from being too neurotic to leave the house into a badass demon-fighter like her Bubby.

Next, in her mind's eye, she summoned up a huge

ד. Abba's lesson about the bent old man finally ringing true on a deeper level, the need to be humble, to make mistakes—one after another, in her case—before learning the truth.

The ring grew hotter, and Orna opened her eyes. Naamah flapped her wings doggedly, whiffing sparks into the air, unable to escape into the coals.

Orna closed her eyes again and imagined י. "Yod. The single point. The unity within the many," she murmured. And thought about the forest, how everything was connected. The rock that grows the soil that grows the grass that grows the deer that grows the mountain lion. Which was all well and good, but where did humans fit in?

The ring was hellfire scorching her finger. Orna opened her eyes, and Naamah thrashed and keened, a monstrous snake frozen in an invisible block of ice. Orna had to be close.

Orna stared at the י on the ring, the single flame. And then at a real-life flame in the campfire. "Yod, the divine spark."

And that's when all became clear.

No divide.

No divide between her and the forest. No divide between her and anyone else. Orna was Abba, was Eemah, was Bubby, was Rowan, was Silvio, was Dougie, was Lottie. Was Naamah.

The ring searing now, Orna caught a whiff of her own flesh cooking. But she wouldn't let go and closed her eyes once more.

If Orna was one with God's creation, then she was one with God. Therefore, was she not God?! And did she not believe in *herself*?!

Orna's mind emptied into black nothing. Then filled with binding light. And went transparent.

Her eyes were closed, but she could see everything: Naamah, Abba, Rowan, Dougie, Lottie, the breathing forest, the weeping sky, the ground furred with needles, three-hundred-sixty degrees as if she stood atop—within—a crystal mountain.

"In the name of Shaddai I bind you!" Orna opened her eyes and belted in a clear strong voice she didn't know she had.

"Orna, no!" Abba bellowed. "Banish her to Sheol!"

But Orna and the delicious power were one; a scratch she could not—would not—stop itching. "Come to me, Naamah!"

From the heart of the blaze Naamah's reptilian form flashed bright and brighter—red to orange to yellow to blue to white—until to look at her was like slivers of glass in Orna's eyes.

"Turn away!" Abba shouted.

Orna did not, only stared and screeched, "We are one!"

An exploding star. A terrible, crashing roar. And a dazzling bolt from the fire sent a numbing shock from the ring up through Orna's hand and body, skin, muscle, and bone. Where Naamah had been, the fire alone blazed.

Terrified, Orna knew she'd gotten swept up in the glory of the moment and gone too far. She needed to rid the Earth of Naamah, not enslave her. Orna tried to yank the ring off, but it had fused with her finger. Slowly, it began rotating, the silver glowing in the full spectrum of a rainbow, whirring faster and faster with a high-pitched, ear-splitting squeal.

The poisonous pain that rushed through Orna's veins was like nothing she'd ever felt before, caking in her marrow like hot coals, wriggling into every molecule until she *was* pain. And pain was *all*.

No way such sanity-rending suffering could last, but it did. Every second a century. Each minute a millennium.

Just when Orna knew she could bear it no longer, when she prayed for the sweet release of oblivion, she passed through to the other side…

No longer crushing misery but the flow of ecstasy, her soul a cosmic orgasm. Pleasure she never even imagined possible cascading through every nerve ending like rivers of pure deliciousness.

Then Abba was beside her, reaching out his hand. But not to help. Small and weak, a flitting ghost who craved Orna's power. Thousands of years of men like him keeping women like her down because of their fear—their jealousy—of the feminine connection to God. But no more.

Like a tremor on the ocean floor, black resentment shook Orna and welled up into a tsunami of hate. She curled her ring hand into a fist.

But Abba, eyes wide, brow gleaming with sweat, grabbed her wrist. And with the wire cutter, neatly, painlessly, snipped off the first knuckle of Orna's little finger. It fell to the ground, ring and all.

And the intoxicating current drained from Orna as if through a breached dam. An empty husk, she fell to her knees, what was left of her pinky finger throbbing and leaking blood.

Abba kicked her severed fingertip and ring into the pyre, which geysered flame a hundred feet into the sky then settled down to a grumbling blaze.

Cored like an apple yet somehow more whole than she'd ever been, Orna reached out with her maimed and bleeding hand for Abba's. He took off his *tallit* and tenderly wrapped the cloth around her wound.

As Orna peered into the frightened, loving eyes of her father, her face reflected back. And for the first time in her life, she experienced pure, undiluted gratitude.

CHAPTER 45

Orna held the bloody *tallit* against her aching pinky. "Thank you, Abba." Not just for freeing her from Naamah. Or for coming up to Charwood to help her. Or for raising her from a little girl to a grown woman. But for being the light that he was in the world.

"My pleasure," Abba said with a weary but brilliant smile and kissed his *tallit*. "Now, let's help your friend."

By the dancing light of the two fires, Orna and Abba slid a quietly moaning—but still living—Silvio onto the sled, and she draped her fleece over him. It was going to be a cold, bumpy ride, but there was no other way. Orna picked up the rope while Abba found a branch from the pile to use as a crutch.

"You've got to save them." Rowan ushered Dougie and Lottie over to Orna, his eyes pleading. Quaintly, Abba hobbled on his stick to stand in front of his daughter.

Orna had no fear of the fallen Tender or his bound guardians, of course, only a nagging urge to push Rowan into the fire.

"She was my buddy." Rowan scratched Lottie's scarred head, and for once the dog—or whatever was inside the animal—didn't seem to mind. "Thirteen and on her last legs. She was the first one I tried the ritual on." He put his arm around slack-faced Dougie's narrow shoulders. "And this guy. I *owe* it to him."

Orna wasn't heartless, but even if she could get the ring from the fire and dared to use it again, what was to say Lottie and Dougie would even make it? After all, Silvio's burns were nowhere near as bad, and he was barely hanging on.

"I know what you're thinking." Rowan's lower lip quivered. "I just want to say goodbye to my friends."

Orna wasn't sure if this was touching or the most selfish thing she'd ever heard. Bring Rowan's childhood pet and sacrificial lamb back from the edge of death, so, what, he could feel like he'd redeemed himself? But it was too dangerous. If she wore the ring again—and, damn, did she want to—this time she might lose herself completely. As much of a *mitzvah* as it would be to try to save Dougie and Lottie, she simply couldn't risk it.

Orna looped the sled's rope around her good hand. "I have to help Silvio."

"Orna, please." Rowan dropped to his knees, hands folded under his beard. "All I'm asking is that you—"

Orna peered into the pyre, and though she couldn't see the ring, somehow she knew exactly where it was. A pang, an almost sexual hunger, burned deep inside her, and she dropped the rope.

A whistle and sickening thud. Lottie fell on her side, the feathered bolt of a crossbow quivering from an eye socket. In the snap of a finger, the German Shepherd was a heap of dust.

Rowan howled but was cut off by a bolt through his shoulder. Staggering, he tried to yank it out, but he was skewered through like a shish kabob.

From out of the frozen dark a dozen people—mostly men but a few women, all dressed in camo—switched on their headlamps. Among them were the two guys she'd met the inn—Young Townie in his wool cap holding a crossbow and Old Townie in his trucker's hat with a pistol—and a few of the other villagers from the Halloween bonfire.

Dougie, meanwhile, had scooped up the shotgun. He aimed and fired. A flare and a bang and Old Townie's bearded face exploded in a spray of blood, the man crumpling like a rag doll to the ground.

Before the guardian could fire again, two of the other camo men grabbed Dougie by the arms, while a third pried away the shotgun. Three more circled a sobbing Rowan, Young Townie aiming the crossbow at the Tender's head.

Orna let out a hundred sighs at once. It was over. Now they could get Silvio to the hospital, Rowan to police, and her and Abba back to their lives.

But Young Townie and a puffy-faced middle-aged man grabbed Orna's forearms, while a couple of grey-haired bruisers took Abba's elbows, one of whom kicked his stick crutch out from under him.

"What're you doing?" Orna asked, jostling Young Townie with an elbow.

"Keep quiet and it'll be over soon." Young Townie dug his fingers into her bicep.

"You're making a mistake!" Abba shouted. "We're not *with* them!"

One of Abba's grizzled keepers slapped him across the face—not viciously but hard enough to silence him.

"You don't underst—" Orna started until the man raised his hand to Abba's face again, and Orna shut her mouth.

After all this, to become someone else's hostages? But one of the townies was propping up Silvio's head on the sled with a hat, while a second checked his pulse. Not something you'd do if you wanted to hurt people.

Then Orna, Abba, and Rowan were being marched

across the clearcut. She turned back, and not far behind, one of the men pulled Silvio on his sled. Phew.

Orna didn't say a word as they trudged along the logging road towards the lodge, her painful finger pretty much clotted thanks to the *tallit* wrapped around her hand. Abba was for the most part carried by the two men, and he didn't struggle or complain. The townies were obviously taking them to the cops. Hell, if Orna had been in their shoes, she'd have done the same.

Everything was going to turn out okay. Technically, she hadn't committed any crimes, since she'd never even run Dougie over in the first place. And Ray, the only guardian she and Abba had personally done away with, was ash now, so there was no evidence. Still, they had a lot of explaining to do, along with some creative editing.

Close to a dozen pickups were parked in a semicircle in the driveway beside Rowan's pickup—tarp blown off the bed, gas cans exposed—Silvio's Prius, and her Subaru, headlights shining on five more townies standing around chatting. The lodge's splintered front door stood open, and from inside, a racket of breaking glass and smashing wood. Not only didn't Orna blame them for ransacking the place, she wished she could've joined in.

Orna, Abba, and Rowan were taken over to the small group, one of whom was Bartender from the inn. The elderly woman, in one of those old-fashioned trapper hats with earflaps, a plaid hunter's jacket, and wool pants, held an axe by her side.

"We stopped them," Orna said to Bartender, who, judging by the way everyone huddled around her, had to be in charge.

Bartender scowled. "You're on their payroll, doll."

Orna's heart sped up. They weren't out of the woods

yet. "I know," Orna said breathlessly. "I was tricked. But we figured it out and took them down."

The temperature was well below freezing now, wind screaming, full moon swallowed by the low grey clouds. A whiff of woodsmoke. Not from the lodge's boiler or chimney, though, but curling from a broken upstairs window.

"Even if it's true." Bartender shook her head. "Doesn't change what happened."

"You don't have to worry," Orna spat out the words quickly as she could, needing to make her case before things got out of control. "Biomass is on its way out."

"Huh?" Bartender gave Orna a squint and sidled up to Rowan. With a finger, she flicked the bolt sticking out of his shoulder, and he hollered. "Know what your beau here did to my brother and sister?"

Orna did not and didn't want to. A crash from upstairs and flames burst through the broken window.

"Burned 'em to death." Bartender spat at Rowan's feet.

Orna didn't want to believe it, but Rowan hung his head. "Only because you killed my parents."

Bartender reached back and punched Rowan hard in the mouth.

Orna thought about saying something, maybe trying to mediate a truce. But clearly all parties had blood on their hands, and there was nothing she could do to fix any of that.

A grunt from somewhere in the night, and one of the townies rolled a thick round log onto the driveway. He set it right side up in front of them.

"Fourteen, all told," Bartender said huskily.

"Fourteen what—" Orna started to ask but then remembered the graveyard in town, and all the deaths in 2005. And the bones in the plantation's ash pile. "Is it true, Rowan?"

Messy hair hanging over his eyes, he nodded.

It was as if Orna's insides had been smeared with tabasco. Not just a murderer, a *mass* murderer. Almost Ted Bundy level. And to think where those hands had been…

Orna sensed Abba looking at her, but she couldn't meet his eyes. Instead, she scanned the roof of the lodge, which was ablaze, heavy gusts blowing flames into the adjacent tree canopy.

One of the men walked an unresisting Dougie over to the log and made him kneel, then slammed his mangled face sideways on top. Bartender sidled up, axe in hand.

Rowan sobbed but didn't try to stop them.

Without further ado, Bartender heaved the axe over her head and chunked it down on the guardian's neck. Before the head could roll off Dougie's body, both were ash.

Orna's knees trembled, but Young Townie and Puffyface held her tight. This could not—*would* not—be her ending! "Don't do this," Orna said in a far calmer voice than she would've thought possible.

A scrape as a townie dragged Silvio's sled onto the driveway. Overhead, the first faint smudge of morning lit the clouds.

Bartender, dragging the axe, blood dripping from the blade onto the driveway, strolled over to Orna.

Abba shouted, "You stay away from her!" trying in vain to break away from his captors.

But Orna still wasn't afraid. Bartender got up close to her ear, so close Orna could smell the whisky on the woman's breath. "If it was up to me, I'd let you go," Bartender whispered. "But it's not. And they want payback."

Rowan's townies brought him over to the log, the Tender making no effort to fight.

This was what Rowan deserved. Or at least had asked for. But Orna's heart still hurt. Because even though he'd been swallowed up by the shadow, he was still as much a part of creation as she was. That whole eye for an eye stuff only worked if humanity—if the universe—wasn't truly one. "You don't have to do this."

Bartender's face was cast iron as she hefted the axe and walked over to the executioner's block.

A small stand of pines had caught fire, and the wind fed the flames. A couple of townies ran coughing out of the lodge's front door and across the porch onto the driveway.

Even if Bartender didn't go all Jack Torrance on Orna and Abba, fierce as the wind was, they'd soon be trapped in the fire. Her car was their only chance. But how?

The matches! Though Young Townie and Puffyface held Orna's arms tight, she was able to pat the front pocket of her jeans and make sure they were still there.

"I gotta pee real bad," Orna pleaded, crossing her thighs. Young Townie and Puffyface looked at each other. "C'mon, it's not like I can outrun you. Just take me behind the pickup real quick." Orna motioned with her head towards Rowan's truck.

Nodding, Young Townie took her over to the far side of the pickup and partly turned his head.

Orna undid the top button of her jeans. "No peeking!" Soon as Young Townie looked away, she plucked the matchbook from her pocket with her good hand, tore out a match, and, balancing the book on her *tallit* bandage, struck it on the strip. A flame sprung to life, and before the wind could snuff it she lit the rest of the book in a sizzling flare.

"Baruch atah Adonai, Eloheinu Melech haolam, asher kid'shanu b'mitzvotav, v'tzivanu l'hadlik ner shel

Hanukkah," she mouthed the candle lighting prayer for Hanukkah as the *tallit* caught fire. Her left hand a ball of agony and flame, she tossed the matchbook into the truck bed and dove under Silvio's Prius a second before the explosion.

The fire from the burning *tallit* ran up the sleeve of her wool sweater, and she frantically beat her broiling arm against the ground. The fire wouldn't go out. In a panic, Orna slithered out from under the Prius and got to her knees, waving her fiery arm. Everyone, including Abba, gaping at the gas cans burning in three columns like the Tree of Life's Ten Sephirot, no one came to help her. Then she remembered the words from childhood and stopped, dropped, and rolled in the dirt, quickly smothering the flames.

Tallit and sleeve smoking, her left arm screamed, badly burned beneath the cotton and wool but otherwise in working order. The townies still mesmerized by the burning pickup, Orna ran to Silvio and dragged the sled with one hand over to the Subaru — Young Townie, with his crossbow, blocking her way. But instead of shooting her, he slung the weapon over a shoulder and lifted Silvio into the backseat.

"Thank you." Orna kissed Young Townie's scruffy cheek. "Now get my dad."

As Orna opened the driver's door, a glacial gust of wind drove flames from the trees to the edge of the meadow, the dry grass instantly igniting.

Young Townie, brandishing his crossbow, stomped over to the two men holding Abba and barked something at them. They immediately let Abba go, and Young Townie helped Abba hop over to the car and ushered him in the passenger side door. Once Orna and Abba were safe inside, both doors shut and locked, Abba handed over the keys to Orna, and with her good hand she punched the ignition.

A half-dozen villagers raced towards the Subaru as Orna did a three-point turn, but Young Townie held them at bay with his crossbow, nailing Puffyface in the thigh with a bolt. As Orna drove off, in the side view mirror she caught a glimpse of the mob tackling Young Townie as if he were a rookie quarterback. Tapping the brake, Orna thought about going back to help, but the fire, driven by the wind, was already halfway across the meadow. Soon there'd be no way out.

As they reached the bend in the driveway, Orna flicked her eyes to the rearview mirror. As she feared, the largest "angel" she'd ever seen loomed in the smoke wafting from Charwood's roof, blending with the clouds glowing red from the flames and the light of the rising sun. None other than Ashmodei, son of Naamah, King of the Children of Darkness.

Orna gazed straight ahead and punched the gas, bucking over ruts and potholes but never slowing down. By the time they reached the end of the driveway, a few dozen snowflakes clung to the windshield like tiny frozen stars.

CHAPTER 46

Orna took in the sweeping, sunny view of the Meadbury mountains through the hospital window. Temperatures in the high thirties, snow still clung to the trees at the base of the red rock slabs, though most of the blizzard's two and a half feet had already melted. According to the news, it had been enough of a dumping to keep the Silvercleft fire from spreading more than a few acres into Charwood's forest, though not enough to save the lodge from burning to the ground.

Giving her bandaged left hand and lightly burned arm a little shake—the itchiness meant it was healing—she drew the shade so Silvio could nap. But first she had something to tell him. She sat in the chair next to his bed and fixed the sheet falling off its side.

"I still can't believe your mom ate the whole thing," Orna said.

Silvio chuckled. His face was shaping up nicely, those burns turning out to be only first-degree, leaving behind pink patches that made him look kind of badass. "I *told* her it was a special brownie."

"And then she pretended she hadn't touched it!" Orna broke down laughing. "Even though it was obvious how high she was!"

Silvio snorted and then winced, gritting his teeth. Getting better every day, he was still in a lot of pain. Thanks to her.

"Sorry, I'll stop." Orna took a breath and let the

giggles fade.

"I love 'em." Silvio pushed the button on his morphine drip. "But thank God they're heading back to Cali tomorrow."

Only two weeks had passed since Orna and Abba brought Silvio to the hospital, yet the grafts on his badly burned stomach and legs healing well. The doctors were so impressed with his recovery they hoped to release him before Christmas, a few days away.

"You really think it was a bluff?" Silvio hadn't been conscious enough to catch Naamah's unhinged lecture, but Orna had filled him in—except, of course, the last bit about the ring and how close she'd come to letting Naamah all the way in. "The whole end of the world thing?"

Orna nodded. "There's still a lot we can do. Protecting forests, for one." Something Silvio had known the whole time, that she'd somehow missed. "We can turn this around if we want to."

Silvio's eyes were glassy from the hit of painkiller. "What if people don't want to?"

Orna shrugged. "All we can do is point out a better way. And hope people catch on before it's too late." She, of course, wasn't brushing off climate change, deforestation, the whole ecological unraveling happening before their eyes. And wasn't even close to giving up. But truth be told, all she could do was her part. Beyond that, it was out of her control. Plus, she had more pleasant things on her mind right then.

Orna set her good hand ever so gently on Silvio's forearm.

Since the morning they'd escaped Charwood—after being treated for her minor burns and snipped finger and Abba had been cleared for his concussion—Orna spent most of every day with Silvio. At first, she'd done it out of crushing guilt. Not only had the guy been brave enough to infiltrate Charwood in the first place, he risked his life to try to warn her. And how had she repaid him? By ratting him out to Rowan and getting him possessed by a demon.

But throughout his stay in the hospital, not one angry outburst, not an ounce of blame, not a single complaint for how it turned out for him. The only thing more surprising than how well his burns were healing was the way Orna was starting to feel about him.

"So, you know I'm leaving in a few weeks," Orna said. The decision to go back to Vermont with Abba hadn't been an easy one, but it felt right. Despite getting along fine on his new prosthetic leg, her father needed her, though he'd never say so. Or maybe it was the other way around, and she needed him. Either way, it would be good to go back east, where the landscape wasn't so rough around the edges and lush as an overgrown garden.

Silvio nodded glumly.

"I want you to come with," Orna said with a smile.

Silvio's lips parted ever so slightly. "Orna, I—"

"Doesn't have to be right away." Orna hoped she wasn't sounding desperate. "I'm okay with long distance for a while if you are."

"I'm flattered, but…"

Silvio was obviously scared, but he'd come around. She squeezed his hand—he didn't squeeze back.

"I can't," he said firmly.

"We're two peas in a pod," she tried to say but could only squeak out, "peas…pod."

He crinkled his forehead. "Then why did you go for him and not me?"

Orna's heart was a wet piece of paper breaking apart.

"I guess it was just the way I felt when I was around him." Or maybe it had to do with Rowan giving her something Abba rarely had: approval. But she'd owned up to the fact that she—and no one but her—had made the wrong choice and would likely pay the price for it with years of trauma. And, as of late, nightmares, mostly of Ashmodei coming for her in the smoke. Along with the occasional dream about the ring buried in the ashes of the bonfire.

But Rowan paid a far steeper toll for his bad decisions, the detective at her half-assed questioning telling her all the "environmentalists" had died in the fire, which inspectors said started from an unattended fireplace. Though Orna knew what had really happened. The townies had killed him. Whether police were helping to cover it up she neither knew nor cared.

"Yeah, well, you blew it, didn't you." Silvio's eyes were hard. "Why didn't you listen to me?"

"I thought you were jealous."

Silvio, brow furrowed, stared out the window. "I was. I was." When he turned back to her, his caramel eyes were kind again. "But that's behind us now."

When he patted her good hand like a brother—not a future lover—she knew she'd never see him again.

"Take care of yourself," Orna whispered, and pulling her hand away, bolted from the room.

Orna stopped at the water cooler in the waiting room and snatched a paper cup from the dispenser. After filling it, she drank the cool, sweet water. And then a second cup. She was alone now, but it wouldn't always be that way. Right? *Right?!*

Downing a third cup, she tossed it into the trash on top of a folded newspaper. A few words catching her eye, she snatched it up and read the headline, DENVER ZOO TO BUILD WASTE-TO-ENERGY

INCINERATOR.

Orna's breath caught, and she felt faint.

CHAPTER 47

Three months later

Orna parked the Forester at the end of the dirt road on the outskirts of Silvercleft and got out of the car. Sun high overhead, air cool but not cold, maybe around forty—typical March mountain weather—she zipped up her fleece and pulled on her gloves. Then around back to pop the trunk.

After living the last couple of months with Abba in her childhood home in Burlington, Vermont, it felt weird to be back in Colorado, the dry air almost harsh in her nose. But she'd needed to get her car from the garage and the rest of her stuff out of storage. Abba had offered to come, but she decided the cross-country drive would give her some much-needed thinking time. She slid a shovel from the back, crammed full of her junk, and then shut the trunk.

She walked up the road to the edge of Charwood's driveway. After a quick look and listen to make sure the coast was clear, she skirted around the metal gate— NO TRESPASSING sign front and center—onto the dirt. The snow all but melted in the latest warm spell, at least she didn't have to worry about footprints.

Though it wasn't the safest thing in the world to come back there, she was pretty sure she wouldn't run into anyone...or any*thing*. Bartender and Young

Townie, after all, knew she'd been brainwashed by the Tenders only to later turn on the group.

From what she'd heard from police, other than poor Old Townie getting shot, none of the Silvercleft residents had died during the fire. Which gave her every reason to believe Young Townie was alive and well. So, there'd be little reason for any of them to hold a grudge against her.

Plus, with Rowan gone, everyone was probably focused on healing and getting back to normal, anyway. The way she was.

And so far as Ashmodei was concerned, so long as she wasn't around any open flames... Besides, it was Purim, yet another holiday celebrating Jews not dying. And that, for some reason, put Orna at ease.

She hadn't gotten far under the canopy before she was panting. Mostly due to the fifteen or so pounds she'd put on—mac and cheese was the best antidepressant— but also because of how tired and low-energy she was lately. Some of it was the bad dreams, but a lot of it had to do with worries about someone finding the ring... and what they might do if they got it.

But she hadn't had a single panic attack in months, and that was kind of a big deal. In hindsight, she realized the episodes, painful as they were, had actually helped. Like the pain you got from touching a hot stove, the attacks were a warning that she was doing something wrong, and if she didn't stop, she'd get hurt for real. And she could only assume their absence meant she was finally on the right track.

Leaving the tree cover, she passed the big meadow, mostly black ash and stubble now, the occasional green sprig pushing up from the soil. At the former lodge site, she stopped to gawk. Nothing left except the stone chimney and foundation—everything else knocked down and carted away. A little sad, she headed around back, the charred ground soft beneath her boots, and followed the logging road.

Though the fire had passed through, most of the pines were barely singed. Of course, hundreds had been torched bare and maybe twice as many on their way to dying, branches stocked with dry, brown needles. Yet the vast majority of the acreage was green as green could be.

It was quiet in the woods, barely a breath of wind to tickle her cheeks. Yet as she reached the old burn, the awful memories of being dragged on that sled got her pulse pounding in her temples. If she hadn't been a hundred percent in favor of the move east before, she sure as heck was now—the further she could get from this place, the better. Indeed, the tightness in her chest told her maybe she shouldn't have come back at all—except it was her responsibility to bury the Naamah-haunted ring so no one could find it again.

Just before the clearcut, a raven—magpie?—croaked. Orna scanned the blackened trunks, but the bird had gone silent, and she couldn't see it anywhere.

The instant she stepped out into the sunny, muddy clearcut she homed in on the two piles of melted ash—one large, the other smaller—where the pyre and campfire had burned out. She put a hand over her heart to keep it from bursting out of her chest.

But it was all right. She'd faced the toughest time of her life and came through the other side stronger and better. It was all over now, that dark night literally turned to day.

Aside from soaring temperatures, melting glaciers and permafrost, and rising sea levels, that is, as she and her fellow humans kept spewing carbon, felling forests, fouling airsheds, poisoning groundwater, overfishing oceans, eroding topsoil, wiping out species faster than they could be discovered, and on and on and on. Even the Denver Zoo was planning to burn animal poop, plastic, and yes, trees, to get in on some of that sweet grant money foundations were handing out for half-baked, techno-fix "solutions" that often did more harm than good—throwing down more towels on the wet floor instead of turning down the tap on the overflowing tub.

So, Naamah ended up being right about one thing, at least—humans no longer needed the influence of demons to do their dirty work. Whether Naamah's prophecy would come true, that humans were destined to toast the planet and bring back the reign of the Children, Orna had no way of knowing.

In the meantime, there were worthwhile acts—*tikkun olam* or "improve the world," as the Jewish tradition called it—and Orna was committed to doing them, having started up an alliance of activists across the country advocating for the preservation of forests on public lands as the best bet to slow climate change. Not the whole answer, of course, but her small piece of the puzzle. Anything beyond that was out of her control.

Gripping the shovel tightly, she made a beeline for the campfire, wanting to get this over with and back to town quickly as possible. She might even get ahold of Silvio, who, she'd gleaned from social media, was living in some cabin outside Meadbury.

It didn't take much scraping to find the ring. Incredibly, the silver had fused to the severed fingerbone, the flesh gone. Squatting, she fished it out of the ashes and dropped it in the palm of her glove. Just as she was about to take off her other glove so she could feel the cool metal against her skin, movement out of the corner of an eye.

Towards the far end of the clearcut, someone lurched out of the woods. The figure was dressed in work clothes and carried some sort of tool—maybe a hoe—over a shoulder. Orna slipped the ring into the breast pocket of her fleece, zipped it up, and stood leaning on the shovel.

Had to be one of the folks from Silvercleft, hopefully a friendly one, maybe even Young Townie. But what were they doing out there? Whoever it was, they had their back to Orna and were hacking at the ground with the hoe.

Throat dry, every fiber in her body telling her to go—run!—back to the car, Orna started forward, shovel in hand, sharp spade-side up. As she got closer, she saw the man—too tall to be a woman—had some sort of sack slung over his back, panniers stuffed with what looked like green brushes hanging to either side.

Halfway across the clearcut Orna noted that the man's long lanky frame was draped in flannel, and she shivered. *It's not him,* she reminded herself. *He's dead.*

The man took one of the brushes from the pouch and set it in the hole he'd dug. Not a brush but a tiny pine sapling. Indeed, as Orna crept closer, hundreds of other baby trees were sticking out from the mud every few feet.

Orna opened her mouth to speak.

A whistle from behind her. Orna whirled around and a small bent-over someone was hustling across the clearcut toting a shotgun. Fingers prickling with adrenalin, Orna dropped the shovel and threw up her hands.

It was Bartender. The grey-haired woman, in the same hunter's jacket and wool pants as the last time Orna had seen her, got within ten feet or so, and, grimacing, aimed the shotgun—Abba's, it looked like—at Orna's chest. "What are you *doing* here?"

"I'm sorry, I just needed…closure," Orna said, truthfully enough.

Orna peeked back over her shoulder, half-expecting the man to have snuck up right behind her. But he was still on his knees by the sapling, lovingly patting the soil around its base.

"What are *you* doing here?" Orna asked, rubbing her belly in wide circles.

"The hell does it look like?" Bartender relaxed her face and lowered the shotgun. "Replanting."

"What for?"

Bartender squinted at Orna like she was the dumbest person in the world. "So it'll be a forest again."

"You mean for biomass?"

Bartender shook her head. "Forest preserve. No logging allowed."

Which came as a surprise from someone Orna assumed was the furthest thing from a tree-hugger. "Aren't you trespassing?"

"Got him to sign the whole kit-and-kaboodle over before…" Bartender's strong eye contact was a dare for Orna to say otherwise. Orna knew this woman—or one of the other townies—had murdered Rowan. But what was the point of dredging all that up again?

A crunch from behind. The man was digging another hole.

Orna went to him. She had to be sure.

The click of a round being chambered. "You turn around right now, missy," Bartender hissed.

Orna didn't. She knew the woman wouldn't shoot her.

A snap as Orna stepped on a twig, and the man

slowly turned his head around.

It *was* Rowan. But not quite. His face was crusty black, like the crud scorched onto the bottom of a pot left too long on the burner. Orna's vision telescoped in and out, and her knees almost buckled.

The former head Tender stared at her with bloodshot eyes, but his expression was blank as if he was facing a wall.

A blast split the air. Orna spun, and Bartender was aiming the shotgun at the sky where she'd fired the warning shot. "Now, git!"

With nothing more for Orna to do, she hurried across the clearcut, the mud sucking her boots as if it wanted her to stay. One last look at Rowan sinking his hoe into the soil, and she slipped back into the woods.

Orna's mind churned as she hustled along under the trees. Rowan was a guardian now—Bartender somehow having learned the ritual and names of the demons. But instead of the terrible tragedy it should've been, it almost felt right. Rowan was still alive—sort of—and on the land he loved. And maybe this time he'd take better care of it.

Orna was most of the way through the forest when the kick came from her belly. It wasn't the first but the strongest she'd felt so far. Rubbing her baby bump, she kept hiking.

Not until Orna had made it to the meadow did she remember the shovel. Oh well, she could pick up another one from the hardware store and bury the ring on the outskirts of Meadbury. Or someplace on the drive back to Vermont, plenty of open country along the way.

Orna fingered her breast pocket, the silver ring cold even through the glove. Or maybe—just maybe—she'd hold onto it for a while.

Josh Schlossberg

Josh Schlossberg's biological horror fiction has been published in numerous magazines and anthologies. He's the author of the Horror Authors Guild award-winning, cosmic folk horror novella, MALINAE (D&T Publishing, 2021), editor of THE JEWISH BOOK OF HORROR (Denver Horror Collective, 2021), lead editor of TERROR AT 5280' (Denver Horror Collective, 2019), co-founding member of Denver Horror Collective (Denver-Horror.com), and creator of Josh's Worst Nightmare (JoshsWorstNightmare.com), where he surveys the dark landscape of biological horror fiction.

Follow him on social media at: facebook.com/joshsworstnightmare, twitter.com/JoshsNightmare, and @joshsworstnightmare on Instagram.

More Books from Aggadah Try It

Treif Magic by John Baltisberger
isbn: 978-1-7348937-0-0

Son of the Right Hand by John Baltisberger
isbn: 978-1-955745-04-8

Sheyd of Gray by John Baltisberger
isbn: 978-1-955745-20-8

Giant Robots of Babael by Maxwell Bauman
isbn: 978-1-955745-07-9

The Mummy of Canaan by Maxwell Bauman
isbn: 978-1-955745-25-3

Graven Image by Maxwell Bauman
isbn: 978-1-955745-52-9

The Revised Anarchist's Kosher Cookbook by Maxwell Bauman
isbn: 978-1-955745-48-2

Scapegoated by Jeff Oliver
isbn: 978-1-955745-14-7

Sightless Among Miracles by Ellyn Bache
isbn: 978-1-955745-34-5

Of the Book: An Anthology of Jewish Horror
isbn: 978-1708473730

The Green Children Help Out by Gillian Polack
isbn: 978-1-955745-03-1

The End of Daze by Andrew Fox
isbn: 978-1-955745-46-8

www.ingramcontent.com/pod-product-compliance
Lightning Source LLC
Chambersburg PA
CBHW051241210726
48287CB00002B/347